For Mom,

Marjorie Jean MacMillan Bradley

July 2, 1929-September 25, 2016

The proofreader that made my life's story shine.

Acknowledgements

Thank you to Debby Gilbert for continuing to work with me on the *Maggie's Montana*. Publishing my *Montana Bound Series* has been a dream come true.

Thank you to Montana friends, cowboys, and wranglers who answered questions, taught me to fly fish, and kept us afloat on the Gallatin River. Thank you to my riding guides Kim, Kim, Amber, and Justin at the 320 Ranch in Gateway who navigated trails and befriended this curious writer. Strolling through fields of sage, riding to the ridge, and meandering through the river is magical when you're on horseback.

A special thank you to my son Trevor who explored the Montana countryside with me. It was truly a blessing experiencing "God's Country" with you. Who knew we were naturals when it came to fly-fishing? I will never forget the foal that befriended you. Seeing her on your heels like a long-lost friend brought an affirmation that horses are spiritual and possess a mysterious understanding for human nature. This joyous memory will never be forgotten.

Thank you Kim Pachy for traipsing through the Montana countryside and visiting the B Bar Ranch in Tom Minor Basin to see the Ancient White Park Cattle. Thank you Trina and Hannibal for taking time out of your day to chat with me about the land that inspires my writing.

Thank you to my parents for taking me on family vacations as a youngster. It was on one of these treks that a sliver of Montana beauty became wedged in my brain. I remember telling myself not to forget the blue sky and now I know why. This book holds a special place in my heart as it was the last book my mom read in the winter of her life. She loved reading and I believe this was her favorite of the three in this series. I can never thank her enough for everything that she has given me and even though she dances amongst the angels in heaven, she will be the voice in my head and the love in my heart.

Thank you to all the readers who have come along for the ride. Pun intended.

Chapter 1

My heart skipped a beat. The Montana sky washed over me as I opened the passenger's side door of the Suburban. Judy'd driven most of the way here while I stared out the window daydreaming about Chloe and John. Ignoring Walter and Harry's tiffs over who ate the last fruit snack or which movie to watch came easily with the distractions clouding my mind, but we'd finally arrived and I couldn't believe my eyes. The 617 Ranch was Chloe and John's new home. Their Michigan house would soon be empty, along with my heart. The Gallatin Valley was the place John had grown up, the place where his father, Winston cultivated cattle and horses, the place John belonged. Sighing, I took in the scene, scents of sage and wildflowers tickled my nose. Chloe's embroidered blue cowboy boots kicked up dirt in her path as she bolted like a wild stallion from the corral to greet me.

"Maggie!" Chloe's voice pierced the air, a freckled horse stuck her nose over the railing of the fence, her dark eyes following the commotion.

I caught Chloe in my arms and held her close. The rim of her Stetson caught on my belly and fell to the ground. My heart tore open as she tugged at my heartstrings like a package on Christmas morning. It was like we'd been apart for the longest time, and I was coming home.

"I can't believe you made it," Chloe said. "I thought for sure you'd change your mind."

"We wouldn't let her." Walter shoved his hands in his

pockets, inspecting the land. "Gosh the mountains are huge here and I sure do like those fancy snaps on your shirt."

"We'll get you a fancy shirt while you're here." Chloe wrapped her arms around her buddy and gave him a squeeze. "Thanks for making sure she got here."

"You're welcome. I might be little, but I have my ways." Walter chuckled, then shook Chloe's hand like they were making a deal.

Judy shut her door then pushed her sunglasses to the top of her head, her black curls pinned back, swaying in the breeze. She tucked her hands in the back pockets of her jeans. Judy's presence eased my nerves as John strolled through the barn door to greet us. The sleeves of his white T-shirt were rolled up, his burly physique more prominent than ever. No one would ever guess a lack of hair beneath his cowboy hat.

Chloe reached down, snatched her hat from the ground, then smacked it across her knee like a pro. "Dang-nab-it."

I took my Ray Bans off, hung them from the collar of my shirt, and smirked at the twang in her voice.

"Dad and Grandpa are teaching me some cowboy *lingo*," she said. "Dad, did I get that right?" she asked, glancing in John's direction.

"Sure did, little lady," he answered, with a grin. He ruffled Walter's curly dark hair. "Glad y'all could make it." He shook Harry's hand.

"Hey, I want to shake, too." Walter stuck his hand out. John shook his hand then squeezed his shoulder like a grown man would greet an old pal. "Thanks, I like that better than the pat on the head. That's for little kids."

"Sorry, cowboy." John's twang complemented his smirk.

The apples of Walter's cheeks bulged. He still had all his baby teeth and I could see each one as he grinned with approval. "I can't wait to see this place." His brown eyes sparkled as he surveyed the property. "Look, Maggie. Cows." He took a deep breath and puffed out his chest. "Mooooo."

Chloe laughed. "You're so funny." She kicked the toe of her boot into the dirt. A pebble grazed my foot. "Sorry, Maggie."

Chloe wrapped her arms around my waist and held tight. Her warm breaths pooled between my cotton shirt and my belly. I peered over to John. His eyes were the color of fresh Irish fields. "I can't believe we made it." Relieved to be out of the car, I stretched out my back.

"Three days and two boys later is a feat," John said.

"You're not kidding." Judy draped her arm around Walter and drew him close. "I haven't gone anywhere without their father since they were born. This is our first adventure without him."

Judy glanced over at me with apologetic eyes. Rubbing her arm, I remembered those grueling car rides with my own little boy. "I think you're too hard on them. Walter and Harry have done a stellar job considering how far we've traveled in the last few days." I wrapped my arm around Harry's shoulder. His messy hair tickled my cheek.

"Walter is kind of a baby," Harry said.

"Hey." Walter scowled and stuck out his tongue.

"Hay is for horses and I have some stalls that need to be mucked out if you two boys would like to spend your energy that way." John gestured toward the barn. Five horses the color of butterscotch milled around nibbling blades of grass in the adjoining pasture.

I squeezed Harry's shoulder.

"Oh, boy." Chloe tugged at the rim of her hat. "You two do not want to clean out stalls. Trust me."

My gaze met John's. He had an ease about him that I hadn't seen in Grosse Pointe, but then again Michigan wasn't his happy place. The 'For Sale' sign adorned his front lawn and I loathed all who toured the McIntyre home thinking it could be someone else's dream. "Any bites on the house?" My gut twisted.

"Not that I know of," John said.

"I still don't want to move." Chloe tugged at her dad's hand. "Can't we go back and forth?"

"Afraid not, darlin'. We're a one-home family." He didn't respond to Chloe's plea when she stuck out her bottom lip. Nor mine, but then again, how could he, since mine was buried deep inside. Reminding myself that everyone's path in life wasn't the same, I thought about my own trek. I'd met plenty of people along the way who'd moved on, but every time I looked into John's eyes, something told me he was part of the journey. My heart held steady as my mind wavered. Getting my bearings proved difficult with the hurt that scraped at the bottom of my heart. We both knew hurt. With my ex-husband it was the sting of reality right between the eyes when he told me he was gay after twenty-something years of marriage. For John, Brook had cheated and left him with Chloe. Even though our situations differed, loss was a factor when it came to trusting others.

"Hey, Harry, come check this out," Chloe said, waving him toward the barn. "Maggie, come look."

Walter wrapped his fingers around my hand and we meandered toward her. I nodded to Judy to join us. The Montana scenery was breathtaking. Michigan had its beautiful spots, but Montana's beauty captivated me. John beamed as he held Chloe's hand. Sun streamed in the opposite end of the barn, and just outside the door was another corral of horses. Their hides shone in the sun, each one beautiful in its own way. Chloe knelt beside a wooden box the size of a milk crate. We all peeked in as she reached down to stroke the back of a black crow.

"This is Frankie," she whispered.

"What's wrong with his wing?" Walter knelt beside Chloe to get a better look.

"He's got a broken wing. I noticed him about a week ago when I was at the pond. I was sitting on the dock dangling my feet over the edge trying to touch the water, and he circled my head. Then I saw him the next day and the next. On the fourth day he was waiting for me on the dock with a bent wing. Dad and me are trying to get him to heal."

"I hope he gets better," Harry said, stroking Frankie's back with a gentle touch.

Harry was gentle with everything and his heart could hold the whole world. His sensitivity was noble and I wished more children with his panache would cross my path. "I hope he gets better, too."

Chloe stared up at me with serious eyes, greener than the finest emeralds.

Chapter 2

Judy sat beside me on the porch.

"I can't believe how beautiful Montana is. So worth the drive." Judy rolled up the sleeves of her T-shirt. "Don't need a farmer's tan."

Smirking at my goofy friend, I sat in awe of the land's grandeur. This was God's country. Lazy mares grazed near the the pond. A river flowed along the property line in the distance. The babbling creek near the house swept my thoughts away. Leaning back in my chair, I took a deep breath. "Thanks for coming with me," I said. "I love your boys."

"Thanks for letting me tag along. This is an incredible opportunity for the kids. Besides, I want to see how things pan out with you and John."

Judy's smirk was incorrigible as I stared at her from under my lashes. "You're supposed to be my friend."

"I am." She put up her hands like she was surrendering. "I'm just saying. You two go together like peanut butter and jelly. Everyone can see it except *you two*."

Exhaling, I raised my eyebrow at her. John's dad walked toward us. Chloe was right. Winston Ludlow McIntyre had the perfect name for this kind of living. His moustache twitched as our gazes met, his love for his ranch flickered in his eyes. He clapped his leather gloves together as he approached. He was all cowboy, tall, broad, and stealth. "Hi there." I gave a little wave, my eyes peering past him at the kids who were tossing pebbles into the creek. Walter's curly black mop-top held my attention.

"Glad you made it." Winston gave a nod. "Nice to see you again," he said to Judy.

"Likewise," she responded. "Thank you for letting us stay with you. You have an incredible place here."

The corner of his mouth lifted. "Wasn't always like this. Wish John's mother was here to see the place now."

Winston's expression reminded me of a story John had told about his mom one night while we nursed beers in the moonlight before he and Chloe left for the ranch. Her love for the land and the animals ran just as deep as his father's. A chill ran down my spine. "I'm sure she's proud."

"Did John show you ladies around?" Winston asked.

"Yes," Judy answered. "We met Chloe's lame bird, Frankie and I believe we were introduced to a pony named Huckleberry."

Winston chuckled as he stepped onto the porch. The fringe of his chaps swayed with his stride. "She's pretty attached to that bird. She's going to wake up some morning and it's gonna be gone."

"You think it'll fly away?" I asked.

"Either that or it'll be dinner for some critter that finds its way into the barn."

I grimaced. "Didn't think about that."

Walter skipped over to the porch.

"Howdy partner," Winston said, giving him a tap on the shoulder.

Walter waved as he looked up into Winston's eyes, then he fluffed the fringe on Winston's chaps. "You sure are big. Thanks for letting me come to your ranch. It's cool." He shaded his eyes from the sun and smiled a thin, irresistible grin before climbing into his momma's lap.

"We don't get many visitors. Just glad you could make it."

Walter gave Winston a thumbs-up. Judy wrapped her arms around her son and held him close. Bradley'd been a momma's boy growing up, too. It seemed like yesterday that I'd held him like Judy held Walter. Walter closed his eyes and whispered, "Do you think I'm a baby?"

"No." Judy stroked his hair.

"Will you tell Harry I'm not a baby? Please?" Walter rested his hand on Judy's arm, their dark summer skin tan and smooth.

"Yes, darling. I will."

Walter nodded off.

"He's pooped," Judy said. "Me, too."

"We could have flown," I said, taking a deep breath.

Judy chimed in. "And miss out on seeing the country. No way."

The airline ticket that Winston slid into my mail slot last spring sat on my dresser, back home. A twinge of guilt nudged me. Now that we'd driven, what was I going to do with his generous gift? By the expression on his face, he didn't seem to mind that I hadn't cashed it in.

"It's important for kids to see the country, their country." Winston settled into the rocking chair next to mine. It creaked as he rocked back and forth. "Chloe's been giving her daddy a fuss about not wanting to move, but she sure does fit here." Winston focused on his granddaughter in the distance as he rubbed his whiskery chin.

I studied Winston's profile, thinking he was a man contemplating a future with an eight-year-old on his heels. "She sure does look like she's having fun." I glanced over to Judy. Her eyes closed as she rocked Walter. It'd been a long haul. The corner of my lip curled up as Chloe held one of the barn cats, its legs flopped, its ears back, and their noses touching. She sauntered across the lawn and up the stairs to the porch.

"Is your furry friend a boy or a girl?" I asked with a nod.

The cat's strange eyes glistened with mischief, and then it began purring like a fine-tuned motor. Chloe's gaze resembled the cat's. A thin smile passed over my lips. I'd never seen a tabby cat with blue eyes, spooky, but beautiful.

"Not sure." Chloe leaned on Winston's shoulder. "Grandpa, is this a boy or a girl?" She held the cat up, trying to decide its gender by inspecting its belly. The cat's shaggy fur tickled her cheek.

"It's a girl," Winston answered. When he crossed his feet, his worn silver spurs jangled.

"Voodoo's going to be jealous," I said. Chloe's boots clicked on the wooden porch as she walked closer. "What's the cat's name?" Mesmerized by the sway of its tail, I stroked its head.

"Grandpa, does this cat have a name?" Chloe squinted in his direction.

"No, come to think of it, none of the barn cats have names." Winston scratched his temple.

Chloe smiled. "That's weird. If you're not going to name them . . . can I name them?"

Winston clicked his tongue, his moustache curling toward the sun. "Might be kind of nice." He reached out to Chloe and she plunked down in his lap.

"I'm going to name her French Fry on account she shared my fries the first night I was here. I was kind of lonely and she kept me company." Chloe put the tabby down, then snuggled back into her grandpa's lap, her head against his chest. "I love you, Grandpa."

Winston closed his eyes, held her tight, and kissed her forehead. Judy snuggled with Walter, and Winston coddled Chloe. I felt a bit left out without a little one to cuddle. Those days were gone. There was always something sacred about holding a child and when I held Bradley, I was whole. I missed the days he'd whisper secrets in my ear and play with the ends of my hair to soothe his weary soul.

Harry scuffled up the steps to join us. He plopped down

in the empty rocker, leaned his head back, and moaned. "I am so tired." He took a deep breath then let it out slowly.

He was a year older than Chloe, yet he seemed more mature with his serious demeanor. He was all about facts and statistics. One word popped into my mind when I thought about Chloe, *ragamuffin*. I could see Harry in a suit and Chloe in her jeans and T-shirt doing whatever it took to pay the bills, although I doubt she'd have to worry about that.

Everyone was accounted for, except John. He'd disappeared into the barn shortly after giving us the tour. Chloe opened her eyes. When our gazes met, my heart beat faster. She was at peace and I could see why, countryside surrounded us, blue sky shrouded us, and the hustle-and-bustle of city life, non-existent. This was what John yearned for. The Montana landscape took my breath away. I couldn't blame him for wanting to leave Michigan to re-root himself. Something I knew nothing about for I'd lived in Michigan all my life. There was no one calling me home.

Chloe's eyelids fluttered shut, her breaths slow and even.

The muscles in my hips ached from the car ride. I stretched my legs, wiggled my feet, and then stood up, trying not to disturb the tired crowd around me. Winston gave me a quick wink as I left the porch. Strolling over to the barn, I passed the horses milling around in the pasture. The split rail fence seemed to stretch for miles. I rested my foot on the bottom plank, then leaned my chin on my hands on the top of the fence. The air smelled different here, aromatic compared to suburbia Detroit. Lean spruce trees streamed down the mountainsides, making green pathways from heaven, the Spanish Peaks streaked with snow rose in the distance.

The sound of cowboy boots against a plank floor broke the solitude. I didn't look over to see who approached. I didn't have to. John stood beside me. A painted pony sporting shades of cocoa, taupe, and sandalwood against a white coat joined us at the rail. John clicked his teeth and the pony nuzzled her head into his side as he rubbed her cheek.

"That's pretty impressive," I said, touching her mane. "What's her name?"

"Pippin."

"I like that," I answered. "She's pretty." Pippin's gentle brown eyes focused on the yellow forget-me-nots growing at the base of the fencepost.

"I can't believe you're really here," John said.

"Me neither."

"Chloe's glad her friends came to visit." John leaned against the fence. Pippin nudged his belly through the gap of the railings. "Thanks for making that happen."

"She seems to fit in here." The hint of sadness tugged at my heart. I wanted John and Chloe to be happy, but not so far away.

"Yup, she sure does." He tugged the front of his Stetson down over his brow with a long sigh.

The late afternoon sun made it difficult to focus.

"We gotta get you a hat," John said.

Pippin bowed before us and gobbled up fresh flowers. "It smells sweeter here." Another horse joined Pippin at the fence. "Wow, that's a big horse."

John reached over to pet the horse's nose. "Starbuck's a Belgian. Seventeen hands high." John pointed across the corral. "Her half-sister, Caribou, is eighteen hands."

I shaded my eyes. The sun skewed my vision even with sunglasses on. John was right. I needed a hat. The top of my head roasted in the afternoon heat. "They're beautiful. What do you use them for?"

"They haul the wagon when needed. Dad rides them occasionally." John smirked. "You should see him when he mounts up. Sometimes I think it's so he can be a little closer to heaven to catch a glimpse of my mom." John's words trailed off into the fragrant Montana air.

A chill ran down my spine. Winston wasn't the only one missing his wife. John's tone may have been a man's, but his eyes were those of a boy's, missing his momma. "I'm sure she's watching over your dad." I took a breath, my chin heavy on my hands. Pippin raised her head and we were nose-to-nose. She snorted and stared at me. I lifted my head then faced John. "And you." He glanced down and kicked at the dirt.

"That's a sorry-looking bunch of people up there on the porch."

I peered over my shoulder. The rocking chairs rhythms like a morose Irish ballad. "Yeah, we're all pretty tired."

"You don't look worse for wear." John took off his leather work gloves and tucked them in his back pocket.

My cheeks warmed. Peering across the field, another chocolate-brown painted pony galloped from one side of the corral to the other. Her hooves pounded the ground, reminding me just how pint-sized I was in comparison. "You're kind, but I feel beat."

"Doesn't matter. You know how I feel."

"Yeah, I do." My gaze met his stare, the stare of a man who knew what he wanted.

Chapter 3

Cheerful sounds of banter outside my door woke me up. The clock read seven a.m., but my internal clock registered nine a.m., Michigan time. I pushed the covers back and swung my legs over the side of the bed, taller than my bed back home, my feet barely touching the floor. Chloe slept through the chatter. She and I had signed on as bunking mates for the duration of my stay.

Her fine blonde hair was strewn across her pillow and she slept curled up like a barn cat on a lazy afternoon. Hesitant to wake her, I took my book from the nightstand and propped myself up against the oversized pine headboard. The room was grand with two double beds and a rustic fireplace framed by a rocky hearth. The ceiling fan spun slowly, just enough to keep us cool.

"Aren't you gonna get up and see what all that racket is about?" she whispered.

I stopped reading and peeked over to Chloe who still had her eyes shut. She stuck her legs out from under the covers and repositioned herself.

"Are you awake?" I asked.

Chloe opened one eye. "Um, yeah. I'm not a sleep talker."

"I was trying not to wake you up."

Chloe rubbed her eyes. "Who can sleep with that noise? Geez." She rolled over and covered her head with a pillow.

I set my book down and tiptoed to the door, then turned the knob to see what Harry and Walter were cooing about.

Harry pretended to draw his gun and shoot Walter. Walter fell on the floor and rolled over as he grabbed his side and gurgled. He held on to his cowboy hat, making sure not to crush it. Stepping into the hallway, I shut the door behind me. "You two look official now."

Harry pointed behind me to a hefty bureau at the end of the hallway. "There's one with your name on it, too."

Touching the rim of the straw Stetson the color of bone, I felt as if I was in another dimension. My hat had a rich, brown leather band with fringe at the back and a circular brass medallion stamped with a floral design. I watched Harry and Walter in the mirror behind me. Walter got up from his dead-man's pose and padded softly back into his bedroom. Judy poked her head out, her messy black curls framed her face.

"There's one for you too," I said.

Judy brushed her hair back from her cheeks and held my stare as she shuffled toward me.

Putting my hat on, I inspected myself in the mirror. "How does it look with pajamas?"

"Not bad." Judy sighed with a raised brow. She tucked messy curls behind her ears then tried her Stetson on, too. "I like it."

Chloe opened the bedroom door and poked her head into the hallway. "We should get down to breakfast," she said with a yawn. "I'd better get dressed. This ranching stuff sure makes me get up early."

"Here, we go. Maybe they'll sleep in tomorrow." Glancing over to Judy, I knew we'd be on the go, especially now that the boys had Chloe to fuel their adventures.

Judy rolled her eyes at me.

I knocked on the door when I heard Chloe rustling around on the other side. "Are you dressed?"

"Almost, be out in a second," she answered.

"Hey, hey, hey." Judy grumbled as she went back into the bedroom she was sharing with Walter and Harry. She shut the door behind her.

Their muffled conversation brought a smile to my lips when I heard the boys whine, "Come on, Mom." I crossed my arms over my stomach, then leaned against the bureau and waited for Chloe to finish whatever she was doing in there.

"You can open the door now," Chloe called.

I went in. Chloe sat on the floor dressed in a red-checkered, button-down shirt, faded jeans with the left knee blown out, and her cowboy hat that matched John's. She picked up one of her blue cowboy boots and put it on. The heel clunked against the floor with a mighty thud. Her long blonde hair knotted from a good night's rest.

"Do you want me to braid your hair?" I wouldn't let Bradley in public without having him cleaned up, and it bugged me when my students came to school with bedheads. I know parents could have hurried mornings, but keeping a child tidy would only help in the process.

"Sure. I'm glad I took a bath last night. All rested and ready to go. Gotta name some cats today," Chloe said under her breath.

She removed her hat as I took the hairbrush from the nightstand. Standing behind her, I gently worked at the tangled tresses. She whimpered.

"Sorry. You really got a number going on here. I'm almost done."

She shifted her weight and tilted her head back so she could see me. "Thanks."

"You're welcome. I just want you to look your best. Now put your head back up please."

"Okeydokey."

Dividing her hair into three equal parts, I worked my

fingers to make a tight braid. She handed me a blue hair tie to finish it off. "Tight enough?"

"What?"

She faced me.

"You know, does it feel like your braid will stay?"

She shrugged. "I still have no clue what you're talking about. My dad never braids my hair."

"When the girls in my class ask me to braid their hair, I try to braid it tight so it doesn't fall out," I explained.

"None of my teachers ever braided hair. Your students are lucky."

Still in my cowboy hat and pajamas, I sat cross-legged on the bed.

"I wish I was in your class," Chloe said.

I raised an eyebrow. "I don't think so. It might be the end of our friendship. Being in the classroom is way different than being the lady next door."

Chloe grimaced at me.

"What?"

Chloe's chin wrinkled. She looked me in the eye and tenderness rimmed her green irises.

"I-" She held her breath.

"Spit it out," I prodded.

"I just think-" She stopped.

"You just think, what?" I could see the wheels turning and my first instinct told me that it was too early in the morning to have a serious conversation, but I held her stare against my better judgement. With all her western garb and spunk, she really emanated mountain living.

"Promise you won't laugh," she said, playing with the frayed denim around the hole in the knee of her pants.

Sitting a little taller, I made the sign of a cross on my heart. "I promise, hope to die, stick a needle in my eye."

She sighed, then stuffed her hands into the pockets of her jeans. "I just think that we're more than friends."

I leaned forward, inspecting her green eyes filled with what I thought was hope. We were almost nose-to-nose. "I'll let you in on a little secret."

"What?" Chloe whispered.

We touched noses. "Me, too." I couldn't see her mouth, but by the twinkle in her gaze I knew she was showing off that toothy grin of hers. She wrapped her arms around my neck and gave a squeeze. I couldn't help but hug her back. "We'd better get going. You know how Walter and Harry get when they have to wait."

Chloe leaned back and fingered her braid. "Yeah, they're probably already down there beating the snot out of each other."

"Really?"

"Yeah, really. It can get ugly. That's the hazard when you have kids," she explained.

Only Chloe would say something like that. "Get going. I have to get dressed." I shooed her toward the door.

"Wear your boots," Chloe ordered. "And that hat. It'll look a lot better with your jeans."

"I think you're right about that." Bending down, I reached for my Frye boots beneath the bed. They were the boots I'd worn when Chloe and I met her mom in Chicago to see her mom's photo shoot. I hadn't heard from Brook's photographer, Booker Thompson, since I turned down his invitation to Los Angeles. "Now get going and see what we're having for breakfast. Something smells delicious."

Chloe turned on a heel, the toe of her boot pointed toward the timber ceiling. "Don't dilly-dally."

I unfolded a fresh pair of faded jeans from my suitcase and a periwinkle T-shirt. "Where did you hear that?"

Chloe peered back over her shoulder as she turned the knob on the door to leave.

"Glad," she answered.

"Sounds about right. She used to say that all the time when I was about your age. Man, you didn't want to mess with her when she was in a hurry."

"Apples don't fall far from the tree." Chloe snickered and winked.

I rolled my eyes as she exited the room.

Even if my mother wasn't here, it felt like she was.

Chloe had a mind like a steel trap, and her ability to remember things astounded me. I stripped off my sleeping pants and tank and then dressed for the day.

My butt slid dangerously close to the edge of the bed as I pulled on my boots. The morning air wafted through the open window. The humidity non-existent, refreshing. Late afternoon was the warmest, then by five I knew a cool breeze would be upon us to squelch the day's heat. The Montana weather appealed to me.

There was a knock at the door. "Yeah."

"Can I come in?" Judy asked.

"Sure," I answered, tugging my pant legs over my boots. I brushed my hair and tied it in a knot at the nape of my neck. Judy was decked out in jeans, a plaid shirt, and cowboy boots. "New boots?"

She wiggled her feet. "No. I've had these since college. I guess they don't go out of style. Haven't worn them since I took Harry to a rodeo a few years ago. He was all about horses, cowboys, and guns. He even got his father to write the word saloon on his playhouse in the backyard. When Pink wasn't paying attention, Harry and the neighbor boys collected empties and filled the shelves inside with beer bottles."

"Impressive." I tugged at the rim of my new Stetson. "Shall we?"

"I'm starving." Judy walked out of the bedroom and into the hallway where she checked herself out in the mirror above the heavy bureau. "Wonder what we're doing today."

"John said something about riding." I stood beside Judy, thinking about how sore my hindquarters would be afterward. "How long do you think it takes a cowboy to get used to riding?"

Judy shrugged. "Not sure. With any luck, our legs won't feel like Jell-O and our knees won't be a wreck."

"I'm not planning on riding that long." I straightened my belt. "What?" I scoffed at her sinister grin.

"I don't think you get a say. Come on. I don't hear any noise downstairs. We better see what the troops are up to."

Chloe, Harry, and Walter waited patiently at the island in the kitchen. Judy's eyebrow arched toward the high ceiling. I shot her a look, then caught John's stare as he flipped pancakes at the griddle. There was a heaping pile of bacon on a platter in front of the kids. Chloe sat on her hands. Walter rested his chin on countertop and Harry fiddled with silverware. There wasn't a word from any of them.

"Interesting. We could have used you in the car on the way here," Judy told John.

John lowered his gaze, an all-knowing grin passing over his lips. He stacked a fresh pile of pancakes on another platter that was half-full.

"I love blueberry pancakes." Walking closer to where he stood, my stomach growled as I smelled the aroma.

"Not blueberry. Huckleberry. We have them everywhere. They're like blueberries, but they grow in the higher altitudes. We put them in everything," John said, popping one in his mouth.

Judy took the pitcher of orange juice from the counter and poured some for the kids.

Chloe studied her dad. "Can I say thank you?" she whispered.

"Of course you can." He stacked another batch of fresh pancakes onto the platter.

While Chloe thanked Judy, I leaned closer to John. "What did you do to them?"

He handed me the platter. His words barely audible, his breath prickled emotion. "I showed them the bottom of the boots just outside the door. I told them if there were any shenanigans, they'd be shoveling fresh horse poop."

"I'm surprised that worked a second time."

"You haven't seen the boots. It's caked on. Smells bad. Gross," he said, holding his nose.

I inspected his feet. His boots were clean besides the few smudges of dust on the toes. "Who do the boots really belong to?" I whispered, glancing over to the kids.

"You're smarter than they are," he muttered. "They belong to Trout."

"Maggie, can we have pancakes now? We've been really, really, really patient," Walter whined.

I took the platter of huckleberry pancakes to the table. Harry beamed with anticipation.

"So who's Trout?" I asked.

"Dad's right-hand man," Chloe answered.

"There's a guy here whose name is Trout?" Harry said, spearing two pancakes before even sitting down in his chair.

"That's not his real name. That's his nickname because anytime he gets time off he's fly-fishing for trout in the Yellowstone River." John slid out a chair for Judy.

"Cool! I want a nickname too." Walter scowled at his brother. "And you don't get to pick it!"

Chloe laughed. John settled in at the table beside me. "He's right you know. You got an extra pair of boots with you?"

Harry munched on his bacon. "Fine." He cut his pancakes into neat pieces.

"Thanks, J.P." Walter said.

Judy looked over to John for approval.

"My friends call me J.P. and I consider Walter good

people. He can call me J.P." John leaned over to Harry and patted his shoulder. "You, too."

"That stands for John Patrick," Chloe reminded us, her mouth stuffed with pancakes. Syrup soaked crumbs fell from her bottom lip as she spoke.

John winked at Walter. "We'll think of something super cool to nickname you."

"Cool," Walter said as Judy helped him cut his pancakes.

Chloe took a swig of juice. "This is delicious. You don't cook this good at our Michigan house."

"What gives?" I raised an eyebrow in John's direction.

He lowered his gaze as if he were a schoolboy caught in a fib. His expression gave him away.

"Fine." John put his two hands in the air as if he were giving up at a shootout. "Chloe's grandpa made the batter. I just fried it up. He showed me how."

"Well, I like it." Walter took a bite and smiled as he chewed. "Can I have more, please?"

"Eat up, partner. Justin is saddling up horses as we speak." John cut his pancakes with the side of his fork and finished his plate.

Chapter 4

John stared into the clear blue sky. "Perfect. The kids are going to stay here with Justin and Ashley while the adults go for a ride up the mountain." He pointed to a tree-covered peak.

"Shouldn't I stay with the boys?" Judy asked.

Harry fidgeted with the slingshot in his hands. "It was part of the deal this morning."

John grinned. "Yup, you two need a break. And these three fine youngsters will be in good hands."

"I want Mom to see me ride a horse, J.P." Walter stuck out his bottom lip.

I frowned at Walter's woeful eyes. Judy picked him up. He wrapped his legs around her waist and hugged her tight.

"I don't care. I'll pick up horse poop," he mumbled.

"How about we watch you ride now and then your mom can go for a ride with Maggie and me?" John coiled the rope that Chloe'd left hanging on the fence.

"We won't be gone too long. Besides once you get on that horse, you're gonna have so much fun you won't even notice I'm gone." Judy put Walter down. "Okay, partner?"

"I bet we can talk J.P. into making s'mores after dinner if you let your mom go for a ride," I said with a wink.

Walter's eyes brightened.

"It's all about the food," Judy added. "Look, there are the horses." She pointed toward the barn.

We resembled a group of *hombres* from a spaghetti western. Walter walked between Judy and me, holding our hands.

"Ashley's a really good wrangler and pretty, too. Walter will love her," John said, nodding to the young lady holding the lead attached to the bridle of a pony just the right size for Walter.

Chloe scooted inside the barn as John introduced Ashley and Justin. "I'll just be in here looking for the cats," she said, peeking into the stalls for furry felines.

"The kids are going to stay in the ring and learn some basics while we take a ride. Maybe we'll see some deer or moose."

Walter's rosy cheeks bulged with his toothy grin. "J.P., I want to see those things, too."

"You just might if you keep your eyes peeled over there." John pointed to an open field across the two-lane road.

"I'll be able to see really good once I get up on that guy." Walter caressed the pony's nose. "His whiskers tickle. Kind of like Daddy's."

Judy laughed.

John picked up Walter with a mighty grunt and plopped him into the saddle. He handed him the reins and told him to hang on to the saddle horn.

Walter leaned forward and petted the horse's mane. "What's his name?"

"Cinnamon. And it's a she. She's as sweet as they come," Ashley answered. "Nice to meet you guys. Winston's been looking forward to your visit." Ashley's long, dark-brown braid hit just below the middle of her back. Her black felt cowboy hat shaded her face. "Let's see if we can shorten these stirrups." Ashley unbuckled the leather strap and tugged upward. "Perfect." She looked Walter in the eye. "You ready?"

Cinnamon craned her neck as if she were checking to see if Walter was ready, too.

"Yes." Walter beamed.

Ashley led Cinnamon into the pasture, and then Justin shut the gate behind them. Harry stood at the split rail fence and watched his brother. Justin tapped Harry on the shoulder.

"You ready?" he asked.

"Sure," Harry said. "Which one am I riding?"

Justin led Harry to a spotted horse. "This paint's name is Freckles 'cause her spots look like Irish freckles." Freckles shifted her weight and her hooves clomped against the ground. "If you climb up on that block, we'll get you going."

Chloe sauntered out of the barn holding a black cat with a white patch on its chest under her arm. "Hey, look what I found. The other cats must be out hunting." She scratched its head. "I think we should name this one Midnight on account of how dark he is."

"And he has a star on his chest," Harry noted from the block.

"He's so cute." Chloe strolled to the fence while Midnight squirmed in her arms. "Hey, look at Walter. He's riding. Woo-hoo!"

Walter waved to Judy and called from across the field. "You can go now. I'm having a great time." His body bobbed up and down in rhythm with Cinnamon's easy stride.

Justin adjusted Harry's stirrups and led him into the pasture. "I promise I won't hold onto you the whole time 'cause you're a big fella."

Harry puffed out his chest, pointed his toes up, and held tight to the reins.

"I'll watch for now," Chloe said. "Midnight and I want to get to know each other, besides, Dad already took me for a ride. I can wait a few more minutes." Chloe beamed as she stared into her father's eyes.

Judy nudged me as Chloe and John exchanged glances. They were two peas in a pod. She was just a shorter version. Her eyes creased in the same places. They had matching dimples and eyes for only each other. Loose strands of hair from her braid swayed in the intermittent breeze that ushered in the day. Judy's grin stirred up all the uncertainties I worried about. I noticed a black feather as I kicked at the dirt with the tip of my boot. Bending down, I picked it up, and knew Chloe needed it for her hat. She gazed up to me with the same smiling eyes she shared with her dad as I tucked the quill behind the leather band on her hat. "Just accessorizing your Stetson."

"Thanks, Maggie. It'll remind me of Frankie when he's gone 'cause you know he's gonna fly home soon. Everybody goes home sooner or later." Midnight jumped from her arms.

"How's Frankie faring with the barn cats?" I asked, wanting to know if he had been eaten for lunch.

"Trout helped me rig up his box so other animals couldn't get in. That Trout is one smart guy. If it weren't for him, Frankie would be some putty-tat's dinner."

"Glad to hear he's doing well," I said, John's stare catching my eye.

Chloe wrapped her fingers around mine, and when I looked, she was holding John's hand, too. She stood between us, a common link.

"Dad, will you help me get on Huckleberry?" she asked. "That way I'll be ready when Justin comes around again." She watched Harry and Walter across the field. "When you get back we can have lunch. Being out here makes me hungry."

Chloe dropped our hands, and we were two separate entities again. John strolled over to a spotted horse and lifted Chloe up as she swung her right leg over the saddle. The stirrups were already set and she took the reins like a pro. John held the lead rope and guided her into the pasture.

Judy shut the gate behind them and leaned in my direction. "Nice picture."

"What picture?" I said, sidestepping horse droppings.

"The one I just took of you three." Judy held out her phone and showed me.

I gazed at the photo of John and me smiling down at Chloe. "Yeah, that's a good one." Goose bumps covered my arms.

Judy tucked her phone in the breast pocket of her western shirt and snapped the flap shut for safekeeping. "Wonder who we're riding?" She meandered closer to the three brown horses wearing black socks. They appeared to be triplets.

John squeezed through the slats of the split rail face. His lips pressed together in thought. "Well, I guess it's our turn. When's the last time you two have been on a horse?"

"I rode about five years ago on Jekyll Island in Georgia. Had a crazy fast horse on the beach." I could almost taste the salt from the Atlantic Ocean on my lips, the memory as fresh as home-baked bread. "What about you, Judy?"

"Well, it was probably the last time I wore these clothes. Maybe two years ago. It was a mellow trail ride." She waved to Walter as he passed by. "What's it like going up this mountain?"

John patted the hindquarter of the horse next to him. "It's slow and easy, just like everything else out here. The horses know what to do." He put his left boot in the stirrup then mounted his horse. "Hold the reins like this. Keep the ball of your foot on the stirrup, toes up. Give 'em a little nudge or a click of your tongue, and we'll be set." He dismounted. "Judy, we'll get you up first. Come over here to the block. Don't walk behind her. Knew a guy once who got his knee cap blown out from one swift kick."

"Ouch." Judy stepped up on the block and mounted the brown beauty. "What kind of horse is this?" She fingered the black mane and patted her neck.

"These three are bays. Meet Charlie's Angels." He snickered. "Trout named them. He's a character, but these girls got your back." Pausing, he nodded for me to climb up on the block. "You're next, neighbor lady."

I stepped up, put my foot in the stirrup, and swung my leg over. John checked the stirrups, making sure they were the proper length then flipped up the flap on the saddle. "Let's make sure this girth is nice and tight. Don't want to lose you." He glanced up and gave me a sexy wink.

"So what *angel* am I riding?" Making sure my feet were in the stirrups correctly, I ran my hand over the braided leather trim on the saddle.

"You're riding Sweet Jaclyn. Judy's on Kick-ass Kate, and I'll be mounting Farrah."

Judy and I both erupted with laughter. John's cheeks quickly changed rosy red.

"Well I guess that didn't come out right. You two are bad, just plain evil." He tugged at the rim of his Stetson trying to hide his embarrassment. "Shame on you, although now you've given me something to think about." John mounted his horse like a seasoned wrangler.

"Keep your eyes on the trail and your mind out of the gutter. We're counting on you, doctor pediatrician man," Judy teased.

"All right, you two, fall in line. Maggie, you're gonna want to be behind me. Keep about a half a horse length between us and we'll be good," John said. "Judy, you follow neighbor lady."

John didn't resemble a pediatrician today. With his plaid shirt, worn Wrangler jeans, and broad shoulders, he was all cowboy. We rode single file. I peered down the trail at the steep, snow-streaked peaks poking their heads above the green mountains ahead of us.

"Man, I love that smell," Judy said, breathing deeply.

John glanced over his shoulder.

"Smells good, clean, fresh. Wish I could bottle it up and take it home." I inspected the profile of a content man and he was more handsome than ever.

"We'll ride to the ridge, take a break, and soak up the scenery. We'll save the rest of the mountain for another day."

"How long we riding, cowboy?" Judy asked.

I glanced back over my shoulder at her. "You worried about the boys?" She had that look only a mother could have.

She shrugged. "Just don't want to come back to mayhem."

John turned around again, the reins lose in his right hand. His left hand rested on the back of his saddle. "Don't you worry, I made sure the kids would be kept busy. Justin is no pushover. Trust me."

"Famous last words," I said.

"Walter is gonna want his s'mores." Judy moved a pine branch out of her way.

"Me, too," I said. "Me, too." The dirt trail rose with the slight incline. Rocks peeked out between roots in the ground mimicking witch's hands. Flecks of sunlight trickled down like stardust. "That fringy moss on those barren trees looks like it belongs in a Dr. Seuss book."

"It's not that whimsical. It's killing the trees. No one is quite sure how to get rid of it." John shifted his weight in the saddle as Farrah maneuvered up the rocky terrain.

I frowned, imagining the loss of trees and habitat. Sweet Jaclyn stopped in her tracks when the sound of falling rocks drifted down the trail ahead of us. Her ears twitched as she peered up the mountainside. The pine trees blocked my view as I strained to see what made her nervous.

"Easy girl," I said, preparing to hold on. Being on a runaway horse was not what I had in mind.

John pointed up the hill. "There are three deer up there."

I leaned forward and searched until I spotted the flighty creatures causing the disruption. They were peering down with caution and curiosity.

"They're beautiful," Judy said just as three white tails disappeared in the flock of trees.

"I'm not sure Sweet Jaclyn likes them." I patted her mane and thanked her for not bolting.

John clicked his tongue and gave Farrah a slight kick. "When we go up this hill, lean forward. It'll help your horse get up incline. When we come down, lean back and let them pick their path." He pointed to a tree that was rubbed clean of its bark. "See that?"

Judy and I both answered, "Yeah."

"Bears do that."

Glancing back over my shoulder at Judy, the thought of meeting up with a bear frightened me, and I remembered seeing a woman at a restaurant along the way with a canister hooked to her belt. I thought it was a fire extinguisher until Harry pointed out it was bear repellent. "I heard that if you think there's a bear around you just make a lot of noise."

"Yeah, that's a good idea. You don't want to sneak up on a bear, especially if she's got cubs. Chances are we won't run across any, but you never know."

We came to the next rocky incline. John's horse maneuvered up the winding path while Judy and I followed.

Chapter 5

"We're almost to the ridge," John called over his shoulder. His horse's hips swayed from side-to-side through the field of tall grass and thistle, a lazy stroll through wicked beauty.

Sweet Jaclyn bowed her head in-between lackadaisical steps smelling blooms in her path as she yearned to snack along the way. My huckleberry pancakes were sticking with me and I was too absorbed in the view to even care about food. And as I looked out over the ridge, it dawned on me how content I felt. Somewhere back in the Dakotas, I'd checked my worries. John dismounted Farrah and tied the lead to a branch then patted her withers. I held the leather horn on my saddle, stood in the stirrups, swung my right leg over the back of Sweet Jaclyn, and then carefully slid down the saddle to steady myself.

John held the bridle, his mouth curled upward. "You feeling a little wobbly? Your knees okay?"

I snickered at his inflection. "I'll be fine." But really I wasn't sure that was the case. John McIntyre was the only man who could make me go weak in the knees, his house was on the market, and most likely by the end of the summer, he'd be heading home to this place permanently. I'd accepted that he was a Montana man, but I couldn't wrap my head around not having him or Chloe in my life back home in Michigan.

John tethered my horse to a branch and then helped Judy off Kick-ass Kate. Kate whinnied, let out a snort, then bowed her head and munched at the thick green patch of grass coated with sunshine as John secured her lead to the tree.

I ran my hand over Sweet Jaclyn's shoulder. Her hide glistened with sweat and I marveled at her muscle definition. These horses were magnificent beasts, creatures to be respected, animals that made it possible for man to explore the west so humans could cultivate the land. John undid his saddlebags then gestured for Judy and me to join him. Judy shook out her legs and I stretched as we meandered to the edge of the ridge. Blue sky shrouded us, making it possible to see for miles.

John pointed to a pasture below us. "See those white specks?"

I nodded, and Judy pulled her phone from her pocket to snap a few pictures. John put his arm around my shoulder and Judy captured our images. His touch reminding me I needed him.

John produced a radio from one of the saddlebags. He adjusted the knob until static pierced the air. "Justin, you there?"

"Yeah, cowboy. I'm here. You at the top of the ridge?"

I leaned over to Judy. "I can't believe I forgot my camera. I could kick myself."

"I'll snap some photos on my phone. Besides, it'll give you a reason to come back up here with John later. Next time, I'll stay home and watch the kids."

I rolled my eyes at her. "Give me your phone and stand over there. I'll take your picture." Golden rays highlighted Judy's dark curls that bobbed when she walked. "Smile." She tucked her thumbs in her back pockets, her dimples prominent. I snapped a few photos then handed the phone back to her. "Check them out. Is there one that you like?" She checked the screen and nodded with approval.

"You can see forever with this view. Who wouldn't want to live here? I think John's got the right idea." Judy glanced over at him as he chatted with Justin. I tuned them out, but Judy went over to listen.

She had a point. Who wouldn't want to live here? The back of my T-shirt stuck to my skin. Riding was hard work.

John joined me while Judy chatted on the radio. "Is she talking to Walter?" I asked, not taking my eyes off the valley.

John nodded. "Yup. She loves those boys more than anything." John's eyes danced in the light.

My heart skipped a beat as a fissure cracked in the depths of my heart like a tremor just before an earthquake rattles the land.

"I suppose, like you love Bradley and I love Chloe despite any breaches of character on any given day."

I laughed. "I suppose." The dip in the front of my hat shaded my face. "Now, what were you going to say about those white specks down there?"

"That's the herd. Those are the Ancient White Park Cattle. Winston's down there somewhere caring for them right now and thanking the heavens that my mom let him stay on this land."

"What are Ancient White Park Cattle? I've never heard of them before."

"They're pretty rare. They're white and have black, ominous horns. We didn't always have them, but Dad dreamed of raising them. I guess dreams really do come true if you work hard enough."

"Or pray enough," I whispered.

"Maybe a little of both." John took off his hat and wiped his brow. "What's your dream, Maggie Abernathy?"

I shifted my weight and crossed my arms in front of me. Before me was a world I hadn't even known existed. Next to me was a man close enough to grab like a golden ring on the carousel. I took my sunglasses off and hung them from the collar of my shirt. "I used to think it was to have a baby. Then I thought it was to make a difference in the world by teaching children. Now I'm not so sure."

"You can have more than one dream, you know."

I soaked up the view of valley below us. "How the hell can you be so sure about what you want?"

A wave of energy passed through his eyes. His electricity drew me closer.

"It's just not fair."

John wrapped his arm around my shoulder. "One day, the moons will align in your world, Maggie, and it'll be fair. Trust me," he said. "This wasn't an easy decision. Chloe's been through enough and I worry about hurting her. I want her to have some stability. This is where we belong."

John kissed the side of my head. I glanced over to Judy who was still talking to Walter on the radio. Embarrassed by the display of affection, my cheeks glowed and my palms sweated. "I think I've spent my time trying not to disappoint people. It's not possible to live life without mistakes." My marriage to Beckett seemed like a lifetime ago and who knows, maybe it was. Maybe it really existed on another plane, in another dimension, and now I'd been awakened. "Chloe will be fine." I squeezed his hand, not knowing if I'd survive their transition.

He wrapped his fingers around mine, and my heart fluttered like the butterflies I'd seen flitting about in the fields along the way.

"I think I finally know that."

"You're a great dad, John McIntyre."

"Thanks, Maggie Abernathy." He chuckled. "Now what do you say to a snack and then a ride down the mountain? I'll show you those cattle up close and personal after we've had some lunch."

John spread out a woolen blanket with brown bison woven into the pattern around the edges. Judy sauntered over, looking pleased as John unpacked some grapes and buttery crackers.

"Everything fine with Walter?" I asked, stretching out my legs to the side and leaning back on my hands to get a better view of the mountains in the distance.

"Yeah, guess I worry about nothing," she said, handing John the radio.

"I suppose we all do," he added.

"I just can't get over how beautiful it is here," Judy gushed. "Gosh." She snapped off a handful of grapes and popped them in her mouth one-by-one. When she was done, she stood and stretched her arms to the sky. "I'm gonna meander over by the horses. Gotta stretch out these legs."

I popped two grapes into my mouth and took off my Stetson, setting it carefully on the blanket, admiring its creamy color and style. I leaned back with my hands behind my head, lowering myself to the ground until my spine touched the earth below me, and then closed my eyes, the scenery etched in my brain, my ears sensitive to buzzing horseflies and a squawking crow overhead. "It's so nice not to hear traffic or the whirr of a siren," I said. "Not to mention the space. It's nice not having house upon house."

"That's part of the draw," John said.

My chest rose and fell to the rhythm of the relaxed country air. "I know you're not a city man, but I'm glad you left this place or I wouldn't have ever met you. Maybe we would've strolled past each other at some point in time, but I feel like I'd always be searching for some missing piece."

"What are you afraid of?"

I opened one eye and stared at him. "Plenty."

"Being happy isn't so bad," he said. "Is that the fear?"

I closed my eye again, and his image replaced the scenery beneath my eyelids. His stare rattled my nerves. *Damn.* I swallowed the knot forming at the back of my throat. "I hate it when you make me think." Sitting up, I took out my ponytail holder and ran my fingers through my hair. The weight against my shoulders grounded me. Something needed to. A soft curl stuck to my cheek as the breeze nudged against me, reminding me of being a child on lazy summer afternoons, staring across the lake back home when dreams came easy and I believed they'd all come true. John wasn't the only thing prodding me to analyze life. Did God do this to everyone?

"You about ready to get back up on Sweet Jaclyn?" John adjusted his cowboy hat. He slapped his gloves against his thigh then brushed away the dragonfly that'd been hovering over him.

"I might need your help. She's bigger when you aren't standing on a mounting block." I folded up the blanket then handed it to the man reeling me in with his invisible line. "I forgot my camera. Will you bring me back up here later so I can get some shots?"

John lowered his head with a flash in his eyes.

"What?"

"You sure you aren't trying to get me alone? Sounds suspicious, ma'am."

I redid my ponytail then put my hat back on. "As much as you'd like that." *As much as we'd both like that.* "Nope. Just want some photos. Who knows, maybe I'll make a coffee table book of Montana hand-colored photos."

John rubbed his chin. "Sounds like a great idea. You're good enough to do that. You know that, don't you?" He stuffed the blanket back into one of the saddlebags, and then hooked the radio on his belt for the ride home.

For me, dreams had become just that, dreams. Was it really possible to grab the golden ring? It'd be just one more thing to carry, or maybe I'd miss as I reached for it and fall flat on my face. "I guess. I never really thought about it. All I've gotten is a stack of rejection letters with my cow photos." Settling for personal satisfaction came easily.

"Maybe you just haven't found the right niche yet."

"Maybe." What was my niche? My niche presently felt like a black hole. Did niches change with time? I supposed they did. And why was I so bound and determined to hang on to things that didn't fill me up like a warm hug or that first sip of hot cocoa on a winter's day?

John ran his fingers across my collarbone and down my arm. Leaning in he whispered in my ear. My breath caught in my chest as his lips grazed my skin.

"I can see you're thinking, Maggie."

His touch sent sparks through my veins, igniting a hot flash. He handed me the canteen. I eagerly took it wanting to extinguish the slow-burn I was feeling.

"I think we've climbed enough mountains for one day, neighbor lady. What do you say we head back to the ranch?" John hooked the saddlebags to his saddle. "You ready to go, Judy?" he called over his shoulder.

"Yup. Better see what those boys are up to." She patted her horse's rump. "Let's go, Kick-ass Kate." Judy ran her fingers through Kate's silky mane. "Can you help me get back up here?" she asked John.

He held the saddle then boosted her up. Judy swung her right leg up and over like a pro. "Thanks."

"I suppose you're gonna need a hand, too," he said, peering back at me.

"Probably, but I can try it on my own. Who knows, I might possess some super human strength." I smirked, put my foot in the stirrup, and hoisted myself up by the horn. My right foot got stuck on the back of the saddle. John nudged it the rest of the way over. The heat from his touch penetrated my jeans. "Thanks, I almost had it."

"Yeah, I'd say you're almost more there."

I wished I was as certain as he was. Feeling like a bumbling fool, I slid my sunglasses back up to the bridge of my nose. I fingered the reins as he untied Sweet Jaclyn from the tree for me. "Thanks, cowboy."

"You're welcome, ma'am." He clicked his tongue as if he were beckoning Farrah to move faster.

John mounted his horse easily. He had enough muscle for the both of us. In the past, working out was not in my regime until Judy and I trained for the Race for the Cure last spring. I'd limited myself to walking Bones around the block and scurrying from my classroom to the copy room on a regular basis. Since then, Judy and I had teamed up for power walks in the neighborhood and short jogs. John's forearms flexed as he hauled himself up. Beckett never had muscle definition like that. I squelched the thought of my ex-husband and focused on John, who directed Farrah to saunter my way. I settled into the saddle and rested my left hand on my thigh. "You ready?"

"I will be in a minute. I just came over here to do one thing."

"What's that?" I questioned John's agenda since we were all packed up, mounted, and ready to go. Laugh lines formed at the corners of his emerald eyes.

"I just wanted to tell you." He glanced down then prodded Farrah to move closer.

His knee grazed mine and we were face-to-face. I lowered my sunglasses to get a better look into his sultry eyes. "What?"

"I just want you to know, you look pretty darn good up on that horse. If I didn't know better, I'd say you were holding out on me."

I clicked my tongue and gave Sweet Jaclyn a nudge with my heels. "Come on, girl." I glanced back over my shoulder at the Montana man who was stealing my heart all over again. "Maybe I am."

Chapter 6

Our horses clomped along at a leisurely pace down the dirt road back to the ranch. The endless sea of green was lined with wooden fences marking off grassy pastures. Chloe and Walter's voices drifted in the breeze, their laughter like a crackling fire. Their jovial banter, infectious. John trotted ahead, got off his horse, and tied Farrah's lead to the post just outside the barn. He peered inside then walked back to help Judy and me dismount our two angels. When Chloe emerged, her cheeks were rosy, her hair was tangled, and broken pieces of hay clung to her clothing.

I held onto the saddle horn and slid down, bracing myself for an unstable landing. My knees ached the last ten minutes of the ride, but my behind felt okay, although tomorrow might be the bearer of bad news.

John took Sweet Jaclyn from me and tied her next to Farrah then he helped Judy down, and led Kick-ass Kate over to her sisters.

"Looks like somebody was in the hay," John said.

Chloe brushed herself off and felt her head. "Guess that braid didn't last very long." Straw littered the ground when John rustled her blonde tresses.

"No worries, we can redo it if you want to." I took off my sunglasses and peeked into the barn. Two small feet stuck out of a pile of hay in the stall closest to the door. "Anyone using that first stall?" I asked, scanning the floor for manure.

"Nope," John said.

"Where's Walter?" Judy asked.

I winked at her over the rim of my sunglasses. "Gosh, maybe he's gone out to pasture with the cattle. That'll be one less kid to make s'mores tonight," I said, smirking at my own joke. "All the more for me."

Judy stepped into the barn and looked around. "Well, I guess he's gone. That'll be one less kid to send to college."

John lugged in a saddle and blanket then placed it on one of the empty saddle racks on the wall. "Man oh, man. Poor Walter. I guess I'll have to eat his dinner too, since he's gone."

The boots wiggled and a grunt came from the pile of hay. Chloe giggled.

Judy pretended not to see her son. "Chloe, are you sure you don't know what happened to Walter? 'Cause I'm sure gonna miss him."

Walter's arms jutted out of the hay and he popped up like a jack-in-the-box. "I'm right here!"

Ashley came in with another saddle and blanket then slung it in onto a rack.

"I'll get the last one." John winked.

"I'll start cleaning the horses up. Is it okay if I leave Chloe and Walter now?" Ashley asked.

"Yeah, I think you've done your penance," John said as he walked by, his heels clicking against the floorboards of the barn. "Thanks, for your help. You can join us for dinner if you don't have plans."

"I'm in." Ashley's dimples emerged from behind her solemn expession.

Chloe ran around in circles like an overly excited puppy. "Yay, Ashley is coming to dinner." She tugged at Ashley's hand. "You can sit by me."

"Okay, okay," she said. "Let's go get Farrah and clean her up." She took a breath and shook her hand free from Chloe. "I'll get you a brush and you can groom her while I clean her hooves."

Judy picked bits of hay out of Walter's curly thick black hair. "Boy, oh boy. This is gonna take a while to get out. Holy moly, Batman." She glanced around the barn. "Hey, where's your brother?"

Walter gazed up at his mother. "He's with that other guy down by the pond learning how to fish for flies. Who wants to catch a fly besides a frog?"

John led Sweet Jaclyn into the barn. "You mean he's fly-fishing?"

"Yeah, that's what I said, and you're really not going to eat my dinner, are you?" Walter asked, his eyes dark rimmed with concern.

"Nah, I was just kidding, but I might eat your brother's dinner," John said jokingly. "I'm so hungry I could eat a horse."

Sweet Jaclyn snorted right on cue.

Walter's face drooped. "I've never eaten horse before. That sounds gross."

Judy ruffled his hair. "John was just kidding. If someone says they could *eat a horse* it just means that they are super-duper hungry."

Walter brushed off the knees of his jeans. "Okay, but you can't have my s'mores." He pointed at John.

"Do you guys need help?" I asked, taking in all of John.

"Nah, you're on vacation. Why don't you two take Mutt and Jeff up to the house and have a rest."

Walter grimaced. "Who are Mutt and Jeff?"

Judy held her son's hand and led him out of the barn. "John is being silly. They are cartoon characters from a long time ago. He means you and Chloe."

"Whatever. Mom, did you really not know I was hiding in the hay?"

"No clue, darling boy, no clue. You are sly as a fox." Judy's boots echoed on the plank floor as she left the barn.

Chloe followed then turned on a dime. "You two go ahead. I have to show Maggie something." She motioned for me to join her in the stall where she and Walter had been playing. "Check this out."

We inspected the box that housed her injured crow, Frankie. He fluttered beneath the chicken wire structure.

"Justin says he's about ready to fly," Chloe said. "Another day or two and we can let him go. Isn't that cool?"

"Sure is." I knelt down to get a better look at the bird, His black eyes glistened, and he didn't seem afraid when Chloe stuck her fingers through the holes to stroke his feathers. "I think Frankie likes you."

"I think so too," she whispered, touching my hand.

I wiped a dark smudge from her cheek. "I sure hope that was dirt." I smelled my finger.

"That's gross." Her brow furrowed with disgust. "I know enough to stay away from the horse and cow poop around here. Stinky."

My eyebrow shot up at her tone.

"Look, I can't even stand Bones' poop. What makes you think I'd get into the stuff around here?" She wrinkled her nose then pinched her nostrils shut. "Gross."

I wiped my hand on my jeans and took another gander at Frankie. "I hope he makes it," I said. Chloe stuck her pointer finger out and gestured for me to come closer to her. I leaned in and we were almost nose-to-nose. "What?"

"Last night when you were asleep, I got up and looked outside. There were millions of stars in the sky, so I made a wish that Frankie would be able to fly again."

"Oh, is that so?" I said. "I thought maybe you'd like to keep him as a pet."

Chloe scratched her head and scrunched up the bridge of her nose as if she hadn't pondered that idea yet. "As much as I'd like that, it wouldn't be fair to him. Sometimes you gotta let go, even if you don't want to. That's what my dad says."

The corner of my lip curled to the sky. "Your dad's a

pretty smart man." Strands of her messy dishwater-blonde hair tickled my cheek as I whispered in her ear.

"I think so, too, but let's not tell him. It's funner this way," she said with a twinkle in her eye.

"I think you said you'd help Ashley comb the horses." I smoothed hair away from her cheek and tucked it behind her ear. The side of her face was streaked with dust, and with the sun cascading through the window, shining all around her, she never looked so beautiful.

Chloe bumped the palm of her hand against her forehead. "Yeah, I do get a little sidetracked, don't I?"

"We all do. I've been sidetracked for years."

Chloe giggled. "See you later, Frankie," she said, putting the homemade birdcage up on the bale of hay.

A spotted brown cat slunk around the corner of the stall and rubbed against my shins. Its nose twitched, its back arched like a witch's cat on Halloween night, and its tail swayed like Vivaldi's metronome keeping tempo to a Baroque concerto. "Is this one of your little buddies?" The feline stared up at me and meowed with disgust. It sat at Chloe's feet. She was becoming the Pied Piper of barn cats.

"I haven't seen this one. I wonder how many cats live here?" She dug a treat out of her pocket, knelt beside the kitty, and stroked its head. She inspected its belly and smiled up at me. "Dad taught me how to tell if it's a girl or a boy. In case you're wondering, it's a girl. I like her spots. She looks like one of the painted horses."

"She sure does." My knees ached and begged for reprieve, so I knelt down beside Chloe. "Her spots remind me of cocoa."

"Yum." Chloe rubbed her stomach. Her brow wrinkled in thought then her lips curled upward. "And the word cocoa reminds me of that designer lady my mom likes. Remember when we went to Chicago and she bought that perfume in that gigantic store where all the ladies walked around wanting to spray us with stuff?"

"How could I forget her Coco Chanel perfume?" I said, scratching the kitty's head although I preferred my four-legged bulldog back home. Chloe was just the opposite. She loved all creatures regardless.

Chloe rolled her eyes at me. "Yeah, boy did we stink after we left that place." She took a deep breath. "This is the kind of smell I like." She stood up, reached down, and picked up the cat. "Her belly sure is fat and bumpy." She stroked the cat's head. "Let's name this one, Cocoa, the hot chocolate kind, 'cause I like that better than perfume." She held the cat out in my direction. "Here, you can hold her."

The cat squirmed and flailed as I tried to hold her close to me. Finally, her belly pressed up against mine.

John peeked into the barn.

"Meet Cocoa," I said.

"Cocoa like hot chocolate, not Mom's smelly perfume," Chloe clarified in a husky tone. "She's got a bumpy belly, Dad."

John reached out for the cat. He held it close to him and felt her stomach. "She's gonna have babies, Chloe."

Chloe's eyes lit up like fireworks on the fourth of July. She clapped her hands then scratched Cocoa's head. "You're gonna be a momma. When do you think the kittens will come, Daddy?"

"Not sure, half-pint, but we'll know when they get here. This momma cat likes the barn. She usually comes around about this time of day for nap." He pointed to the corner where Chloe and Walter played in the hay.

I crossed my arms in front of me and watched, amazed at Chloe's charisma. John set the cat down on the ground. Cocoa trotted to the corner of the stall and curled up in the sun. Within seconds, her eyes were closed and she was purring like a well-oiled machine.

Chloe sat on the bale of hay next to Frankie's cage. "Cocoa's gonna be a mom. That's so neat. Maybe that's why she's so tired."

"Probably." I thought back to the days I carried Bradley and the sleepless nights of colic and feedings. "Um, do you think Ashley is waiting for you?"

"Oh my gosh, I almost forgot. Good thing you're here, Maggie."

"Yeah, you're like a chicken with its head cut off," I said, exiting the stall.

"You sound like Glad. I sure do miss that woman." Chloe grabbed my hand and led me over to the horses being groomed by Ashley and Justin.

"Me, too," I said. "Maybe we should call her tonight."

Chapter 7

With a belly full of s'mores, I sat with my back against the heavy headboard with my eyes shut, reminiscing the day as I listened to Chloe talk to my mom on the phone. She lay on her bed, knee bent, one foot crossed over, and one hand behind her head.

Chloe told Mom all about the cats and Frankie, the injured crow. She told Mom about our dinner with Ashley, how Harry stared at her the whole time, and how he was being a dumb boy.

When I glanced over, Chloe's dishwater-blonde hair was fanned out around her head on her pillow. She giggled into the phone and told Mom she missed her. I missed her, too, but I knew she'd be there waiting for me when I got home.

"Yeah, she's right here, Glad. Just a sec." Chloe held the phone out in my direction.

I got off my bed and took it from her. "Hi, Mom," I said. "How are you? Is Bones doing okay? He dug a hole in the backyard. Figures."

Chloe stretched out on her side with her hands tucked under her head. Her bright eyes faded like the distant sun. Her eyelids fluttered, and I hoped she'd dream about her new friend, Cocoa.

"Yes, Mom. We'll call again. Give Bones a hug and a kiss for me."

"For me, too," Chloe said with a big yawn.

I clicked off the hand held receiver, set it on the nightstand, and gazed over at Chloe. The lack of service to my cell phone was not a hardship. In fact, it was kind of nice not receiving text, updates, and messages from the carrier about usage or upcoming deals. "You about ready to turn off the light?" I asked.

"Yeah, I'm tired." Chloe yawned again then tugged the sheet up to her chin. Her eyes flitted beneath her eyelids as if they were searching for the perfect dream. "I'm glad we called Glad." Chloe kicked at the covers. "I sure do love that lady. You are so lucky to have a mom like that." She scrunched up into a fetal position and stopped fidgeting.

"Definitely," I said, shutting off the lamp.

Dusky hues filtered between the slats of the shades. I tiptoed over to Chloe's bed to tuck her in. Brook nagged at the back of my mind. I smoothed Chloe's hair back from her face, kissed my pointer finger, and then touched her freckled cheek.

I glanced toward the door as the knob turned. Walter's hair preceded his entry. I smiled at him then motioned for him to come in. He crept over to the bed, and in the tiniest of whispers, said goodnight and kissed Chloe on the cheek.

She half-smiled. "Goodnight, see you in the morning. I'm sure we haven't found all the cats."

Walter grinned, his baby teeth perfectly straight with a tiny gap between his top incisors. He motioned for me to follow him into the hallway, so I did. I latched the door behind me, trying to avoid a disturbance. His brown eyes twinkled in the dim light.

"I like your Spiderman pajamas."

He held out his arms and showed me the fabric webbing below his armpits. "Thanks." He tapped his chin with his pointer finger. "I was supposed to tell you something, but now I can't remember." His dark curls bounced up and down as he scratched his head.

"It's okay. I'll just go ask your mom."

John came up the stairs, treading lightly in his socks.

"Okay," Walter said, heading back to his room. "Moms and Dads shouldn't ask us kids to remember too much stuff. Don't they know we have other things on our mind?" he said, shaking his curly mop-top.

John's smile was the perfect ending to the perfect day.

"I'd shoot you a text, but that doesn't always work here. Thought you might like to come down and have a beer with me."

"Sounds good. Don't know how much longer I'll last though. I'm pretty tired."

John leaned closer to me. "I just think you're pretty." He kissed the side of my head. "Let me check on Chloe and I'll meet you in the kitchen."

"See you in a few." Ignoring the fact that his lips were just on my right temple, I pretended like it was everyday business to share such pleasantries. Poking my head into Judy's room, Harry was already asleep, and Walter was curled up next to Judy like a sleeping cat holding a comic book between its paws. Judy peered over the rim of her glasses.

I shook my head apologetically. "Walter couldn't remember the message so I'm here in person. Didn't mean to bug you."

Judy lowered her book and held the page with her finger. "I just wanted you to know that I'm in for the night. I'm beat. We'll see you guys in the morning."

"Sleep tight." I closed the door then padded down the stairs carefully as not to awaken sleeping children. It'd been quite a day with horseback riding, meeting the animals, and learning to fly-fish. I held the thick pine banister and gazed around the great room with its high ceilings, heavy furniture, and Montana charm.

"It wasn't always like this," John whispered in my ear. "The house I grew up in is down the way. Trout lives there now. Dad built this a few years back when he started making money. It's not as big as some of the other places around here, but he's proud of it. We all are."

John stepped down from the last stair and stood next to me.

"It's beautiful. He's worked hard." I thought about my job back home and couldn't correlate the two worlds if I tried.

John took my hand and led me to the kitchen.

"How'd the ranch get its name?" I asked, leaning against the counter.

John smiled. "Dad chose the name. Thought the number 617 might make my mom love it even more." He popped the top of a Beltian White and handed it to me. "Try this. I think you'll like it."

"So what's 617 stand for?" I pictured the sign hanging from the timbers that marked the drive when we pulled in. 617 was painted in black block numbers just above the word ranch that was written in matching capital letters.

"They were married on June seventeenth."

"The 617 Ranch," I said, liking how it sounded. "I thought maybe it was the number of cattle they had or the number of children your mom wanted to get even with your dad at some point in this venture." I sipped at my beer.

John popped the top to his beer and took a healthy swig. "How about we get a couple more of these and go sit by the fire? I think it's still going. Trout and Dad were out there last time I checked."

"I should get my jacket." I set my beer on the counter.

"There's an extra flannel hanging by the back door." John opened the fridge and placed four cans of beer in a fabric cooler on the counter. "Need chocolate?"

Picking up my beer, I took a long drink. "Good idea," I said, packing leftover Hersey Bars in with the beer.

The mudroom smelled like leather and hay. I slid on my

boots, and John helped me into a flannel jacket that hung on a silver hook.

"Thanks," I said. His closeness stirred my feelings like a poker to glowing embers. The green plaid collar brushed against my cheek. It smelled like John and I liked having his scent wrapped around me.

John wiggled into his boots, put on his jacket, and held the door for me. I stepped outside and stared into the sky. "Don't see this many stars in Grosse Pointe," he said beneath his breath. "Not sure why I ever left this place. Young and stupid I suppose. Guess I learned the hard way about following my own dreams."

"We all do." Beckett scratched at the corner of my mind. "When you're young, it's easy to get lost."

White lights twinkled overhead in the big sky that reached down around us. We were wrapped in a blanket of constellations. John took my hand in his. Holding tight, I searched the heavens for an answer written in the stars.

"I've never seen anything like this," I said. "There are stars in-between the stars. There must be a bazillion of them. Think about how many wishes that could be."

"You sound like Chloe," he said, taking the cooler from me. "Watch your step." He flashed a light at my feet. "I'm not ashamed to admit . . . I make a wish every night." His eyes flickered just as brightly as the stars overhead.

Emotion singed the edges of my heart. "Let's go see about that fire."

"That's just like you."

"What?" The heels of my boots clicked as I meandered along the wooden planked walkway that led away from the house, past the creek, and to the fire pit.

"You think if you avoid something that makes you uncomfortable, it'll just go away." John's light ricocheted from left to right with his stride.

"No, I don't," I said, glancing over to him, his eyes intense in the dark night. I sipped my beer and raked my hand through my messy waves.

"Yes, you do. It took you forever to even talk about the night we slept together."

My beer went down the wrong way, causing me to hack. I choked back the erupting coughing fit while John patted me on the back.

"Breathe. You'll be okay, Maggie."

I took a sip of my beer, swallowed, and then cleared my throat. When I recomposed myself, I stood nose-to-nose with John. "Why do you do that?" I asked with conviction, sure that he understood his perfect timing to pick on me. His smug expression irritated me even more. His eyes held a secret, one that I'd only find out with time, or maybe never at all. "Seriously?" I drew my jacket shut to block the chill wafting through the night air.

"It's a gift," he answered with a tilt of his head.

I shook my head at him. "I'm not the only one that sounds like Chloe tonight. "Good grief."

"Good grief is right." John paused. "It's not a bad thing that we grew close. It's not a bad thing that just maybe we have something that could go somewhere. What's so bad about investigating our feelings, anyway?" He finished his beer and stuffed the empty can into the cooler.

"I know what you're thinking," I said.

"I bet you don't." He inched closer, his gaze fixated on mine.

He was right. I didn't, but I wasn't going to let him win. I pinched my mouth shut. *Damn you.* John's lips grazed my cheek, his breath hot on my neck like his fiery touch had been so many nights ago. I closed my eyes and clenched my fist. The almost empty beer can crinkled with the pressure.

"Has it whispered to you yet?" he asked. "Because once it has burrowed its silent voice into your heart, there's no love greater than the one hidden in the mountains under the fields of wildflowers. And if you find a rosebush, it's extra special. The treasure just may be golden."

With a deep breath, I swallowed his words. What called to me was more than a whisper. I held his wicked stare.

"Back in the day, it was said that miners used to plant a rosebush close to the place where they struck gold. When I'm out riding, I hunt for them, but I know where my treasure really lies." John turned off the flashlight.

My voice quivered as I spoke. "That's the thing. You are so sure and I hear other callings."

"They aren't callings, Maggie, they're unfinished tasks that you feel obligated to complete."

His hand grazed mine. His warm touch ignited veins of truth. "I suppose that makes me weak," I said.

John wrapped his fingers around my hand. "No. That makes you human."

I squeezed his hand.

"You'll find the way," he said.

I teetered on the balls of my feet. My cheek brushed against his stubbly chin. "I wish I was as sure as you are."

Moonlight reflected in his green eyes. Huge clouds drifted in the night sky, his face lit by more than Mother Nature.

"A little faith goes a long way." His words were drawn out, his tone deep and seductive.

This John McIntyre was different from the one who lived next door to me back in Grosse Pointe, and I wasn't so sure how long I could beat him away, no matter the size, nor the number of invisible sticks I possessed.

Chapter 8

Winston and Trout excused themselves when the fire died down. It'd been an evening of ranching stories and stories about John's childhood. The crackling flames licked the Montana air and sprinkled glowing ashes over the ground as the wood popped and burned.

"You ready to head back?" John asked as Winston and Trout headed toward Trout's house. John's gaze followed the two men as they walked in stride, conversing about running the horses at the crack of dawn.

"Yeah, my eyelids are getting kind of heavy." As much as I wanted to stay up with John, my body wouldn't allow me. The porch light glowed in the distance. "If you want to go with your dad, I can find my way back." I pushed myself out of the Adirondack chair that anchored me. John's proximity made my heart beat faster in the darkness, making the night air alive with prospect. I dropped my empty beer can into the cooler, and then peered to the heavens, found a faint star, and contemplated making a wish. Unsure of what to wish for, I hesitated. Tired of hesitating, I mulled over how much of life I'd missed in those moments of introspection.

John wrapped his arm around my shoulder. "What did you wish for?" He turned on the flashlight and we meandered toward the house, our boot heels clicking against the wooden walkway, echoing in the night.

"First of all, you're not supposed to tell your wish or it doesn't come true. Second of all, I couldn't decide. I didn't quite get that far."

John stopped in his tracks and switched off his flashlight.

"Close your eyes."

I narrowed my gaze as I peered over to him. "Why?"

"Because that's where you start. Just close your eyes."

My legs wobbled as the darkness beneath my eyelids felt ominous compared to the Montana night sky. I took a deep breath, trying to steady myself, trying to loosen the threads that held me tight against the breast of the unknown like that of a fly upon a spider's web.

"Think about the stars. Picture the sky above you," John said.

It was hard not to think about his seductive voice. What guy would hold a woman beneath a blanket of stars and teach her how to make a wish?

"Focus, Maggie."

I peeked at him from under my eyelashes.

He smiled. "I know it's hard, but just focus. Don't tell me what you see, but think about the first thing that pops into your mind. Picture it in the stars and make your wish."

Pinpricks of light appeared behind my eyelids and I felt a grin pass over my lips. I settled into John's body and found my balance. Taking a deep breath, I opened my eyes and made a wish.

John whispered into the darkness, "You can make a thousand wishes in a thousand nights. One of them is bound to come true."

"I suppose you're right about that."

John faced me. "My mom used to say that to me when I was a boy."

A chill ran down my spine as the words left his lips and I felt her presence like wispy strands of hair that stroke your face in the summer breeze. "Tell me her name again."

"Ida May." The sorrow behind his eyes cut deep. "Her name was Ida May."

Touching his cheek, I couldn't ignore the feeling that she

drifted through the Montana sky like the scent of pine and leather that lulled me. "She's with you. You know that, right?"

John wrapped his fingers around my hand, the one that caressed his cheek. "Montana may have whispered to my dad, but she was the one that drew me back home. This is the place I feel closest to her."

"I know." I thought about Mom, back home. I thought about how Chloe said I was lucky to have Glad, and she was right. I couldn't imagine my life without her. I couldn't imagine not having her by my side for major milestones and monumental heartbreaks. She'd been my beacon, but my heart ached for John's world.

"She would have liked you, Maggie. I think you would've made each other laugh, mostly at me, but nonetheless, she would have liked you."

"I would've liked to have known her." I squeezed John's hand.

"Yeah, I think my mom and your mom could have hatched some pretty good plots."

My mouth curled toward the heavens. Another chill danced across the nape of my neck. "Yeah, I bet you're right."

John's smile disappeared. His expression grew serious, and for the first time, I wasn't afraid. He wrapped his arms around me, our gazes focused upon the other, our breathing in sync. His words were seductive and warm. "See, it doesn't hurt so far, does it?"

I shook my head *no,* then John kissed my forehead. Feeling unsure of my footing, I rested my hands on his shoulders to steady myself. I stood on the balls of my feet, my boot heels not touching the wooden walkway as John held me close.

"It's all about balance, Maggie."

The corners of his lips rose. John cradled my face in his hands as his soft lips mingled with mine. Sweet "somethings" passed between us. His hands moved from my face to the nape of my neck, and then down to the small of my back. Our kiss lasted until my feet were planted back on the ground.

"We'd better go in. The morning will be here before you know it and kids show no mercy," John said.

We strolled hand-in-hand back to the house.

I crept into the bedroom trying not to wake Chloe. She had one leg out of the covers and she held Voodoo close to her chest as she slept. She mumbled something in her sleep as I folded the covers back on my bed. The clock shone in the dark and I closed my eyes. My usual list of prayers scrolled through my head, asking Him to show me the way, and then I silently said "The Lord's Prayer" as I pictured the Montana stars sparkling overhead.

Chloe mumbled something in her sleep again. Ignoring her, I rolled over. She was rearranging the covers, her slurred speech inaudible. She cleared her throat and said my name. I froze when she said my name again.

Reluctant to answer, I finally answered, "Yeah?"

"It's okay if you like my dad."

"Okay." I closed my eyes deliberating unlikely scenarios.

"Maggie?" Chloe said.

"Yeah," I answered, not knowing if she was sleep talking.

"If you want to kiss him, you can," she said in her slow, sleepy speech.

Hoping she wouldn't remember this conversation in the morning, I concentrated on moon shadows drifting across the ceiling. I fluffed my pillow before shutting my eyes.

"Maybe you can be my mom."

My eyes popped open and there it was, hanging in the air between us. *Be her mom*, what? I was Maggie Abernathy, annoying neighbor lady, woman of indecision, and queen of treats when thwarted. My mouth ran dry and I wiped my sweaty palms on the sheet. Nowhere in my plan did I foresee being a mother to someone else's child, let alone an eight-year-old. Bradley was my charge and he was happily in Boston getting over the trauma that Beckett and I caused throughout his childhood. I thought about sending him a text and explaining my offer of reimbursement should he need a therapist.

Voodoo fell from Chloe's bed with a thud, but she held tight to his leash. This time, when John and I had held each other, Chloe hadn't entered my mind. It was about him and me. Chloe'd just thrown me a curveball and I didn't know which way to duck. "Crap," I said under my breath.

"I heard that. You shouldn't swear," Chloe said. She exhaled, yanked Voodoo up from the floor by his purple cord, turned her back on me, and then curled up like a purring, barn cat.

I asked God to please not let her remember our sleepy conversation in the morning. Arranging my pillow, I assumed the fetal position and closed my eyes. John's kiss was fresh on my lips. Chloe's words even fresher. She was like a mute button on the remote control. She rendered me speechless.

Shutting my eyes, I was pretty sure sleep wouldn't be my friend, so I pictured the stars in the sky like John told me to. I focused hard until I thought they were all present. John's mom would have loved Chloe to pieces, just as I did, just as my mom did, but probably more. It was easy for me to believe that the love in this family ran deeper than veins of Montana gold.

Chapter 9

Rubbing sleep from my eyes, I wondered what time it was. The sheets rumpled beneath me as I rolled over and noticed Chloe wasn't in her bed. Craning my neck to read the clock on the nightstand, I saw it was past nine o'clock. Eleven o'clock Michigan time. Unexpectedly, I'd slept through the night . . . a feat I hadn't accomplished in months. I stretched out, my legs preparing for sharp cramps in my calves, something new my aging body did on a regular basis now that I was in menopause thanks to the cancer medication. When the cramps didn't come, I stretched my arms over my head then cupped my hands behind my head and stared at the ceiling.

There were no voices in the hallway. No Walter and Harry jibing at each other. No sweet Judy shushing them and no Chloe to jar me into reality. I touched my left temple. I couldn't feel the scar any more from bumping heads with her last summer. Chloe hadn't quoted Cesar, The Dog Whisperer, since my arrival, but then again, Bones wasn't here. He was back home, probably eating table scraps and sleeping on the bed. Chloe didn't have classmates picking on her either. Her content demeanor trumped rolling tumbleweeds that left her unsettled.

The only voices I heard were the voices in my memory from last night. I tried to sort out what really happened, but found myself in that state of mind that's foggy like the early morning, and I wasn't really sure what transpired. Rubbing my eyes, the veil lifted, leaving me capable of seeing the landscape hidden beneath mystical haze. I searched the corners of my mind, trying to remember my dreams, but nothing surfaced. I'd been here two nights and slept for two nights without having one of my Stephen King dreams, as I referred to them.

There was a knock at the door. "Come in," I said, hoisting myself up so I could rest my back against the hefty wooden headboard.

Chloe peeked in. "Are you awake?"

"I guess so. Is Judy still asleep?" I asked as Chloe entered the room with a tray of food.

"No, everyone is up, except you. I thought you might need some food. Dad is cleaning up the kitchen." Chloe stepped carefully toward me, a breakfast tray in hand. The juice teetered and sloshed over the edge of the glass. She stopped in her tracks and worry creased at the corners of her mouth. "Walter's mom carried this up the stairs and I made it this far. Maybe you should take it from here."

I kicked off the covers, got up, and took the morning's offerings from her. "This is really nice, but you guys could have gotten me up."

Chloe sat on the bed next to me. "You were sawing logs as my grandpa says."

"I guess I was pretty tired."

"That's what you get for staying up late with J.P."

She sounded more like a girlfriend at a slumber party than an eight-year-old with missing teeth when she smiled. I inspected the plate.

"Don't worry, Trout helped make the eggs, Dad made the bacon, and Walter's mom helped with the toast."

"Did you help?" I asked.

"Yeah, I stayed out of the way." Chloe giggled. "Me, Harry, and Walter watched cartoons while the grown-ups cooked."

Chloe gestured for me to eat. "Go ahead, you deserve a break."

Balancing the tray on my legs, I scooted closer to the headboard. I nibbled at a slice of bacon as Chloe sat Indian style at the foot of my bed. My stomach rumbled. Suddenly, I was painfully aware that she was inspecting me. The muscles in my belly pinched as I bit into the toast.

"Try the huckleberry jam. It's delish." She pointed to the jar of preserves next to my plate.

Chloe smiled, her eyes wild with curiosity.

After smearing jam on my toast, I gobbled up the rest of my breakfast. "There. All done." I put the tray in front of her and got out of bed. Her stare followed me as I moved through the room to gather my clothes for the day. My nerves prickled. I bent over to retrieve my socks next to the bed and when I glanced up, she was standing right beside me grinning. When I turned my head to see her better, my hair fell across my face. Chloe tucked it behind my ear. Her proximity unraveled the threads of uncertainty I'd neatly stored away deep inside myself, the way Mom stored her yarn in her knitting bag, smashed and pushed to the bottom.

"What?" I closed my eyes and swallowed when I heard my harsh tone.

"Sorry. I didn't mean to be in your space." A slight frown nipped at the corners of Chloe's innocent pink lips.

"So, we might as well get this out in the open if we're going to have any sort of day, today."

Chloe's brow furrowed as I spoke.

Prepared to talk about her dad and me, I sat at the edge of the bed searching for words.

"I'm not sure what you mean, but can I tell you my news first?" she asked.

"Sure. Go for it."

"I just wanted to tell you that Cocoa had her kittens. That's why the house is so quiet. Harry and Walter are in the barn now. I only brought up breakfast so you could get moving a little quicker and get out there to see them."

I felt like a schmuck. "Oh."

Chloe's eyes twitched as she investigated the lines on my forehead. She leaned closer to scrutinize my face. "I know those lines. What are you worried about?" she asked. "You get them every time Bones goes near the garden or runs loose on the front yard." Stray strands of blonde hair brushed against Chloe's cheeks as she tilted her head.

"Nothing, just a little upset that I missed the morning festivities." A shred of relief passed over me when I realized I wouldn't have to explain anything to Chloe about her father and me. I hadn't even fathomed that John and I might form an alliance, and a romantic one at that. A to-do list in Michigan flashed before me. Finish my career was at the top. Being an Abernathy meant I was expected to finish what I started. "Why don't I get cleaned up and I'll meet you in the barn? I promise I won't be long."

The seam of Chloe's lips curled toward the ceiling. She touched the ends of my hair as her eyes searched my face. "I like how you look when you get up."

My cheeks flushed with embarrassment, thinking I'd look much better after a hairbrush and a skosh of makeup to cover the imperfections.

"I can see your freckles. They look like mine."

I touched Chloe's nose with my pointer finger. "I suppose they do."

She played dot-to-dot on my forehead. "I think we have more in common than you think, even if you're older. Maybe we were sisters in another life."

I narrowed my eyes as our gazes connected.

"I know what you're thinking," Chloe said.

"You do? I think your dad and I played *this* game last night." I wasn't so sure about playing again.

Chloe giggled. "My mom explained it to me once when I heard her talking with her friend on the phone. She thinks

I don't get grown-up talk, but a lot of times I think I do. It's a gift," she boasted as she hooked her thumbs in her back pockets.

"So what else do we have in common?" Somehow Chloe had stifled my angst and sucked me back in with her precocious charm.

"Well, we both love Glad. We both like jeans and T-shirts." Chloe scratched her head. "We both know my mom is a little kooky, but she's still my mom." She paused and fingered the heart on her Tiffany necklace Brook had given her. Chloe's eyes rolled to the ceiling in thought and she tapped her lips with her finger. "We both love Bones. Um—" She took a deep breath. "We both love my dad, s'mores, and a good book."

Her words charmingly innocent, Chloe patted my shoulder. "I could go on and on, but I'd really like to show you those kittens. They looked kind of gross at first, but now that they're cleaned up, they're really cute. Their eyes are still closed." She stopped and the lines in her brow deepened. "Do you think my eyes were closed when I was born?"

I shook my head. "No, I think your eyes were wide open ready to see the world." And she was seeing the world through her own eyes unaware of the precise interpretation. Part of me missed being eight-years-old. Maybe I'd never really experienced the age of eight. Being born a serious soul, ready for business had its consequences.

Chloe had thrown "it" out there in a laundry list of comparison and not batted an eye once or smirked like an audacious teenager. She was right. We had a lot in common.

Chloe stood up and opened the dresser drawer, and then pulled out one of my white T-shirts. "It matches mine. I'd kind of like to be like you today, if that's okay."

I took the tee from her with a smile. "That's definitely okay. Let me get cleaned up and I'll be down."

"I hate to be a pest, but I don't trust myself with that tray." Chloe pointed to the dirty breakfast dishes. "Can you carry that down to the kitchen?" She scrunched the bridge of her nose and her shoulders.

"No worries. I'll get it."

"Thanks, you're the best." Chloe faced the door then stopped to stare at me over her right shoulder. "Make sure you wear your boots. Oh, and the girls are fly-fishing today."

John rinsed morning plates smudged with sticky jam at the kitchen sink. I admired the hanging rack of pots and pans over the butcher block island.

"Thanks for the breakfast," I said, setting the tray on the counter. "I can finish up in here if you want."

"You're a bit of a sleepyhead this morning." The dishes clanked together as John set them on the counter. He turned off the water then leaned against the counter.

His gaze washed over me. "What?" I asked, crossing my arms in front of me.

"You look like you belong," he said. "You've got the jeans, the boots, the hat, the belt buckle, and the attitude of a rancher."

I smiled. "I'm not sure I've ever belonged anywhere." Truth was I only knew Grosse Pointe, hadn't really lived anywhere else, and I always went back to it, because that's where my family was.

"I think we all feel that way from time to time," John said, arranging the dishes in the dishwasher. "You know when you're on the highway cruising along, then all of a sudden panic strikes because you've lost track of the mile markers and you're certain you've lost your way. Life is a highway. Exits come and exits go, but you really don't know you're home until you reach your destination, which most likely will turn into just a pit stop because you've got other places to be."

"Yeah, that decision to stay on or get off can be a bitch."

John raised his eyebrows at me.

"What?"

"We should take that sass out to barn and see those kittens Chloe's gonna want to keep."

"Thought you'd be with Winston today."

"Nope. He has Trout and Justin. I said I'd stay here to help with the kids. Besides, we never got around to seeing those cattle yesterday. I'll drive you out there later."

"I'd like that," I told him.

John closed the dishwasher and wiped down the counter. "Chloe says the girls are fly-fishing today."

"Yup. Pretend you're cracking that whip from ten to two, and you'll do just fine." John flicked his wrist in midair pretending he was casting.

"Yeah, okay. We'll see about that."

John stepped closer to me, and I tucked my hands in my jean pockets.

"Have a little faith, Maggie."

The hair stood up on the nape of my neck. "And a lot of balance."

"And a little bit of balance." He tucked his fingertips into his back pockets.

His suddenly serious nature rattled me. "What is it?"

"I've had an offer on the house."

"That's good, right?" *Damn it.*

"Yeah, but it makes this all a bit more real," he said.

"Not sure I understand what you're getting at." I shifted my weight and crossed one leg over the other as I leaned against the counter.

"Damn it, Maggie, how hard are you going to make me work?"

I held my breath, thinking that we'd never actually be having this conversation. John's tone was gruff and impatient. It hurt to even think that we'd go our separate ways. And yeah, if he wanted something more from me than what we had, he was going to have to lay it on the line. "You're going to have to be a bit more specific." I narrowed my gaze and averted my stare out the kitchen window. The kids knelt beside the stream, plucking rocks from the cool mountain water. Chloe's hair fell around her shoulders as she tilted her head back to check the horizon. I wondered what she was searching for.

"Maggie, I think you know what I'm asking you. Is there any way you can be a part of our lives here, too? I want to be with you."

My insides quivered. John's emerald gaze focused on me.

"I'm not sure how. Montana is a hell of a long way from Michigan. Not to mention, I really want to finish my career."

John's shoulders slumped as he stuffed his hands deeper into his jean pockets. We'd had this discussion before. What didn't he understand?

"Long-distant relationships never work out," I said, not sure I believed my own words. His stare questioned my line of bullshit.

John faced the window, his profile almost identical to his daughter's. I touched his forearm.

His eyes filled with hurt as he turned in my direction. "Please, Maggie. I think we belong together. I think you'd be happy here 'cause you sure as hell aren't happy living in your stone house working like a dog day in and day out. Dreams change." His voice trailed off.

Stepping closer to him, I took off my Stetson, touched his cheek, and then kissed his lips hunting for certainty. *It* was there. I just didn't know how to harness it, how to admit I needed him, how to say goodbye to the place I knew as home. This was one of those moments when I wanted to veer off the highway of life, but was petrified of crashing. "I think I love you," I whispered.

John's fingers caressed my cheek, our connection held strong and fierce.

"I have to come back to Michigan to finalize the paperwork and clean out the house," John said. "I've given official notice to my partners. I've actually spoken to the guy who runs the local clinic. I can practice here if I want and work with my dad."

"Sounds like you'll have the best of both worlds. Does Chloe know yet?"

"No." His eyes dimmed. "Sorry, I was going tell you when I came back to Grosse Pointe, but it's been eating at me. I didn't want to ruin your trip."

Trying to wash away the lump at the back of my throat, I swallowed. "It's okay. It was bound to happen sooner or later, and to be perfectly honest, it'll make the time we have left sweeter. I'm glad you told me."

"You lie," John said.

The corner of my mouth curled up. My eyes met his. "Yeah, you're right. I was just trying to make you feel better."

"Well, it didn't work. Your eyes give you away, along with those creases in your forehead."

I rubbed my forehead as Chloe's words replayed in my mind. "Damn it. Maybe we should quit standing around here feeling sorry for ourselves and go see those kittens."

"Maggie, you don't have to pretend." John's touch was warm.

"Unfortunately, that's one thing I'm pretty good at. I did it for over twenty years with Beckett. Practice makes perfect." Sarcasm trickled from my tongue in eloquent fashion.

John held my hand. "I've spent a lot of my life pretending, too."

My cheeks went hot and my eyes welled. I begged myself not to cry. This was not the time, nor the place.

John sighed. His burly chest heaved with hope.

Chloe skipped into the kitchen with a handful of pebbles. I turned my back to her so she couldn't see my eyes and put my Stetson back on. John lifted her up and sat her on the counter.

"Hi, Dad, can I have something to put my rocks in?"

"Sure, peanut." John searched under the counter in a cupboard overflowing with plastic containers. "Here, this looks just about right size. Do Walter and Harry need one, too?"

"Yup."

I inhaled, held my breath, and then counted to ten, trying to find my courage. Forcing a smile, I faced Chloe. "I think I'm ready to see those kittens," I said happily, but my heart ached when I saw the expression on John's face. How was I going to leave him behind without regretting what just might be the most monumental mistake of my life, even bigger than marrying Beckett?

Chapter 10

Cocoa and her kittens nestled in the hay, in the exact spot where she'd curled up yesterday. The morning sun peeked into the barn, making Chloe's green eyes sparkle. She knelt beside the family of cats, her hands on her knees with her feet firmly planted and her balance impeccable. She lowered her chin so it touched her knees. "Look at them," she whispered.

Emotion flooded the air, and a wave of tears escaped from the corners of my eyes. Lowering my gaze, I hoped my cowboy hat would disguise the sudden rush of foolishness. I swiped at the corner of my left eye then tried to smile as John's stare caught my attention. I knelt down to count the tiny bodies woven together like one of Mom's hats she made for the babies at the hospital. Pink noses dotted the pelts of gray, white, burnt sienna, black, and tan. They suckled at their mother's tummy while she dozed, not minding the spectators.

"How many are there, Chloe?" I asked, not wanting to disturb the bond.

Chloe tilted her head in my direction, her gaze sent chills down my spine, and another unexpected wave of emotion through me. My level of sensitivity rattled my nerves. This unusual reaction made me wonder if my inner core of strength that I prided myself on was deteriorating. Chloe possessed a wholesomeness that was crushing me. Something I was unprepared for.

"Six, I think." She peered up to her dad.

He nodded. "Pretty exciting stuff," he said. "Maybe we should let them have some time."

Walter rested his hand on my shoulder then leaned over for a better look. "Wow," he said. "I've never seen anything like that. They're so tiny and squirmy. Was I like that when I was a baby?"

Judy knelt beside me. "Yup, pretty much," she said, winking at Harry who was leaning against the wall with his arms crossed over his chest, trying to fit in with John, Justin, Winston, and Trout. He was a man trapped in a boy's body.

"Was Bradley wiggly?" Chloe asked.

I smirked. "Yeah, really wiggly, but I held him tight."

Walter leaned closer, his cheek skimming mine like a smooth stone skipping across the lake back home. Chloe's smile penetrated my guarded heart. Walter's touch imbedded her passion for life deep below my surface in that magical way that children sometimes do. All without saying a word. Soft patches of tingles bubbled to my surface, reminding me that I was once a child, too.

John rested his hand on my shoulder, sending me his own message. We were no different than the helpless kittens matted together fighting for that one thing to fill us up and keep us warm. I pondered the scene around me as if I were studying the world through the viewfinder of my camera. Frame-by-frame, images linked to tell a story, a story that I desperately wanted to finish, but feared the ending. The smell of leather, horses, and hay drifted past. The barn had become a sanctuary.

Walter leaned against his mom and I stood up next to John, our elbows touching. I pursed my lips as his eyes beamed with prospect. I glanced back at Chloe who had mumbled in her sleep, *"Maybe you could be my mom."* A familiar pang nipped at the seams of my heart.

Wrapping my arms around my middle, I pressed my fingers into my flesh. "Maybe we should leave them alone."

Harry smirked at me like a proud papa. Judy held Walter's hand and led him out of the stall. John and I lingered a moment longer, our eyes focused on Chloe still crouched in awe, admiring the miracle of life.

"She's a good momma," Chloe said, cocking her head to the side and adjusting her cowboy hat. She stood, shook out her legs, sauntered over to us, and took John's hand.

She held my hand, too then led us out of the stall. John glanced down, fine creases at the corners of his eyes conveyed the gentleness in his heart. I held tight, knowing I was like the tail, the end of a game I used to play on the frozen Michigan waters with my childhood friends called Crack the Whip. Nothing good could come from letting go.

Harry's fifth-grade impatience seeped through his calm exterior. "Can we fish now?" His voice cracked.

Chloe held tight and squinted into the sun. The vast Montana sky washed over us. We each grabbed a pole from the bunch lined up against the fence. The image of Cocoa hovering over her babies gave me goose bumps.

John scuffled back into the barn to get the box of flies, a bucket, and a towel. "Somebody better catch some fish today. So far my luck hasn't been so good."

John was talking about me and Judy's expression confirmed it. Sliding my sunglasses up to the bridge of my nose, I hid behind the dark lenses and strolled behind Chloe and the boys, pretending to listen to their banter. John caught up to them and Judy trailed in-between. I felt like that one lonely kitten unable to find her place in the brood. John stood with the kids on the bank of the pond, showing them how to maneuver the rod. Inspecting his every move, his fluid movement drew me in. Chloe and Walter stayed close to John, but Harry went to the far side of the water and Judy followed. I sat in an Adirondack chair in the shade, watching the brown mare with white socks and her foal meander across the field.

Chloe's voice echoed in the still Montana air. "She's coming this way."

John cast his line into the pond. He and Chloe chatted as they swung their poles back and forth, and back and forth. Chloe hooked her fly on John's hat. He dislodged the non-barbed hook and handed it back to her with ease. "Come on over, neighbor lady. Let's see what you can do."

I marveled at his casual tone. The conversation in the kitchen still stuck in my craw. Lowering my sunglasses, I got up from my chair. With pole in hand, I crinkled my nose, like Chloe did when she was unsure, and joined them.

"Show me again what I'm supposed to do." I held the pole out. It seemed unusually long and the line was thick. The tiny threaded fly tickled my finger as I unhooked it from the reel. John's muscles flexed in the golden glow from the sky as he reeled in his line.

"Watch. Ten and two, ten and two," he chanted as he swung the rod with his right hand and letting out more line with his left. His line dropped onto the surface of the calm water. "Let it sit for a few seconds then tug then repeat."

Chloe swung her rod and hooked the grass. She bent down to get the fly. "Dang it. I'm not ever going to get this."

Swinging my pole from ten and two, I focused on the fly twittering back and forth while my eyes struggled to keep up with the sway of the line. Before I knew it, John's arms were around me, guiding my movements. I extended the line then let it fall into the water. I could feel my tongue between my lips like a child struggling to reach that bag of cookies on the top shelf. John's touch was more enticing than the summer sun, undeniably wanting more than I could give. I stepped away from him. "I don't want to get you," I said, reeling in my line, ready to cast again.

"You sure you haven't done this before?" John asked.

I peered over at him, knowing that fleeting bursts of flirtations didn't equate to lifelong relationships.

He smirked.

I smirked back as Chloe's fly hooked the back of his shirt.

"Oh brother." Chloe sighed. "Sorry, Dad."

Gray skies floated overhead, and dense clouds drifted to the east. I took off my sunglasses and hooked them to the collar of my white T-shirt that matched Chloe's. Drops of water fell like a leaky faucet. Chloe set her fishing rod on the ground. Her Stetson came lose when she tilted her head back, checking the sky. It hung from the chum hooked to the back of her shirt collar. She stuck out her tongue like she was catching snowflakes. Lost in her innocence, I studied the fly at the end of my line as I cast it over the pond's surface. A fish flopped out of the water when John jerked his pole. He reeled it in, and then dislodged the hook from the fish's mouth as I watched from the corner of my eye as not to miss my own nibble. Harry let out a holler as he too wrestled with his own catch.

John released the fish into the bucket. "We just might be having trout for dinner," he said. "Looks like it's your turn, neighbor lady."

Harry trotted around the pond, holding his fish in one hand and his pole in the other. Judy's line flew across the pond and landed with the plunking raindrops. Walter knelt beside the bucket trying to pet the fish.

Hoping to get a bite, I tugged at my line. The lazy drips from above doubled in size. John came closer to where I stood. "Um, are we going to get soaked?" I peered into the horizon that grew dark.

John pondered the skies. "Don't know. You afraid of a little rain?"

I scowled at him. "No." Though his smirk irritated me, I still found it humorous.

"Can't have smooth sailing until you go through a few rough patches," he said.

I rolled my eyes at him. My T-shirt stuck to my shoulders with the wetness. Chloe put on her Stetson and ran toward the ancient shade tree. The foal ran after her in what she must have thought was a game of chase. "Oh, my gosh," I said, feeling light-hearted.

"Yeah, that's Sunnyside Up. She's like that about this time of day." John rested his pole on the ground and cupped his hands around his mouth. "Chloe, Sunny's right behind you. Head's up!"

Sunny's mom sauntered with her muzzle close to the ground nibbling as she neared the tree, the rain dripping from her withers. Chloe stood with her back against the tree trunk, the foliage her shelter while John and I weathered out the spurts of drizzle. I reeled in my line. "I reckon there's no fish in my future."

John's dimples appeared. "Not so sure about that. There's one standing right beside you." He wiped the drops of water from the rim of my cowboy hat. "Why don't you go stand with Chloe? It'll stop soon." He pointed to the west where light peeked through the clouds.

Judy jogged around the pond and stood with Chloe under the tree. I weighed my options, and then whipped my pole back and forth from ten and two, from ten and two. My fly landed like a droplet from heaven upon the water's surface. John patted me on the back then set his pole.

"That's my girl," he said as he moved his pole back and forth, back and forth, making the perfect cast.

"What's Sunnyside Up's momma's name?" I asked, focusing on the task at hand.

"Sun Ray. Ray for short," he explained as if she had a preference.

Ray slowly made her way to the tree then paced the perimeter while her charge nuzzled up against Chloe. Chloe patted her neck as Sunnyside Up nuzzled her black nose into Chloe's belly.

"Chloe sure does have a way with animals," I said, giving my line a gentle tug.

"She sure does." John beamed with pride. "Probably kind of like the way you have with your students."

The rain morphed into mist. I thought about my students and how each class came with its own make-up. There were always the handful of behavior problems, the kids in the middle who plugged along like blue-collar workers heading for the line at General Motors, the few who excelled, and the growing group of students with needs, not all special needs, but needs that they didn't get fulfilled at home to bridge the gap between survival and conformity.

"Not sure about that," I said. "But, I'll agree with you there. Occasionally, some of my students are like wild animals," I said. "They're left to their own devices." I tugged at my fishing line. "But everyone's purpose isn't defined in the early years. I think everyone has a calling."

"I guess I never really thought of it that way."

"It's kind of like natural selection." I glanced in John's direction, taking my eye off my fly just for a second. "There are some who make it and some who don't and no matter how hard you try to save them all, it might not be possible with the given circumstances. Those are the souls you pray for, right after you evaluate your competency as an educator."

John frowned.

"What?" I said with a shrug. "That's just how it is, and when you can't save them, it makes you realize that you're human, too. That's when you just do the best you can and hope like hell it's enough to make a difference. Everyone has a purpose, not the same purpose, but nonetheless a purpose. If all children grew up to be doctors and lawyers, this world would be a pretty boring place."

"Hey," he said.

"Fine. If everyone grew up to be lawyers and congressmen, this world would be a pretty boring place.

Somebody's got to deliver the mail. Someone's got to bag the groceries and lay the bricks. That's all I'm saying."

I glanced over to Chloe who was showing Walter and Harry how to pick long strands of grass, hold it between her fingers, and blow to make sharp whistling sounds, loud enough to drive home the cattle.

"Somebody's got to paint the pictures and make the music. Personally, painting the pictures would make my heart sing. Chloe could make the music," I said, wincing at the piercing sounds cutting the air in intermittent bouts. "Where'd she learn how to do that?"

"Not sure. Some things they just learn on their own."

The corner of my mouth curled toward the sun. "You're right about that." His eyes glimmered in the light breaking through the clouds.

"I like how your eyes shine," I said, holding his stare.

"I think I get that from Chloe." Clenching his teeth, he reeled in another fish.

Sun Ray nibbled at the low-hanging branches.

Chloe ran back to the bank of the pond. "Hey, Dad, we're gonna go back to check on the kittens then Judy is going to make us some grub." She scratched her head as she said the word *grub*. "That just sounds too much like dirt to have anything to do with food, but whatever."

"Okay. Maggie and I will clean up here and meet you at the house. Take your poles back to the barn and tell Judy thanks."

"Okeydokey." Chloe trotted off.

I flipped my line into the pond. "Casting is more fun than catching."

"I like the catching part. Makes me feel like I accomplished something," John said.

Sun warmed the back of my neck and dried my shirt. "Yeah, but once you catch the fish, you have to touch it. I'm not so sure I can do that." I yanked my fly out of the water and it stuck on the grass. "See, I scared myself just thinking about it."

"You'll never know until you do it." John's deep voice, filled with conviction. "Just might be up your alley. There is nothing about you that says sissy."

Laughing, I wound the line up then narrowed my gaze at him. John tugged at his line and reeled in another fish. It flopped back and forth as he snagged it with a net. Water splashed as the dorsal fin wiggled to and fro, desperately trying to free itself.

"Natural selection," John said.

"*Touché*."

"Want to try and get it off the hook?" John grasped the trout with one hand and held it in my direction. It wiggled and I raised my eyebrow at him. Sticking my hand out, I tried to be brave, but when it wiggled again, I jerked my hand back to my side. I couldn't do it.

"Maybe another day," he said, retrieving the hook from the fish's mouth.

Stepping closer, I inspected the process. The fish's gills heaved in the air. "Um, I'm thinking no."

"It's okay, not everyone can grow up to be a doctor or a fisherman," he said. "Somebody's got to make the music." John put the fish into the bucket. "Keep them or let them go?" he asked, staring up at me.

I knelt beside him. "That's a good question. I don't know. How bad do you want to eat them?"

John tipped the bucket and the five trout sloshed back into the pond. "We'll save this bunch for later." He tickled the water with his fingertips then flicked some at me, his grin growing mischievous. "I liked you better in a wet T-shirt."

My cheeks burned, but not from the sun.

He glanced around. "Good, they're all gone."

"What's all gone?" John's wild stare bristled my intuition.

I backed away as his eyes flashed with determination. He wiped his hands on his thighs and stepped toward me.

My palms grew clammy and sweat formed on my brow. I knew this game. "This is silly. We're adults."

"Um, I believe the words you used were *natural selection*." He lowered his gaze and reached out.

Squealing like a schoolgirl, I ran for cover. Out of breath, and his feet thundering behind me, I darted around the back of the mighty willow. I shrieked again as John caught me by the hand and pinned me up against the hearty trunk.

"You are one hard girl to catch, Maggie Abernathy, but the chase is worth it."

Chapter 11

"Eat up," John said, biting into his second peanut butter and jelly sandwich.

"I haven't had one of these in a long time." I took another bite. "Thanks, Judy."

Walter's cheeks bulged as he shoveled his lunch into his mouth.

Judy touched his hand. "Slow down."

When he smiled, crumbs fell from his lips.

Chloe and Harry talked about fishing and collecting more rocks down by the creek.

"Ashley's gonna get you three back up on those horses this afternoon." John finished off his sandwich then guzzled down the last of his lemonade.

"Woo-hoo," Walter said, lifting his arms overhead like a prizefighter.

"Maggie and I are going to see the cattle. Judy, you want to come?" John asked.

"As much as I'd like to see the cattle, I think I'd better stay here with the boys and give Ashley a hand."

"John, how far away are they?" I asked.

"Not far. Give me a second, I have an idea." He scooted his chair back from the table, got his radio from the counter, and then called Justin over the crackling line. He left the dining room to continue the conversation.

I nibbled on grapes as I listened to the kids' conversation. Judy's sideways glance caught my attention. "What?"

"You don't need any tagalongs. Just go. We'll be fine."

She bit off a hunk of her sandwich. "These do taste so much better in Montana."

"You are so lucky," Walter said, poking her in the arm.

Suspicion tugged at the corner of my mouth. I wasn't seeing a kid opposed to moving eighteen hundred miles away from my quiet Michigan lake town. Maybe she'd feel differently when Harry and Walter were gone, but for now that wasn't the case.

"Dad says I'll probably get to come back to see you guys once in a while." Chloe nibbled at the end of a strawberry. "Maggie, that means you, too."

"What?" Walter asked, sipping his milk.

Chloe sighed. "I'm just so glad you're here, but part of me feels bad."

"Why?" Walter said, making his milk moustache twitch from side-to-side.

"Promise you won't be mad," she said.

Walter made the peace sign with his pointer and index fingers. "Promise. Stick a needle in my eye."

Judy grimaced at the exchange.

My mind flashed back to the day Chloe and I sat on the kitchen floor moping about her and John's move, her letter tucked away in my desk back home. My heart cracked like worn leather at the notion that she'd become a distant thought, kind of like those students in my class that I'd grown attached to over the years, but somehow all that's left is a smudged crayon picture or letter telling me how much I meant when the school year ended.

Chloe's eyes flashed in my direction. "Well, as much as I don't want to leave you guys, I think I actually kind of love it here," she said.

Walter smashed his lips together and his brow furrowed.

Harry munched on chips acting as if he wasn't at all surprised.

Chloe set her elbows on the table and clasped her hands in front of her. "I feel bad, like I'm not supposed to want to stay here."

My heart sank. Out of the lot of us, she seemed to be handling it better than me. Her green stare met mine. "I knew you'd like it once you got here," I said.

"Anyway, let's not borrow trouble," Chloe said.

"Where did that phrase come from?" I asked.

"Grandpa. He told me that the other day when I told him I thought you weren't coming. He's a great listener." Chloe showed her teeth like the horses did before they got a treat, then she finished her lunch.

John joined us at the table. "We can all go," he said. "The fun way."

"Woo-hoo." Walter tilted his head and gave John a fist bump. "What exactly is the fun way?"

"What a dodo brain. He's a weirdo." Harry rolled his eyes and shook his head in dismay.

"Well that weirdo is my son, too, and I'd appreciate it if you didn't call him names." Judy collected empty plates from the table.

Chloe nibbled her sandwich down to the crust then left the remaining sliver of bread on her plate. She shrugged at her dad who was inspecting her technique. "What? I only like the insides."

"So tell us what the fun way is." Walter batted his eyelashes and begged. "Please."

"Justin is going to hook up Starbuck and Caribou to the wagon. You guys can sit in the back and enjoy the scenery."

"Woo-hoo." Walter raised fists in approval.

Harry rolled his eyes at his brother. "Excellent." His smooth intonation made him sound like one cool cat.

"Thank you," Judy said, reaching for Harry's plate. "See, that's not so hard."

"Yeah, whatever, but Walter's still—"

Judy cut Harry off before he could finish the insult. "He's still your brother."

Walter grinned wildly and touched his mom's hand. "Thanks, Mom."

Harry moaned.

"Do you want to stay here with Ashley?" John asked. "She could probably use some help in the barn."

Harry leaned back and rested his arm on his chair.

Chloe inspected him as he thought. "She's too old for you," she said, finishing her milk. "But cleaning up horse poop is fun."

Harry glared at her. "You're supposed to be my friend."

Chloe lapped up the last drops of milk that trickled down the outside of the glass. "I am your friend. Friends don't lie to each other."

Taking a handful of dirty dishes to the sink, I couldn't help but laugh to myself. Judy stood beside me at the counter, cleaning off plates and enjoying the wit. She leaned over and whispered in my ear, "Seriously, you two need some alone time."

I pushed the food scraps down into the garbage disposal, and then checked over my shoulder for big ears. "Um, really we don't."

Judy sighed then bumped me with her hip. "Really you do. I saw you by the tree."

I ignored her, my cheeks hot like glowing embers.

"Oh, come on, you wouldn't have dragged yourself out here if you didn't think there was a chance in hell that you two had something," she said under her breath.

"I'm not talking about this now," I said between clenched teeth.

Judy threw the dishtowel on the counter and planted her hands on her hips. "You can't be serious."

"What are you two arguing about?" Chloe asked, handing me her empty milk glass.

"Nothing," I answered.

"It's not nothing. Maggie is stubborn and won't listen to me," Judy said, tilting of her head.

"What's the problem? Maybe I can help." Chloe wiped her mouth with the back of her hand.

"It's fine." I took a deep breath.

"Chloe, let's just say that she's closed for business," Judy said.

Chloe's nose wrinkled in its usual fashion. "What?"

"Now we know where Harry gets it from," I said, closing the dishwasher.

Chloe stuck her hands in her pockets and raised her eyebrows in exasperation. "Must be a grown-up thing, 'cause I'm not getting it."

"Thank you," I said, resting my hand on her shoulder. "You got that right." I caressed her sticky cheek. "We can argue later. Let's go find our wagon ride to see those cattle."

Judy raised her left eyebrow at me. "Whatever."

"What's going on over here?" John asked.

"Nothing." I dropped the dishtowel on the clean counter.

A glint of curiosity flashed in his cowboy eyes.

Walking away, I didn't look back. Chloe's boots clicked behind me, through the mudroom, and out the door. I stormed off toward the creek and sat on the boulder next to the one-man bridge that crossed it. Chloe came over and sat next to me. This time she wasn't having the melt down, I was. Too afraid to touch the truth, I focused on the gurgling stream.

"What's the matter, Maggie? I'm sure Judy didn't mean to make you mad." Chloe found a pebble and tossed it into the water.

Running my tongue across my teeth, I glanced over at her from under my lashes.

Chloe shrugged her shoulders at me. "What were you *really* fighting about?" She stared across the field, her eyes soaking up the landscape.

"It's stupid. Nothing."

"Must not be nothing if you're mad."

"Okay, Dr. Phil," I said.

Chloe draped her arm around my slumped shoulders. "Remember that one time when my mom left without me?"

I closed my eyes ashamed at my reaction. "How could I forget?" It was just last year that I cradled her as she sobbed for the mother who left her behind after promising to take her to Hollywood.

"Is it worse than that?" She took a deep breath. "Are you going to run away?"

"No, this is a little different." I leaned my head against hers. "You ran away 'cause you were sad and hurt."

"Well you don't seem so happy."

With my left elbow on my knee, I lowered my head to rub the tension from my brow. "You know when someone says something that's not really their business?"

"Do I ever." Chloe glanced over her shoulder at the sound of heavy boots scuffling behind us. "Hey, Dad."

"Great," I uttered under my breath.

John cleared his throat. "Chloe, why don't you go see how Justin's coming with the wagon and horses? Maybe Walter and Harry can go with you."

Chloe rested her head on my shoulder. "Whatever Judy said, don't let it wreck your day. That's what Glad would tell you and I'm sure that's what you'd tell me if I was moping around."

Her warm cheek pressed up against mine and I knew she was right. "I guess. The only difference is I'd have to find you in the bushes."

Chloe giggled then stared up into her dad's face. "I'm going." She hopped off the rock and kicked her heels against the ground as she sauntered away. "Geez."

John sat beside me. "Since Judy wouldn't say what that was all about, you want to?"

Pressing my lips together, I felt my brow crease. "Not really." I turned my head to see him better. The front of his Stetson curved over his forehead and hung just above his brow line. The muscles in his temple twitched.

"You can keep it to yourself, but it's gonna gnaw at you until you come unraveled."

"Isn't that what this is?" The hair stood up on the nape of my neck as his words brushed against my cheek.

"Eventually, you're going to have to let something go."

Thinking about our kiss under the willow tree warmed me through. Resting my head on John's shoulder, I knew Judy had my best interest at heart. "Tonight when the stars come out, I'm going to find the brightest one and make a wish." John's lips were soft against my cheek.

"Me, too," he said, holding me close.

Chapter 12

Caribou and Starbuck clopped along the dirt path that paralleled the main road. To the west, mammoth green pastures separated the two. Chloe leaned against me. Golden strands of sun-bleached hair highlighted her braid. "Are we almost there?" she asked her dad.

"Yes. You'll see them in a minute." His temples twitched as he focus on the terrain. "Pretty soon you'll hear them."

"Chloe, lean over next to your dad." Pointing my camera in their direction, I snapped a photo. John's narrow gaze depicted someone deep in thought while Chloe's haphazard grin complemented her father's solemn façade. Justin commanded the horses, clicked his tongue, and maneuvered the reins like a pro, his feet resting against rectangular metal pedals. I snapped a photo of the horses hauling the wagon. Their flanks flexed with each step, showing off their muscular builds and power, Justin's profile in the foreground anchored the image.

"They have big horns," Chloe said, sitting up on her knees and peeking over Justin's shoulder. She steadied herself then pulled herself up, leaning against him. His eyes warmed as he glanced back at her and the creases at the corner of his mouth indicated he didn't mind having her so close.

John scooted closer to me. "She is something," he said, shaking his head.

Chills ran down my arms. "Yeah, you're right about that." Chloe's way with animals and people was a gift. Touch was natural for her, her eyes an invitation to unconditional acceptance.

Chloe rested her hands on Justin's broad shoulders as the wagon bumped along. She reached down to pluck something from the bale of hay behind the driver's seat. I smiled, realizing it was a feather. Chloe tucked it into the leather strap of Justin's cowboy hat.

The dusty road wound through a patch of trees that towered overhead like a covered bridge of greenery. The dark woody patch was cool like my thoughts. John leaned over and told me the cattle were just ahead.

Chloe held on to her hat and pointed toward the break in the tree line. "Squint your eyes," she said. "Those specks of white are the cattle. They almost look like fireflies when the trees move."

John draped his arm around my shoulder. "Who knew cattle could be magical?" he said into my ear.

Chloe could apply her spin to anything and reel you in. Her imagination wildly connected to real life, very much like Bradley when he was her age. Children were different at home than they were at school. Every once in a while I'd get a glimpse of true personalities when we took a break from the rigor.

Huge branches bent overhead in the breeze. Chloe was right. White dots filtered through the swaying leaves that lined the horizon. Justin snapped the reins, letting Starbuck and Caribou know it was time to giddy up. I tugged at the rim of my cowboy hat as not to lose it. John produced a chum from his front shirt pocket then hooked one end to my Stetson and the other end to the collar of my T-shirt at the base of my neck. His fingers grazed my skin, sending electric tremors down my spine.

"Thanks," I said.

"Wouldn't want you to lose your hat." John peered straight ahead, and then broke his stare to glance at me. "Or anything else."

I grinned then gave him a nod. I hadn't met anyone like him before. John and I had shared some tender moments in the past year like the time he took the stitches out of my head after Chloe and I banged noggins. He'd pitched a tent in my living room so Chloe and I could have a campout without the rain. Once he even brought me lilacs in the middle of the night to apologize, but the times I cherished most were when he was just himself and we sat side-by-side enjoying a beer over trite conversation as nightfall muted daily drama. John squeezed my shoulder as if he were remembering those times, too. Blinking away the daydreams, I yearned for more.

The mooing grew louder. White cattle with painted ears of black and snouts of coal peered at us. I snapped a few photos. Winston trotted across the pasture to greet us while Trout rode behind him, his hand holding leads to two saddled horses without riders.

"Hey, Grandpa." Chloe knelt on the bench beside me. "Did you lose some guys?"

He laughed. "Nope. Those are for your dad and Maggie. Thought she'd like to get up closer and personal to take some photos."

"Really?" My breath caught in my chest. What did I know about riding with cattle?

"Yup, we're going to ride with herd today. Just for a little while."

Judy glanced over her shoulder, the creases at the corner of her mouth filled with mischief. "Did you know I was going to get dumped off in the middle of this place?"

"Yup. The kids and I are staying for a bit, but then we're heading back. We'll see you two later."

"Dad says I have to be older to ride with the cattle," Chloe said.

"We're heading over there." Winston pointed to a dark-green field in the distance at the base of a mountain lined with pines.

"I'm not sure, I can ride with the cows," I said. "I've never done that. I've been on a horse, but never with other animals."

John held out his hand. "Well then, I think it's about time you rode with the big boys. Come on, neighbor lady."

I balked at the invitation, but then held out my hand.

John yanked me up from my respective seat.

"Ride with the big boys. That's funny," Walter said.

"What do I do?" I asked.

Trout grinned. "Get on this horse and just ride."

John lowered the step on the back of the wagon. "You can stand here and get yourself mounted."

Trout dismounted his horse and led a painted pony toward me. Her chocolate-brown spots dotted her creamy hide. Her mane and eyes reminded me of midnight. "This girl got a name?"

John hopped off the back of the wagon and patted her neck. "She's as sweet as they come. I call her Neighbor Lady 'cause her freckles remind me of you."

"You're funny," I said. "Really, what's her name?"

Trout checked my stirrups and girth. "That ought to do it. Her name is Peaches 'cause she's that sweet, just like John said. We're gonna put J.P. on Mocha cause she's got a bite that gets the cattle going."

"I don't know how you keep all these horses' names straight," I said.

John positioned his left foot in the stirrup, swung his right leg over in one swift movement, and then hauled himself up using the horn of black leather. "No different than you learning thirty names in a year and learning their likes and dislikes." He gave Mocha a jab with the heels of his boots. "Come on now, give Peaches a nudge."

I buckled the saddlebag on her right hindquarter. Winston sat slouched in his saddle, his hands on his thighs, watching me get settled. He gave me a nod and steered his horse to the right with a smidge of a kick.

"Come on, girl." I followed his lead.

Peaches craned her neck to see me. She batted her eyelashes and the muscles in her neck twitched as a breeze washed over us. Patting her neck, I leaned forward. Holding her stare, I clicked my tongue and she fell in line with Mocha. Winston and Trout galloped ahead. The cattle strolled at a leisurely pace with their horns pointing toward their destination. Glancing at John, my grin grew wider. "I've never seen cattle like this." Their white hides sacred as a white dove.

"Dad likes them because of the ancestry. Guess he can relate to their Celtic roots."

My ears perked up. "Celtic?" I never thought of Montana cattle having roots that distant.

"Yeah, people think the cattle were imported here from England just before World War II to protect them from the Nazi invasion. They were sent to the zoos, but someone had the right mind to put them on a Texas ranch. Over time, they were sold and eventually made their way up here. This is what it's all about. Living on the land and raising them organic."

Winston's body moved in time with his horse. They were one. Trout circled behind. John focused on me as I bumped along, trying to move in stride with Peach's gait.

"Everything has roots, Maggie." John's body bobbed as Mocha sauntered along, the grass ankle high. "Just 'cause you get uprooted, doesn't mean you can't adapt."

His green stare glowed beneath the shade of his hat. Part of that Celtic charm brimmed within the man beside me. A momma and her babe ran past us like thunder. My gaze followed their path. I gave Peaches a kick and we trotted after them. John rode beside me. My confidence brewed.

"You sure you're not a cowgirl?" he asked. "'Cause you kind of ride like one."

"Maybe in a former life" I couldn't help but smile. Something about this Montana living was weaseling its way into my heart.

Chapter 13

As we neared the grazing ground, I studied the three wranglers riding alongside me. Pressing my lips together, I tried to hold my smile to a casual grin, but there was nothing casual about the day. I wasn't just out on a ride with John and his dad to shoot some photos. John's ulterior motive thrived in-between the trot and the canter across the countryside. With the lush pasture and rich mountain terrain, he knew I didn't have a chance, but I held steady as Winston sized me up. This was John fighting harder, and I was coming unglued.

When Winston nudged his hat back from his forehead, I suspected he needed to get a better look at me. He mopped his brow with a bandana and shoved it back in his rear pocket. Then he directed his horse to walk beside mine, their strides at an even pace.

"How you holding up?" Winston asked.

"I'm good." I suspected the glint in his expression reflected my joy. Even with the thought of aches and pains to follow, I didn't care. I licked my dry lips.

"You have water in your left saddlebag."

I pulled back on the reins. Peaches bobbed her head forward, loosening the reins to rub her nose against the tall grass.

"Go ahead grab a drink. She'll wait." Winston stopped beside me to drink from his own canteen. "There's a creek up there for the cattle, but you can't see it from here. A good place to soak your feet if you ask me."

"John said these cattle have Celtic roots." Resting my canteen on the saddle horn, I savored the swig of water.

"The best kind," he said. "You ought to know that with a last name like Abernathy." Winston screwed the canteen top closed and tied it back in place next to his horse's saddlebag.

"Guess I would," I said, feeling my Irish flare. "With a little Scotch mixed in."

"Sounds like a drink hearty enough for a cowboy." Winston's moustache twitched, the dimple in his left cheek deep as Crater Lake.

The delivery of his message loud and clear. My cheeks smoldered beneath my hat. "Years ago we went to a dude ranch." The cattle lollygagged across the land. "But it was nothing like this."

Winston leaned forward in his saddle. "Yeah, when I'm not sure about life, all I have to do is mount up and ride off. Sometimes I can feel—"

Clouds washed over Winston's expression as a gust of wind pushed at our backs.

"You what?"

"I'm just an old man. You'd think I was crazy," he said, fiddling with his saddle.

John and Trout rode up ahead in the distance. I couldn't help but pry. "You feel what?" I asked, leaning forward to let the air hit my sweaty backside.

"I feel John's mom in the breeze."

I studied Winston's profile. Another gust of wind brushed over my shoulders. I imagined it was her, beckoning us to move forward. Winston tugged his hat down and settled back into his saddle. The toes of his boots pointed toward the baby blue sky.

The creases at the corners of his eyes, a road map to his past.

"What's your horse's name?" I asked, trying to make conversation with a man obviously distracted by another place and time.

Winston clicked his tongue with the curl of his lips. "Forget-Me-Not." Her golden ears perked up as her muscles twitched with urgency, her gaze a window to her glimmering soul. "Ida May loved them as much as I love this horse."

I rubbed Peaches's neck and set my feet in the stirrups. She whinnied at Forget-Me-Not's movement as she sidestepped to the sound of Winston's voice. The clouds overhead moved swiftly as the breeze picked up. I swear I heard Winston's voice clearly as he trotted away, *"I'm going, Ida May, I'm going."*

Chills ran up my arms and down my legs. The unexpected presence kissed my cheek and I wondered if it was Ida May introducing herself, or if it was my dad drifting by to say *get on with it girl, don't just sit there, follow him.*

John dismounted Mocha then led her to the creek. She nibbled at the earth's offerings as she pressed her nose to the ground. "You gonna be able to get down from there without falling over?" John asked me as Peaches and I joined them.

"I'm not sure. I think my right knee is asleep." I dropped my feet from the stirrups and moved my toes in circles.

John tied Mocha to a fallen tree branch. "I'll catch you."

"Sounds like a fairy tale," I said, trying to maneuver my right leg over the backside of Peaches. I pressed my belly against the saddle and slid down slowly until my feet met the ground.

John's hands rested on my waist. "Could be if you let it."

"Nothing is a fairy tale. Besides, they usually involve poison and ugly women who possess magical powers."

"Maybe, but there's always a happy ending."

I gaped over my shoulder. His marriage to Brook didn't have a happy ending. His career choice didn't have a happy ending. He floundered through life just like the rest of us. There was no guaranteed happy ending. "Not without consequence," I said.

"Maggie Abernathy, how on God's green Earth did you get so jaded?"

Peaches let out a long sigh as she shook her head.

"Traitor," I said. Peaches stared back at me. I thought I saw a glint of hurt in her eyes. "Sorry, you're a good horse." I ran my fingers through her tangled mane. "Yeah, my legs feel like rubber bands."

John tied Peaches next to Mocha. Her eyes fluttered shut.

"Looks like she's napping." I spied a place to sit at the end of the dead tree.

John sipped water from his canteen. "Want a drink?" John's temple twitched when he swallowed.

"You're not afraid of cooties?"

"Nope," he said, holding the canteen out in my direction.

I took a swig, wiped the drip at the corner of my mouth, then took another gulp and handed it back to him. "Your dad said he thinks he hears your mom in the breeze."

"He's not the only one." His cheeks smoldered as he fidgeted with his gloves. "Pretty silly, huh?"

A dragonfly buzzed my nose. "Not at all." Studying John's profile, I took a deep breath in an attempt to ward off emotion. I picked a yellow flower that resembled a daisy and caressed the pedals as I reminisced about the cane they'd found at the cancer center with my dad's name on it. "I knew I'd be okay. I knew I'd make it through radiation." I tugged at the rim of my Stetson. "I knew it was my dad and he was with me." The hair prickled on the back of my neck. "It's not silly at all."

John took the flower from me and tucked it in the leather band on my hat, just like Chloe had done with the feather as Justin drove the wagon. "Yeah, I guess it's not silly."

A clear vision of his mother floated through my mind. Her blonde hair flowed in the wind, her blue eyes filled with pride for her boy, her spirit embracing her son as she'd done in a black-and-white photograph that Chloe shared with me.

Even if they weren't with us, they *were* with us. I took a deep breath, wondering what the rest of the afternoon entailed. "So, what's next?"

"I thought you might want to get that camera out and take some shots. Then—" John pointed to a dirt trail that led into a grove of trees. "Then we can take the scenic route home. We can ride up that trail, across the ridge, and back down."

"Is that a challenge?" I asked, feeling my legs come back to life.

"Or we can ride back the way we came." John peered over his shoulder across the flat land. "You can see a lot more from up there."

"I don't think you even have to ask. Scenic route." I patted Peaches's shoulder then got out my camera. I strolled through the pasture, with one hand on my camera and one eye peering through the viewfinder, careful not to get too close to the cattle. I didn't just see another world, I was beginning to understand another way of life.

John slipped down off the log and sat with his back to the downed tree trunk, his hat covering his resting eyes. I zoomed in and shot a couple of frames before he noticed what I was doing.

"Didn't mean to wake you."

"I'm not sleeping," he said, "just daydreaming."

My head felt like I'd been in a dream since we left Judy and the kids back at the wagon. "Your dad and Trout are heading back to the ranch. Just let me know when you're ready."

After John closed his eyes, I knelt beside the stream to wet my fingertips. The cool rush exhilarated me. Everything seemed simple out here. Big Sky. Mountains. Grass. Cattle. Peaches shifted her weight as I secured my camera in the saddlebag. The snap of the plastic buckle echoed in the still air. John came up behind me, his breath on my neck, his father and Trout off in the distance, his words in my ear. I shut my eyes, pushing John's message deep down inside, trying my best not to lose control in the Montana breeze when we made our way back home.

"I know she's calling to you, Maggie Abernathy."

When I opened my eyes, I was still standing beside a horse at the base of a mountain and next to a man with wild green eyes laced with true intention. The rims of our hats touched as he turned me around. We stood toe-to-toe and nose-to-nose.

"I'm not one of your Ancient White Park Cattle," I said.

The epic blue sky tugged at the corner of his mouth. "Maybe not, Maggie, but I know you have to be thinking about us."

"How do you know?" I whispered, his hands on my hips, his warm touch radiating through my jeans.

"'Cause I see it in your face. I hear it in your voice." He nudged his hat back from his brow.

His eyes flickered, and I could see how John's mother, Ida May, would've been drawn to follow Winston all those years ago. I covered John's hands with mine. Thinking about my job back home, I tossed it to the side. I thought about my house, my mother, and the usual day back in Michigan. With a bat of an eye, I pretended it was gone.

"Maybe we should head out." I sighed and made no mention of that nagging list of obstacles I felt were obligations.

John squeezed my hips and drew me closer. My Stetson fell back and hung by the chum against my back. "You can have the fairy tale, neighbor lady."

My breath caught in my chest. His lips covered mine and in a matter of seconds, I entertained the thought of purging everything I knew and selling anything that wasn't a family heirloom at the yearly neighborhood garage sale.

Chapter 14

Chloe met us as Mocha and Peaches moseyed out of the trees and onto the trail leading to the barn. "He flew away." She yelled through cupped hands. "Frankie flew away."

John dismounted Mocha, flipped the reins over her head, and tied them to a post. "What's this all about, short stuff?"

Chloe followed on her dad's heels as he led Peaches by the bridle to another hitching post. He patted her sweaty shoulder as I held the leather horn and lowered myself to the ground, his hand on the small of my back.

"What's going on?" I asked.

Chloe flitted around. "Frankie flew away."

"Maybe it was all those kittens making eyes at him, got him nervous, and scared him away," John said, sliding his hand up my back. "How sore are you?"

I shook out my legs. "I guess we'll find out tomorrow," I answered. "I'm not really sore from yesterday's ride."

Chloe tugged at her dad's hand. "Ashley and I were in the barn. I took the top part of the cage off to give Frankie some bugs and he just started flapping his wings. He hopped out the barn door and off he went. It was like a miracle." Chloe couldn't contain her excitement.

Ashley appeared in the barn doorway. "Was it better than Harry tripping over the shovel and landing in a pile of manure?"

John's eyebrow shot up. "Really?"

Ashley nodded and crossed her arms in front of her as she leaned against the doorjamb.

Chloe laughed and slapped her knee as if she were part of a vaudeville show. She let out a snort and we all mused at Harry's misfortune.

"He's inside getting cleaned up. I showed Judy where the washing machine is." Chloe caught her breath and let out a big sigh. "That was hilarious. It stunk." She held her nose and grinned at Ashley. "But I don't think he thought it was so funny. He turned all red."

"Oh my," I said. "Maybe we shouldn't be laughing about it."

Chloe skipped over and dust billowed into the air like tiny puffs of smoke just before a volcano blows. She yanked at my hand and whispered in my ear. "That's what he gets for trying to impress a girl."

A smidge of guilt came over me for finding humor at Harry's expense, but Chloe's observation was priceless. John and Ashley led the horses into the barn.

Ashley called over her shoulder to Chloe, "Hey, you want to help me?"

Chloe skipped into the barn behind her, staying clear of Mocha's back end. She went over to the shelves and grabbed a brush to groom Mocha's freckled hide. John took the saddle from her back as Ashley slid a halter over her head. Chloe stroked Peaches's nose while Ashley showed Chloe how to get the mud out of the horse's hoof.

"You should face your horse," Ashley said in soft, yet firm voice, picking up the horse's hoof. "Looks like you guys went through some mud."

"A little bit at the bottom of the trail," John said. "At least there wasn't standing water like last week. That was a mud bath."

Ashley looked up with a smile. "But it sure was fun getting dirty."

Chloe brushed Peaches's coat and as she did, Peaches's eyes softened and her tense muscles relaxed. Walter skipped into the barn holding an orange Popsicle in one hand and a grape one in the other hand.

"Harry's just about clean. Mom said we shouldn't laugh at him anymore when we get back to the house. You want a Popsicle, Chloe?"

Chloe raised an eyebrow as she inspected the treat. "No, I'll get one later. I'd rather brush Peaches."

Walter skipped over to where I sat.

"You want one?" he asked.

"I think I do," I said. "What color do you think I would like?"

Walter held out the purple Popsicle.

"Good choice. And thank you."

He sat beside me licking his cold treat while I nibbled on mine, thankful for the snack. My stomach grumbled.

Ashley cleaned Mocha's feet while John fiddled with her bridle. Her shiny coat shimmered as the sun filtered through the dark barn.

"What else happened besides Harry's little problem?" I asked.

Walter inspected the orange drips on his pants. "Nothing much."

I finished my Popsicle and tossed the stick into the trash.

Chloe appeared to be disgusted. "You didn't even read me the riddle on the stick," she said.

"Sorry."

"Remember how I couldn't read those last summer?"

"How could I forget? Remember how many *Junie B. Jones* books we read together?"

"How could I forget?" She giggled to herself. "I love that girl."

"My nieces read those stories."

Chloe stroked Peaches's neck with the brush. The horse raised her chin in the air with a heavy sigh. Chloe scooted in and brushed her chest. Peaches closed her eyes and relaxed her hindquarters. "Yeah," Chloe told Ashley, "Maggie helped me read better. Actually, she's helped me do a lot of things better."

Walter picked up a chunk of orange ice from his jeans, plopped it into his mouth, and then sucked on it until it was gone. "I'd read you mine, but I can't read that good yet."

"It's okay. They're usually stupid anyway," Chloe said, taking a comb to Peaches's mane.

Leaning back against the wall, I watched Walter toss his stick into the trash.

"I may not be able to read so well, but I can make a basket." He licked orange drips from the back of his hand.

"Maybe we should get you cleaned up for dinner," I said.

"Whatever you say, but it's really just my hands." He held up his sticky fingers. "See."

"Yeah, okay." I stood up, stretched my legs, and walked over to the corral where John leaned up against the fence. I rested my arms on the split rail then laid my chin on my hands. "I think I'm going to take Walter in and get him cleaned up for dinner."

"You glad you went to see the cattle today?"

"Yeah, I got more than I bargained for."

Sunnyside Up came to the fence and nudged me with her nose.

"In a good way, I hope," John said, running his fingers through her mane.

"Yeah, in a good way." I winked.

"So what are you waiting for?" He took a deep breath.

I shrugged. "I don't know." I sighed, taking in his whole body that pressed up against mine just hours ago. A cool breeze picked up as I thought about our afternoon kiss.

John tugged at the front of his Stetson. "Did you feel that?"

Tiny goose bumps prickled my arms. "Yeah."

"Good," he said.

Chloe came out of the barn and wiggled her way through the slats of the fence to see Sunnyside Up, brush still in hand. "Thought she might like a good brushing, too."

Leaning against the fence, I marveled at her charm. Sunny loved the attention. Her momma Ray watched from a distance. "Must be magic."

John rubbed his stubbly chin that was looking more and more like his dad's each day. "That, and a little bit of trust."

"Yeah, must be."

Chloe spoke to Sunny as she worked her way around her. "I think I'm getting better at this. Wish I had someone to brush my hair every day. Maggie did my braid today." Chloe showed Sunny her braid. "It looked way better this morning, but like anything, it gets wrecked and you just have to do it over again."

Sunny pawed the ground with her hoof.

"Okay, I'll get back to brushing," Chloe said.

I repeated Chloe's words in my head. *Just like anything, it gets wrecked and you have to do it over again.*

Chloe produced a sugar cube from her pocket and held it in the palm of her hand just like John showed her. While Sunnyside Up devoured her treat, Chloe's belly shook with laughter. "Your lips tickle." Sunnyside Up nudged Chloe. "Okay, okay, you can have another one." Chloe dug into her pocket. Sunny swished her tail with delight when Chloe showed her the treat. Sunnyside snatched up the treat then whinnied.

"So do you think my lips tickle when I kiss you?" John whispered in my ear.

I peered at him out of the corner of my eye. "Truth?" Scrunching my lips together, I thought about how nothing seems to matter when he's kissing me.

"Truth." He rested his foot up on the bottom rail.

My belly tingled when I thought about his touch.

"So do they?"

"You're not going to let this go, are you?"

"Nope."

"Fine," I said. "Kind of, but in a different way."

John's brow furrowed as he studied Chloe and Sunny. "What's that mean?"

"Promise you won't laugh?" I asked.

"Scout's honor," he said, holding up three fingers.

I scowled at him. "Were you even a scout?"

He frowned.

"You were never a scout."

"Okay, okay, so you're not the only liar around here."

"Hey, don't judge. I only fib when it's necessary."

John smirked. "Okay, neighbor lady," he said with a laugh.

"Geez," I said, picking at my thumbnail.

"So . . .?"

"So what?" I shot back.

"Come on, you were going to tell me a secret about how you feel when I kiss you."

His eyes sparked with excitement. I wondered if I had that same infectious aura. "It doesn't tickle. It . . ." I took a deep breath and held his gaze. Why was it so difficult to just say the words? Why was it so damn difficult to just feel? I covered my eyes with my hand and put my head down like an embarrassed child. John poked my side making me jump. His cackle, a deeper version of Chloe's laugh. "All right." I composed myself then reminded myself to breathe.

"Geez, you're a mess." John rubbed his jaw.

"Thanks for the boost of confidence." I said. "Not everyone is as outgoing as you."

"Seriously," he said with a straight face.

"Seriously." I looked away then swallowed the foolishness at the back of my throat. "It makes me feel alive. I haven't felt that in years."

John touched my cheek.

"There, I said it. Now what?" I asked, lowering my gaze.

"That was a good first step." He seemed quite pleased with himself. "I think I heard someone say that everyone blooms in their own time."

I wrinkled my nose at him. "Um, I think that was me."

John pressed his lips together and brushed the end of my nose with his forefinger. "You should listen to yourself. You're a pretty smart lady. Your time will come."

The corner of my mouth lifted as the sun struck our backs. His words lingered in my head just like all the other silly ideas, fears, and notions that came my way, the emphasis on the word, *trust.*

Chapter 15

While staring out the window at the kids, I rinsed off dinner dishes in the kitchen sink. Outside, the boys played and skipped rocks across the creek. Chloe snuggled with French Fry in a chair. I was feeling the ride in my hindquarters, but ignored the ache in my backside. Judy brought me a Beltian White.

"I love this beer," I said. "We need to take some back to Michigan with us."

"It's a peace offering," she said, "in case I needed one."

"You don't need one. I think I'm over it."

"I didn't mean to push you. Obviously, you need your space." Judy sipped at her beer.

I cleared my throat, wiped my hands on the dishtowel, and then took a long swig of the ice-cold beer. "Damn, this stuff is good." *Good enough to move out here for.* I kept that tidbit to myself. Getting Judy started again was not my intention.

"Come on, finish those up already," Judy prodded. "It's getting dark and John's making a bonfire."

"I'm going as fast as I can. This is the first time in—" I stopped to think. "Forever that I've actually been able to slow down, enjoy the days."

Judy leaned against the counter. The curve of her back hugged the edge of the granite. "Yeah, it's different out here. The air, the tick of the clock."

"I know," I said. "Pure nature sure does beat fertilizer for the perfect lawn, pollution, people, and cars. Even the thistle is pretty. Things seem slower and in a good way." I loaded the last of the silverware in the dishwasher, added the soap, and then closed the door and started it.

"You're thinking about it, aren't you?" Judy asked pointedly. "I'm sure it's scary, Maggie, but damn it's real."

Sipping my beer, I raised an eyebrow at her. "We got any more of these in the refrigerator?"

"Yeah, lots. John heard you say you liked these and bought a bunch when he went out to check the ditches yesterday." Judy inspected my every move. "Just tell me you're at least thinking about it."

I picked at my thumbnail. "Whatever I say stays between us."

Judy scooted closer as I spoke.

"I mean it," I said.

She put up her free hand and backed away. "All right. Must be serious if you're so testy about it."

I sipped my beer in silence.

"Doesn't it get tiring beating the same old drum?" Judy whispered.

I pinched her bicep. She had muscular arms for a petite woman. I held my breath and thought about her wealth of gumption. She could handle a Suburban, two boys, and a frisky husband without batting an eyelash.

"Yeah, it kind of does." The admission, lightening my load.

Judy choked on her beer. A few drops even came out her nose.

"Excellent. That was a better reaction than I imagined."

Judy wiped her nose with the back of her hand.

"Oh, now I know where Walter gets it from," I said.

Judy wrinkled her brow and grabbed a napkin from the basket on the island. "You know, you're kind of mean," she said with a glint in her eye.

"Well, when you hang out every day with seven-year-olds, you learn a thing or two. It's not always a bed of roses, or a bowl of cherries, lots of times you get the thorns or just the pits," I said.

"I know you love your students, or you wouldn't get so worked up about everything. They're lucky to have you."

"Maybe, but in some cases, I just wish I knew my efforts made a dent."

Judy pinched my bicep as I flexed my muscle. "I think you're getting buff hanging around here. Ashley told me that your metabolism works harder here cause of the elevation."

I finished my beer. "Maybe that's why I'm so hungry." I put the can in the sink and asked for another.

"Have as many as you like. I think John might enjoy seeing you tipsy. Maybe you just might let that guard down of yours just a teensy bit."

I popped the top and sipped the foam from the lid. "Ha-ha. You're so funny. I don't think so. I don't know how to even do that."

Judy cleared her throat. "From what I saw, I beg to differ."

My stomach flip-flopped. "Yeah, maybe I need a few more of these." I jumped when Walter's piercing squeal resonated through the kitchen.

Judy set her beer down and rushed to his side. "What's the matter?" She pushed his hair back, inspected his face, checked for blood, but only discovered leftover orange Popsicle residue. "What's the matter?"

Walter's lower lip quivered. "Harry said he was going to put horse poop in my shoes when I go to bed. Can I sleep with my shoes on?"

"Why would he do that? What did you do to him?" Judy asked.

"Good question," I said.

Walter's dark glare warned me.

I lifted the beer to my lips and sipped slowly.

"I didn't do anything," Walter said. "Harry's just mean."

"He isn't going to put horse manure in your shoes and, no, you can't sleep with your shoes on. I'll talk to him when I get out there."

Walter surveyed the clean counter. "I'm hungry."

"Me, too." I set my beer down and checked the cupboard next to the refrigerator. "Maybe we better have a s'more before bed."

Walter's mood lightened at the mention of food. "Good idea, Maggie."

Judy went outside. I could see her talking to Harry who was pleading his case by the look of his hand gestures and creased expression. I knelt down beside Walter. "Seriously, what did you do to make him mad?"

Walter's sheepish grin validated my instincts. "Promise you won't tell? Stick a needle in your eye?"

"Sure," I said.

He stuck his balled-up hand in my direction with his pinky pointing directly at me. "You have to pinky swear."

He eyed me like a hot fudge sundae. *Crap.* He was going for the gusto. I hesitated, but then stuck out my pinky and hooked it with his. "Now, what did you do?"

"I told Ashley that Harry loved her," Walter said proudly.

I raised my eyebrow at him.

"What? It's true. He tries to act all grown up around her and that's no fun. It's just stupid. Even Chloe thinks so. Do I still get a s'more?"

I thought about rewarding him with two, but I decided against abiding a midget criminal mind at work. His capability exceeded his size and he had Judy wrapped around her little finger. "Sure."

Judy came back in. "He says you started it, Walter." She planted her hands on her hips.

I pretended to zip my lips behind her back then I reached around her to get the graham crackers, chocolate, and marshmallows.

"I did not. Are you going to punish me for telling the truth? Is that what they do to you in court when you tell the truth?"

Judy grunted. "You've been listening to your father too much. Could you do me a favor and just stay out of Harry's business?"

"What?" Walter's voice squeaked. "He really does *love* Ashley." He pressed his lips together and pouted like a puppy dog.

"Thanks for the info. You just indicted yourself," Judy informed him.

"Oh man," he said, shoving a marshmallow in his mouth.

I handed him another marshmallow. "Better luck next time," I said. "You almost got away with it."

Judy grabbed his ear and he stared up into her dark eyes. She meant business. "Look, mister, you are going to apologize to your brother, then when he's not around, you are going to apologize to Ashley for embarrassing her, too. Someday you're going to feel the same way about someone and you're not gonna want me around announcing it to the public, or do you? 'Cause I can remember this for a long, long time." Her voice grew deeper and more serious with each word.

I stepped back.

Walter grimaced. "Okay, okay, I get it. Can you let go now? That kind of hurts."

Judy bent down and met her youngest son on his level. "Oh, you have no idea the damage I can do."

Walter stepped back then glanced over at me. I pretended to zip my lips for other reasons now.

"All right. I'll apologize," he said.

Judy patted him on his rear-end and sent him out the door.

"Nice job," I said, clinking my can with hers. "I might be mean, but you are a little scary. I like it."

Her wicked smile, infectious. "We'll see if it works."

"Nothing is ever foolproof," I said.

"Yeah, you're right about that. I have to say, they've been pretty good."

"Harry's so mesmerized by Ashley he doesn't dare be a dork or she'll think he *is* a dork," I said, making sure no little ears were listening.

Judy's left eyebrow shot up. "Who calls anyone a dork anymore?"

I smiled. "Me."

"So not cool," Judy said. "So you really are thinking about this John thing, right?"

I pressed my lips together in disgust.

"Good girl. Not everyone would be able to pull it off, but I think you have the stamina and talent to pull off anything you want to."

"Thanks, but let's not push it."

Chloe gestured for me to sit by her when we neared the fire pit. Walter wanted me to sit by him, too. John motioned to me to join him.

"Man, I should walk around with treats more often." Judy drained her beer and opened another one.

Winston sat on a stump, strumming his guitar.

Chloe burped. Harry's faint smile of pride made me chuckle. French Fry jumped from Chloe's lap and ran into the dusky haze of the early evening as the stars began to shine in the night sky. Harry snubbed his approval of Chloe's belch and his brother's apology while I relished the one, big happy group around me that I considered family.

Judy raised her beer can toward the fire. "Here's to Montana."

Winston winked and began playing John Denver's "Wild Montana Skies." Goose bumps covered my arms. Winston was proving to be a very interesting individual. There was nothing city about him. He sang the words as he strummed the cords. "It's his favorite tune," John said, blowing out the flames of his burning marshmallow.

"Well, I like it," Chloe said.

"Me too." Walter concurred with a nod of his head, stuffing his mouth with gooey pillows of melted sugar.

Judy raised her beer can toward the heavens. "To Montana," she said even louder, then Harry punched his little brother in the arm.

Chapter 16

Feeling the need for some alone time, I crept back outside, and leisurely sashayed down the path that led to the fire pit.

"I thought I heard someone coming."

Winston picked at the strings on his guitar as I emerged into the light of the glowing embers.

His rendition of "Leaving on a Jet Plane" danced in the Montana night, the stars the tambourine, the crickets the chorus. I settled into the Adirondack chair next to him then propped my feet up on a log. The heat warmed my toes while Winston's tune cheered me up, even if I'd hoped to wallow in self-pity alone.

"Whatcha doing out here? Thought you'd be long asleep by now with all that riding you did." Winston leaned his guitar against the chair on the other side of him. Moonlight shone across his face, highlighting years of hard work and determination.

"Restless, I guess."

"I suppose you would be," he said, peering in my direction, wisdom glistening in his night eyes.

Everyone could read me better than I could read myself. *Damn it.* I tugged my jacket closed, John's scent embedded in the fabric. Curious of Winston's intention and the conversation we shared earlier in the day, I felt safe in asking, "What do you mean?"

"I've seen it before and I see it in you."

I stared into Winston's midnight eyes as he rubbed his whiskery chin. His demeanor gentle and wise. I suspected he could talk his way out of a bear's den without batting an eyelash.

"If you don't mind me asking, what do you see?" My head tingled with the slight beer buzz from the evening, leading me to believe I should have kept my mouth zipped.

Winston poked the fire with a long stick. Yellow flames licked the dying logs like the lake back home when it kissed the shore. He propped his foot up on the log next to mine and crossed his legs. With his elbows resting on the armrests, he clasped his hands under his chin. "I see it in so many who pass this way. They're unsettled, kicking like a bronco, stirring up dust so they can't see what's right in front of them."

The night air kissed my neck like John's lips and the only sound between Winston and I was the snapping fire that sang its own tune. I breathed in slowly letting his words settle.

"I saw it when I first met you, I see it now. There isn't anything wrong with making peace with your true calling. Fear breeds fools," he said, nudging his Stetson back from his brow.

Narrowing my gaze, I peered into the fire hoping it could tell the future like a crystal ball. "Do you know when you see something and it seems impossible?"

"Yep, that's what this place was many moons ago, a dream. You're talking about a dream."

"I suppose I am."

"Nobody can dictate your future. Some will think you're foolish no matter which fork in the road you choose. Those who don't follow their hearts are the dunderheads. I think you already know this, but all forks in the road lead home."

Leaning back in my chair, I crossed my arms over my belly. His words coaxed me to scrutinize the decisions I struggled with. Sleepy notions swept away my words.

"It's getting late and this old wrangler has an early morning. Will I see you on a horse tomorrow?"

The moon tugged at the corner of my mouth.

"That's what I'm talking about."

I felt the creases in my brow form. "What?"

"Your britches might be a little sore, but your head's telling you to saddle up tomorrow 'cause it's calling you. That's the hard part 'bout making decisions. You can't see your own face."

I swallowed away the foolishness that lingered on my tongue. "What exactly do my eyes say?"

Winston leaned forward and so did I. "You're yearning, dear girl. You're yearning." Winston touched his chest. "Pay attention to what your gut is telling you."

I leaned back in my chair then smoothed the hair away from my face, knowing that fear stifled rationalization. Winston stood, reached for his guitar, and bid me a goodnight.

"Night," I said.

He looked over his shoulder before leaving me by myself.

"Yeah, I'll be back up on that horse."

He clicked his tongue, his eyes like midnight emeralds. "Good, 'cause you sure look like you belong up there." Winston strolled toward the house, his footsteps echoing through the Montana shadows.

My eyelids grew heavy and the fire dimmed, but I pulled another beer from my pocket, cracked it open, and then dug for the Hershey bar in my other pocket. My mental laundry list of responsibilities reeled in my head, but I folded it up to enjoy what was left of the night and this unforgettable vacation. Tilting my chin to the sky, I searched for the perfect Montana star. Dreams seemed greater in this spectacular landscape, not dampened by career expectations, neighbors, and roads filled with people bogging me down.

I threw my Hershey wrapper into the fire, admiring its last flicker in the night. With half a beer left, I couldn't drink one more drop of Montana ale. The echo of a slow stride caught my attention. A tall, dark silhouette standing with his thumbs hooked in his front pockets greeted me. "You look like the Marlboro Man," I said, raking my fingers through my hair.

"Dad said you were out here. I didn't hear you leave."

"Chloe's not the only sneaky one around here," I said with a grin, poking the burnt embers with Winston's stick, hoping for one last burst of energy.

John pulled me out of my chair. We stood toe-to-toe in the moonlight where hazy light washed over us like a fairy tale, I supposed the one that John spoke of earlier. His hands rested on my hips. His eyes sparkled like jewels at nightfall. My heart fluttered like Frankie's wings as he flew away. I swallowed hard, reminding myself that I was human.

John rested his hand on my chest. His fingers caressed my collarbone. "Your heart is racing," he said.

"I know. I'm not sure what to do about that?" I hooked my fingers in his front pockets.

"Dad said you might need some company."

"I think he told you just the opposite."

"Yeah, he said you needed some time alone."

I imagined someday John might have a rougher exterior, one that matched the mountain ridges aged by time and weather. John's crooked grin harnessed me and Winston's words were etched in my mind. "I guess all this *thinking* is making my heart beat faster."

John kissed my cheek. "I think that's good."

"Me too." I touched his face, tracing his jawline with my fingers, memorizing the glimmer in his eyes. "I like how you look in your Stetson and jeans."

"I like how you look riding in front of me perched in a saddle. No one would guess you're a city girl."

"I like how it feels to be in the saddle. I like the horses," I whispered.

"I know," he said.

"You had a city girl before. What makes you think it could be different this time?"

John's warm touch caressed my cheek. "You giving me a chance?" he asked, holding my face in his hands. "What's with the sad eyes?"

"Just a lot to figure out." I covered his hands with mine. "I guess there's part of me that wants to stay and I know I can't." I traced John's lips with my finger. "This is so hard."

Winston's words grew louder in my head.

"You know how I feel," John said.

"I know."

The fire died out and we stood in the darkness as the moon hid behind massive clouds. Heat lightning flashed low in the sky behind the pines in the distant.

"Maybe we're just the calm," John said.

The boat rocked beneath my feet and John's strong arms steadied me. "I'd like to think there won't be any storms."

"That's a nice thought, Maggie Abernathy, but without the rain and storms, there wouldn't be foggy mornings, the fresh scent of pine, and the reminder that there are some things bigger than we'll ever be."

My eyes closed just for a second. In that blip of time, John kissed the side of my head and scooped me up like I'd seen him do to Chloe so many times before back home.

"I think someone needs to find her way home," he whispered.

"Yeah, home. Are you taking me to bed?" I asked, wrapping my arms around his neck.

"I wish, darlin', I wish."

"That's not what I meant." I rested my head against his shoulder. He smelled of leather and sage.

"I know, darlin', I know."

Chapter 17

Even with my eyes closed and being half-asleep, I had the eerie feeling that I was being watched. When I forced away the dream in my sub-conscious, I peeked through squinted eyes. Daylight streamed into the room, and Chloe stood just inches away from my face.

"What time is it?" I asked her.

"About eight o'clock. Are you awake?"

She leaned in closer to my face. I covered my head with the patchwork comforter. "Ugh." A moan escaped my lips. My head was in a fog. "Just let me sleep for a few more minutes. I'll pay you."

Chloe peeked under the covers.

"What? How much do you want?"

"Not that much. I guess. I've been waiting for you to get up," she said with a grimace. "I guess I can wait a little longer if you really want me to."

Folding the covers back, I scooted over so she could nuzzle in next to me. Bradley used to keep me company when I wanted to stay in bed and he felt the need to be by my side. Chloe's urgency to start the day stumped me. "You can crawl in if you want," I said to her, rubbing my forehead and closing my eyes again.

"Really?"

I opened one eye and turned my head to see her better. "Really. Just climb in." I scooted over a smidge more. "It's too early to get up."

"You got up this early the other day, not that day that you overslept, but before then, remember?"

"Yes, you made me breakfast, remember?" I covered my face with the back of my hand.

"Dad made you breakfast and sent me up here to give it to you."

"Do you think you can go back to sleep for a bit?" I asked, hoping like hell she could. What was the rush anyway? I dozed off for a brief second, but woke when Chloe shifted her weight and rearranged the covers. When I opened my eyes, she was lying on her side facing me, her clasped hands under the right side of her face, her eyes closed, and a grin on her face. Soft breaths escaped her lips. She sighed like Bones did when he had given up. Glad for the reprieve, I focused on falling back asleep, even if it were only for five minutes. My mind wandered back in time to last night. Heat moved through me like wildfire. I kicked my leg out from underneath the covers and raised my arms over my head. God, I loathed these hot flashes. What did men have that even equate to this phenomenon?

Chloe felt my forehead with her clammy hand. "Holy crap," she said. "Are you okay?"

I opened my eyes. "You shouldn't swear. But, yeah, I'm fine. It's just part of getting older," I explained without going into depth.

"You feel like you just ran a race. You're all sweaty. Do you need a cold washcloth? Sometimes my dad gives me a cold washcloth when I have a fever." She jumped out of bed and ran out the bedroom door.

"But I don't have a fever," I said to nobody. I kicked the other leg out from under the covers and used the bottom of my T-shirt to wipe the band of sweat form my forehead. Chloe came back in and dabbed my forehead with a damp washcloth. A drip of cool water ran down my cheek, across my neck, and into my shirt making me shiver.

"What? Now you're cold?" she asked, feeling my cheek.

"No." I held the washcloth to my head. "Thanks," I said. "I think this helps. I should remember this for the future."

Chloe sat on the bed, cross-legged, staring at me. "If this is what it's like to grow up, I think I'll stay eight. You don't look so good."

"Thanks."

"How often does this happen to you? I don't think it happens to my mom, but how would I really know since I'm never really around her."

Chloe babbled while I unfolded the washcloth to cover my face. When the heat subsided, I removed the terry towel and checked the clock on the night table. It was barely a few minutes past eight o'clock. Chloe's binoculars were next to the clock. "Have you been looking for animals or birds? I bet it's a little different than spying on the neighbors back home."

"Actually . . ." She slowly enunciated at a sloth's pace.

My T-shirt stuck to my back as I propped myself up against the headboard. Leaning forward against my knees, I worked it free. If Chloe hadn't been here, I would've whipped it off at the first sign of inferno. "Actually, what?" I asked. "If you're not going to tell me then I'll go take a shower and brush my teeth." The grit from beer and chocolate made me wince. I swung my legs over the side of the bed, but Chloe caught my arm. Her eyes were filled with question, her creased brow filled with curiosity.

"Um, well, don't get mad at me, but last night when you snuck out . . ."

"Yeah, but I don't think that since I'm an adult, going outside after dark is *technically* sneaking." I wondered where she was going with this. "And—" I motioned with my hand for her to continue. "Get there faster," I urged, "I really have to go to the bathroom."

Chloe rolled her eyes. "Fine, go to the bathroom. This might take some time." She shooed me away.

Hurrying into the hallway, I tiptoed to the bathroom, trying not to wake the boys or Judy, then slowly closed the door, and hurried to do my business. I washed my hands and splashed my face with cool water. When I opened the door, Chloe was standing there with her arms crossed, tapping her foot against the wood floor. I put my finger to my lips to remind her to be quiet. Her bare feet padded quietly behind me as I went back into the bedroom.

"Do you have any other business to do before we get started?" she asked.

I lifted my right eyebrow as she questioned me then sat on the bed, leaned back against the headboard, and crossed my legs. "So what's this all about?"

"I don't know, you tell me," she said, making herself comfortable by my feet.

I shrugged. "Not sure what you're getting at. Does this have to do with Harry or Walter?"

"No."

"Then who?" I asked.

"You know," Chloe said, narrowing her gaze.

"Not really? You wanna clue me in?" My shoulders tightened up as I watched frustration build in her stare.

Chloe reached over the edge of the bed, grabbing Voodoo from the floor. She toppled over and landed with a thud.

"Are you okay?" I asked, reaching down trying to grab her, but missed. She rolled over, stood up, and moaned before pressing her lips together in disgust.

"Well that was embarrassing. Will I ever not be a dork?" she said, her cheeks a rosy pink.

"I told Judy kids still use that word. She didn't believe me," I said. "And to answer your question, we're all dorks. Now what's this about?"

Chloe took a deep breath. "I saw my dad carry you in last night through my binoculars. He only does that for me."

Her tone bristled my nerves. "I was super tired from all that riding and I stayed up too late." I didn't mention all the beer I drank. "Your grandpa and I got to talking." I wished for a diary and a pen to jot down some of the things he said. "I guess I wasn't ready for bed and just wanted a few more minutes by the fire." I pressed my lips together. "You know what it feels like when you don't want the day to end." The corner of Chloe's mouth went up and a slow grin erupted.

"Yeah, that happens to me a lot," she said, tapping her finger against her cheek.

There was a knock on the door.

Chloe and I both whispered, "Come in."

Then in unison we chimed, "Jinx, you owe me a Coke."

John stuck his head inside the room. It wasn't the first time he'd seen me in my pajamas. I'd been caught several times chasing Bones in the morning hours or hunting for little girls who hide beneath the bushes.

"Just wanted to see if my girls were up," he whispered.

Chloe smiled and gestured for him to come in. He was dressed for the day in his jeans and plaid shirt. His silver belt buckle caught my eye. "Did you get a new belt?"

"Nope. Dad found it. My mom gave me this for my birthday a long time ago. I wanted the biggest belt buckle in Montana. Funny how things look bigger when you're ten. It's pretty cool."

John moved closer to the bed.

I wrapped my arms around my knees. "Are the others up yet?"

"Nope," John answered, "and they went to bed before you.

Chloe brushed the hair away from her face. "That was nice of you to carry Maggie in last night. I'm glad you didn't leave her outside."

John picked up the binoculars, a slight frown etched into his expression. "What did I tell you about spying?"

A shadow crossed Chloe's face. "Sorry, Dad. I just can't

help it. I know I'm not supposed to, but—" She took a deep breath. "I'm sorry."

I patted her knee.

John sat down beside her and wrapped his arm around her shoulder. "Maybe I should just take the binoculars, so you're not tempted."

Worry flashed at the corners of her mouth. "Oh, I don't know."

"Spying isn't a skill you're going to need in the near future," he said.

"I would make a good spy?" Chloe perked up.

John wrinkled his brow. "I'm thinking, no."

"What if I promise not to use them for spying?" she asked.

John stared at me.

I made a face at him. "Not my department." I wasn't sure I wanted it to be my department and if I decided to have a relationship with him, Chloe would be more than my neighbor, more than just an eight-year-old friend. She would be my boyfriend's daughter. *My boyfriend's daughter!* My mind went berserk. I was too old to have a boyfriend. I studied John and Chloe as they discussed the binoculars and rules. Being on the outside suited me just fine. John squeezed Chloe tight. She wrinkled her nose and groaned.

Then he winked at me. "Maybe you two should get dressed. Maggie's gonna get back up on a horse and we're going to ride by the creek today. Maybe we'll see some elk."

"Are Walter and Harry and Judy gonna come, too?" Chloe asked.

"If they want, Walter can ride with me. I thought maybe you could handle an adventure outside the corral."

Chloe beamed. "Really?"

"Yeah, but we'll put a helmet on you," John said.

John's gaze met mine. His eyes pleaded for affirmation.

"Your dad knows best," I said.

"Whoopee, this is gonna be great," Chloe said.

I wasn't sure if John's energy originated from his daughter's excitement for the day or from the fact that he thought that I was one of *his* girls. He referred to Chloe and me as *his girls*, and I relished how the words warmed me through.

Chapter 18

We rode single file along the riverbank, and Ashley and Harry led the way. Judy's horse fell in line behind her son's and I brought up the rear, the perfect position to watch John ride. He straddled Walter in the saddle in front of him. Chloe was sandwiched in the middle of the pack, her favorite place to be. I couldn't imagine Chloe anywhere else.

"Walter, do you think you can help me take the reins?" John asked.

"Sure."

John handed the reins to Walter then rested his hands on the horn, encasing Judy's treasure.

"You're doing just fine. Let Breeze do all the work, she knows the routine," John said, patting Breeze's neck. "Good girl."

Walter glanced over at me. He held the reins with pride, one in each hand. His feet dangled at John's knees, his knobby knees peeking through the holes of his blue jeans. I wasn't the only teacher in the group. His patience tugged at my heart. There was something about a man holding a child that my senses couldn't resist.

"Looks like we got ourselves a wrangler in training," John said.

Chloe held on to the saddle horn then glanced over her shoulder. The sun sparkled across her cheeks. "How am I doing, Dad?"

"Looking good, darlin'," John answered.

Ashley slowed Sweet Jaclyn's stride and we all stopped behind her. She pointed up the hill. Pippin's ears twitched at the sound of falling rocks. She danced sideways and I tensed up, sensing her angst. I knew the signs. I was the master.

"It's all right, girl," I said under my breath. "I know how you feel."

Pippin peered back at me, her ears twitching. She stopped prancing and I figured if she was gonna go, she'd go, regardless of what I wanted to do.

Chloe leaned over her horse's neck and peered up the hill.

"What's up there?" I asked John. "'Cause Pippin doesn't like it."

"Hold steady. She'll be okay. There's a moose up on the ridge."

Peering through the dense pines, I couldn't see the beast and really wished it would flee so Pippin would relax. While silently lecturing myself to remain calm, Pippin's head jerked at the reins and she whinnied. She kicked her back legs out from behind her. I wrapped my left hand in her slick mane like a tether, praying like hell she wasn't going to run.

"There it goes," Chloe said.

Pippin reared up and I held steady, not giving way to her intentions.

Rocks trickled down the side of the hill in front of us. I glanced up, the moose leaping into the trees with a mighty bellow.

"That thing was huge." Chloe's eyes filled with panic when she saw Pippin bucking. "Whoa, Maggie."

Pippin stumbled and then bolted toward the ranch. I hugged her belly with my calves, struggling to pull back on the reins as she galloped full speed. "Whoa, girl. Settle down." While I reasoned with a runaway horse, part of me wanted to hunker down and keep on going. Not sure if my instincts were correct, I let her settle down in her own time, and then guided her to a patch of bright purple forget-me-nots near the river where she sniffed the tall grass and chomped on a mouthful of sweet greens for comfort.

My hands shook as I squeezed my calves against her belly, trying to get my bearings. Relaxing back into my saddle, I let go of her mane. Pippin craned her neck to see me. I coaxed her into a trot then rode back to the others. Walter's brown eyes stared at me in awe. As I eased up on Pippin, she transitioned into an easy gait.

Chloe's jaw hung open. "Wow, that didn't look like much fun." Huckleberry's nose touched Pippin's as if she was comforting her. "Huckleberry didn't even move."

"I'm glad," I said, stroking Pippin's damp neck.

"And that's why you have a helmet on," John told Chloe.

"Maggie, you want my helmet?" she asked. "Wouldn't want you to get another set of stitches like last summer."

With a deep breath, I lowered my shoulders, releasing the strain. "Nice try," I said. John glared at her.

"It was worth a try. Anything's worth a try."

"My girl's got a point," John said, conveying an all-knowing expression.

The sky tugged at the corners of my mouth, knowing he wasn't talking about a helmet. Walter gave me a thumbs-up. His free-spirited attitude lightened my heart. Leaning over, I patted his knee as he and John circled around to get back in line as Ashley waited for the high sign that we were moving on.

"That was some good riding, neighbor lady. You okay?" John asked, letting Breeze fall in stride beside Peaches and me.

Judy's stare caught my attention. She was picturing some storybook ending while sweat crept across my brow and dripped down my back. I felt like a wreck.

"Yeah, I'm fine." I patted Pippin's neck. "We all get a little spooked from time-to-time." I wasn't sure if the pit in my stomach was caused by my own trepidation where John was concerned, or the fact that the wild ride scared the hell out of me. Maybe they were one and the same. "You're a good girl."

I wanted to believe that heavy sigh meant that the rest of our ride would be slow and easy.

"I thought I was going to have to come after you." John swayed in stride with Breeze's nonchalant stride.

Glancing over at him, his eyes conveyed a deeper concern than the one he'd exhibited in front of the kids. "I'm fine," I said in my true *Maggie* fashion.

John winked. "I wouldn't expect anything less. That was something. Dad would have been proud," he said. "If Trout would've seen you in action, he'd be asking you to wrangle full time."

"Not sure I'm up for that." I kept my eye on a squawking crow overhead.

"Dad, look over there, in that dead tree on the other side of the river. Maybe it's Frankie." Chloe shaded her eyes.

"I was thinking the same thing," I said, inspecting my white knuckles.

John trotted ahead to catch up with Ashley. Walter bounced up and down as he held on to the saddle horn, John's arms securely held Walter in place. "Yee-ha," he hollered as black curls bobbed up and down.

A twinge of envy sparked as I watched Chloe sway in stride with Huckleberry. Why couldn't I switch gears that easily? If she could accept Montana, why couldn't I? Her focus intent on the horizon made me think she could see something in the future that I couldn't. "Hey girlie-girl, you doing okay?"

Happy creases formed at the corners of her eyes when she spoke. "I'm good. I love this little girl," she said, rubbing Huckleberry's neck. "Some of her black spots look purple. That's why they call her Huckleberry. That's what Grandpa said."

"It's a great name. I love huckleberries. Wish we had them back home." I removed my right foot from the stirrup and stretched it out, hoping to alleviate the ache. "I think we're almost to the place where your dad said we could put our feet in the water."

Chloe smiled. "That sounds fun." She perked up eagerly looking for the stream near the shady knoll as John looped back around, herding us like stray sheep. "What do you think Glad is doing today?" Chloe asked. "I miss her."

"Me too." I thought about her back home, which seemed to be another dimension of time compared to what we were experiencing here. "Maybe she's knitting or driving around in her convertible with Bones."

"I hope she's having as much fun as we are."

"Wouldn't that be something to see her on a pretty pony like Huckleberry?"

Chloe giggled. "Yeah, that would be something."

"How are *my girls* doing back here?" John said as he strode up beside us.

There was that phrase again. I was one of *his girls*. Trying to stifle the brash thoughts of living miles apart made my heart throb.

"Good, Dad. Are we stopping up there?" Chloe pointed not too far ahead.

"Yup. Justin brought us some lunch. You guys can wade in the water after you eat."

"Woo-hoo," Walter called out.

John dismounted Breeze. "Hold on for a second, cowboy," he said to Walter as he tied Breeze to a low hanging branch, then he held out his arms and Walter slid out of the saddle as John guided his feet to the ground. "Look up," he said.

Walter tilted his head back before John unbuckled his helmet. He shook his hair free while galloping to meet his mom.

"Whoa, my legs are wobbly." Chloe goofed around, pretending to be a ragdoll after John helped her down, too.

John guided Pippin into the shade. Pippin's eyes shimmered in the sun that found its way through the dense greenery. I thought about what we must have looked like running away from that moose. I was no different than Pippin. It was easier to flee than face my demons. How did I ever let myself get like that? Protecting myself didn't seem to come without unforeseen consequences.

"You ready?" John held out his hand to help me.

"I think I got it." I hoisted my butt high enough to swing my right leg over Pippin's hindquarters. Leaning my belly against her saddle, I slid down until the toes of my boots met the ground. John was there to steady me. "I think my knee is asleep." I shook my right leg then rubbed my kneecap.

Ashley helped Judy while Harry insisted on getting down and tying his horse up by himself.

John gave me a nod. "He sure is hellbent on being a man while he's here," he whispered.

"I'm sure boys all go through that when there's a pretty girl around. Bradley was no different."

"Suppose you're right about that," John said. "Once we get our sights set on something with hips and a pretty smile, it's hard to thwart our motives."

"Did you say, *thwart*?" I asked. "That doesn't sound like cowboy lingo to me."

John cleared his throat.

What he didn't know was that I was totally turned on by his cowboy appearance and extensive vocabulary. Every part of me wanted him.

"What? It's a word," he said.

I poked him in the bicep. "I know. It just sounds funny, that's all."

We inspected the blanket and picnic basket that Harry was ogling over like he hadn't eaten in days.

Chloe skipped up to John and grabbed his hand. "Can I eat on the rock by the river, over there?"

"Don't see why not. Make sure your trash gets back in the basket."

"Come on, we can eat over there," she said to Harry and Walter.

Judy helped the kids organize their lunches while I meandered to the edge of the stream. Bending down, I splashed cold water on my cheeks. Judy reminded Harry and Walter about using their manners and no bickering. Harry forced a smile showing all his teeth.

"Guess he's not over that whole Ashley thing yet," Judy said, patting my shoulder.

She handed me a sandwich and I sat down, hoping the sound of the river would drown the day's drama. "How sore are you?"

Judy rubbed her knees. "My butt hurts and my legs feel like I've run a marathon, and we all know that didn't happen. How come you're not complaining? How do you do it?"

"I'm not that sore now, but we'll see tomorrow after Pippin's little episode back there. Boy, can she run fast." I inspected my lunch. "Yum, more peanut butter and huckleberry jam."

"Sorry, I guess I should've made something more mature for the grown-ups." Judy unwrapped her sandwich and took a big bite. "So Chloe says she saw her dad carrying you in last night."

John sauntered over to the rock to check on the charges.

"I see that look in your eye. What gives?" Judy asked with a mouthful.

The concern at the corner of her mouth melted my insides.

"Just let it go, Maggie. This is your journey and no one else's. I know you. Worrying is going to kill you before some runaway horse or wrangler."

Judy squeezed my hand, but didn't let go.

"Fine." The well of tears burned behind my eyes when Judy touched my hand. "What if it doesn't work? I don't know if my heart can survive that. What if I decide to be part of this world and it falls apart? What would I have then?"

"Is that what you're worried about? You'll have everything you had before. For Pete's sake girl, don't throw another log on the fire."

"But I don't want it to hurt." My lip quivered and I couldn't wrap my head around why I was unraveling now.

"It doesn't have to and if you and John decide to part ways, you'll know that you fought for what you wanted."

"That's the problem. What I want and what I can have are two separate entities."

"You listen to me, Maggie Abernathy." Judy scooted closer. "You can have it all. You can be the fairy princess. You survived Beckett. You kicked cancer's ass. You deserve it."

Something snapped inside. "I'm not sure I want to be a princess, but I would like to kiss the prince. Every night, all night."

"Now we're talking."

Avoiding Judy's stare, I checked to see where Ashley was. My insides tensed with predicament, my heart torn between two worlds, my head spinning with scenarios.

"You'll figure it out. You're pretty resourceful. If you can handle Pippin, not to mention all those second graders year-after-year, you can handle this. I hate to be trite, but where there's a will there's a way. Fight."

I glanced over to the kids. Chloe had her boots off. One sock went flying above her head and she tugged at the other one as she rested her foot over the opposite leg. Harry meandered along the riverbank tossing stones into the water. Walter followed behind, his jabber muddled in the air. Something out of the corner of my eye caught my attention. Walter tipped toward the water.

"Oh, no," I yelled.

Judy followed my stare. She jumped up and ran toward the squeal. I ran after her.

John stepped into the river and hauled Walter up by his collar. "He's not going anywhere. We could walk across the river at this point and barely get our feet wet. Look how shallow it is." John tried to ease the panic.

I watched the silent exchange between the boys. Walter surveyed the crowd for attention while Chloe stood close to me with her hand over her mouth.

"Are you okay?" John asked, kneeling beside the dripping munchkin.

Walter rolled his eyes. "It was my own fault," he said with narrowed gaze and a dark flash in Harry's direction. "I slipped and just fell in." Walter took a deep breath. "I'm fine."

Chapter 19

Chloe read *Tales of a Fourth Grade Nothing* at the kitchen counter while I started dinner. Judy was coddling Walter somewhere and Harry had gone to the barn with John and Winston. Chloe put a tie-dye piece of cloth in her book to hold her place as she munched on crackers and cheese. "I've been thinking," she said with bulging cheeks.

The sweet tang of barbeque sauce made my stomach growl as I licked my finger. Dinner wouldn't come soon enough. The mountain altitude was making me ravenous. When Chloe didn't continue, I glanced back to see if she was still there. She swallowed hard and rested her arms on the counter. Her eyes glowed with that expression students get when they really don't want to tell me something, but have to because they're being interrogated or they know it's the right thing to do and they obviously fear the consequences, usually a rift in a friendship. *Good Lord, what now?* Moving the cutting board closer to her, I waited.

"Well." She paused and looked around. "Well, it's like this."

I chopped up some onion for the bean salad and waited. She was going to have to spit it out on her own terms, terms she could accept. I didn't have the energy to pry.

"So, I was talking to—" She stopped, again. "Let's not say who." She sighed then rested her chin on clasped hands. "So, I guess I was thinking that my dad really likes you."

I piled minced onions to the side of my board and started dicing celery. "I like him, too."

Chloe grunted. "No, not like that. You know, really, really, likes you."

I scooped the pile of diced celery into the bowl then added the onions in with the cannellini beans. The loss of words stupefied me. What was I supposed to say? Chloe's exaggerated exhale released any butterflies she held hostage within herself.

"When we move here, he's going to be sad 'cause you're not going to be around."

I sidestepped the whole *like* thing. "I'll miss you guys, too."

Chloe blew a strand of hair away from her face. "Maggie, Harry said—" Chloe stopped and covered her face.

I touched her hands when she didn't surface. Peeling her fingers away from her eyes, I leaned closer. "What is so bad that you can't say what Harry said? I won't be mad."

"Cross your fingers, hope to die, stick a needle in your eye," she whispered through pursed lips.

"Yeah, promise."

"You know that sounds really gross," Chloe said.

"Yes, it does. Now what is bugging you?" I asked, trying to lighten her somber mood.

"He said that you two were in love." Chloe covered her face again.

"Oh boy," I said, tucking my hair behind my ears.

Chloe gawked through her fingers at me. Her green eyes filled with what looked like hope.

I waited for her to continue while squeezing limejuice into the bowl to fill the void.

"Aren't you gonna say anything?" Chloe asked.

"I don't know what to say," I said, wiping my hands off. I did a look-see into the living room to see what Judy and Walter were up to. Judy was curled up at the one end of the sofa napping and Walter was curled up at the other end.

I took Chloe's hand. "Let's go outside," I whispered. "They're sleeping and we wouldn't want to wake them."

Chloe sat up, her eyes fixated on my hand touching hers. She covered my hand with her free hand, her fingers soft against my skin. She wiggled out of her chair and came around the counter. I reached out to her and she melted into me. It'd been a long time since I picked up a child, but instinct prompted me to scoop her up and carry her on my hip, so I did. She wrapped her arms around my neck, her breath brushed my neck like a lake breeze.

I set her down on the boulder next to the creek. "Why are you so sad?"

Chloe looked away and tucked her knees up against her chest, her toes each painted a different color.

I sat next to her.

"Are we telling the truth, or are we doing that thing where we fib so the other person doesn't feel bad?" she said, tugging the hair tie from the bottom of her braid. Her fingers worked at her dishwater-blonde hair until it was loose enough for her to shake her tresses free. Blonde streaks fell over her shoulders like a crimped horse's tail.

The corner of my mouth tugged downward. I leaned back on the palms of my hands. "I guess we aren't fibbing." I sighed, knowing I couldn't have escaped the topic much longer. Chloe's pensive profile captivated me.

She inhaled deeply. Her chest held the breath like a leaking balloon. "I don't want my dad to be sad."

"I don't want him to be sad either." I didn't want myself to be sad. This unexpected conversation made my head zing with all the things I had to sort out, and not wanting to share it with Chloe added a whole new dimension.

"This is going to be a hard transition for all of us," I said. The muscles in my chest tightened, leaving me wondering if suffocation could be induced by the onset of reality.

"This sucks," Chloe said.

"Yeah, it does."

"What are we gonna do?"

"I don't think there is anything we can do." A shadow drifted across Chloe's emerald eyes as I spoke. I forced myself to breathe then pulled my legs up onto the rock, and crossed them like I was listening to a story when in all actuality, I was living a story, a story that I desperately wanted to have a happy ending, but didn't know if that was possible.

Chloe took a deep breath. "Is Harry right?"

Damn him. "I don't know." That was as honest as I could be. Gravity wrested at the corners of my mouth and my shoulders fell forward. Chloe's stare riveted me. The air went into and out of my lungs like it might be my last breath. The babbling creek muted the world around us.

"I think he is," Chloe said under her breath.

John strolled toward us, his physique defined and brooding. Chloe rested her chin on her knees. John's boots scuffed across the rocky path, his face mirrored our melancholy. He unbuttoned his plaid shirt, took it off then flipped it over his right shoulder. His white tee clung to his body in all the right places. I studied Chloe's face as she stared through him. Her eyes connected with mine briefly, but her attention focused on the man who'd gone country.

"Boy, you two look like a sorry bunch. What died?" John asked, crossing the quaint bridge.

"Nothing," Chloe said, her tone flat.

Concern twitched in his temples. I tried to smile. Harry brought this on and now it was me who wanted to dunk him into the creek.

"You mad at the boys?" John asked.

Sitting quietly like the stunned passenger in a skidding car, I wondered if the invisible guardrail I careened toward would give way.

"Nope," Chloe snapped.

I raised an eyebrow in response, letting her know it was her move.

John lifted her chin with his pointer finger. "Then what gives?"

Chloe held steady. "I don't really think I should say."

"Well, if you don't say, I can't help you." John cupped her chin in the palm of his hand. "I think Maggie might agree."

Holding my breath, I wasn't so sure this time. If he only knew.

Chloe stretched out her legs in front of her. "It's nothing, just girl stuff," she said, picking at the fray in her jeans.

I've seen those eyes before and I knew that John wasn't buying what she was selling. He stared through me. What did Chloe want me to do? "Maybe we should finish dinner. A little food might do us all some good. I bet your dad is hungry." I wiggled off the rock then faced Chloe.

Her eyes had gone pale and drooped, and then she reached out for her dad. John gobbled her up and we went inside.

Giving the bean salad a stir, I drizzled salsa over the colorful mixture to give it zip. Chloe picked up her book and stared at me. Her expression reminded me of Bones and the way he pouted when I didn't walk him before settling in for the night.

Chloe finally meandered out of the kitchen. "I'll be outside reading," she said. "Let me know when dinner is ready."

John scrubbed his hands in the sink. "What is going on?" he asked, eating a spoonful of beans.

"I'm not sure you want to know, and I'm not sure it's my place to say anything."

John tossed his spoon into the sink. The thud startled me. "Well, I can't help if you don't tell me," he said, slumping against the counter.

I rubbed my temples. "True, but—" I rinsed out the empty salsa jar and sprinkled the bean salad with cherry tomatoes and avocado.

John took off his cowboy hat and fidgeted with the rim while I cleaned the counter, covered the salad, and put it in the refrigerator. The blast of cool air slowed the oncoming hot flash. I wiped my forehead with the back of my hand before shutting the fridge door. "We just need to put the chicken on the grill and brush it with some sauce."

"Fine, have it your way, but it's going to come out sooner or later and probably when we're at the dinner table with everyone watching."

I glared at him while imagining the uncomfortable scene. "Why do you have to be so difficult?"

"Me? I highly doubt this has anything to do with me." John opened the refrigerator and popped open a beer. "Want one?"

I shook my head. "No, but a needle in my eye right now might hurt less." We were bickering all ready and I hated that.

"What did Chloe do to you? Does it involve blackmail?"

"I wish it did. That would be easier to deal with. And just so you know, it has everything to do with you," I said, helping myself to his beer. "I changed my mind. You might want to get yourself another beer." I showed him my teeth.

John groaned. "I hate that fake smile. Nothing ever good comes from a face like that," he said, twisting off the top to another frosty beer. "You're not going to take this one, too, are you?" he asked. "Can't picture you being a double-fisted drinker."

"I'm not, although that sounds like a great idea."

"Come on, neighbor lady, let's go sit on the front porch."

Chapter 20

The rocking chair anchored me to the porch as the story unfolded. John sat beside me, jaw slightly ajar.

"Yeah, it's all about you," I said. "Chloe doesn't want you to be sad." The pang in my heart stung. "Remind me to thank Harry before he goes to bed."

"Forget about Harry." Disgust crossed John's mouth. "You know what I mean, Maggie. At least there is one honest person on this ranch."

Oh my God, John really loves me. I sucked down a long draw of beer, my nerves bristled at the truth. Unable to handle the truth, I drained my bottle and set it on the floor of the porch. Rocking deliberately, I caressed the smooth arms of the chair. My heart skipped a beat when he reached over and wrapped his fingers around mine. John stared across the pasture and into the mountains, squeezing my hand. "She loves you so much," I whispered, shrugging off my own feelings, my throat raw.

"I know, but I can't make you do something you don't want to do."

"It's not that I don't want to do it. I just don't know how to do it," I said as the beer penetrated my veins, calming my nerves.

"People live crazy lives all the time," John said. "I'm hoping like hell that you come to your senses."

Hot tears brimmed. *You have no idea.* The words haunted me as I sat in silence feeling his warmth in our innocent touch, electricity raging between us. He stood, leaned in my direction, and kissed the side of my head. I closed my eyes memorizing the touch of his lips. The aroma of mountain air and every day grit consumed me.

"Judy and I will finish dinner," John said.

I closed my eyes as I bantered with myself. In silence, the obligations I'd committed to nagged at me. I peered into the future, to a time when I'd be retired and then what? I imagined my world without rift and hurt. I imagined a world with John, and Chloe. I reminded myself that things change and with usual predictability comes complacency.

Boots shuffling up the porch steps jarred me from the plight within.

Winston greeted me with a nod and sat down in the chair beside me. "If you're out here, who's in there making dinner? You didn't leave it up to J.P., did you?"

I smirked. "No, he's got Judy. I was just going inside to help."

"Good, 'cause that boy needs some direction."

I could use some, too. Smiling at Winston, I fidgeted with the hem of my shirt.

"It sure did get warm today," Winston took off his cowboy hat. He set it on the chair next to him and mopped his brow with a bandana from his shirt pocket.

"Sure did," I said. "I better go help with dinner."

Chloe opened the front door and peeked out. Her eyes brightened as she made eye contact with her grandpa. She scooted through the door and hopped into his lap.

I went inside, feeling the pit in my stomach expand. Walter moped past me as I made my way to the kitchen. "What's wrong?" I asked.

"Mom told me to go wash up. I'd rather stay dirty. It's easier."

I mussed his crown of soft curls. He had a red mark, the size of a summer peach on his cheek from sleeping. "She didn't think your swim in the river was good enough?"

Walter narrowed his gaze at me.

"You didn't fall in the river, did you?" I asked.

Walter shook his head and frowned.

"Harry pushed you, didn't he?"

Walter shook his head no, but his eyes said, *Yes.*

"It's hard, isn't it?" I asked, sitting on the bottom step leading upstairs. Walter sat beside me.

"Yup." His lips popped.

"Is Harry still mad at you?" My shoulders slumped forward as I thought about my own problems.

"Nope." He sighed, mimicking my sad posture.

"That's good."

"I guess so." He smacked his forehead with the palm of his hand. "Sure wish I didn't have to do stupid stuff to get him to forgive me."

"Dinner will be in a little while. You'd better get going. Do you want me to help you?"

Walter's dark eyes peered through me as I spoke.

"No, but it's nice of you to ask." Walter tilted, then shook his head. "I think I got water in my ear." He grabbed his earlobe and jiggled it like an old man. "Brothers," he said quietly.

I watched him trudge up the stairs like the world weighed him down. Resting my elbows on my knees, I cradled my head in my hands then squeezed my eyes shut, begging for the future to reveal itself, but I knew the only way to see the future was to open my eyes and step into it. I'd been born in control and loosening the reins made my heart beat double-time.

My chest heaved with lust for Montana living. Winston worked diligent long hours to maintain his dream, John followed in his footsteps with his heart on *my* sleeve, while I hid my heart *up* my sleeve. I wandered day-to-day, wondering if I had the guts to admit I even had a dream. Getting up, I went back outside and headed toward the barn, wishing I could saddle up and ride off into the sunset.

The barn door, barely ajar, captured my attention as I moseyed down the dirt road. When I peeked inside, sunshine washed over me from the opposite end of the barn. The menagerie of saddle blankets, saddles, and tack lined the walls just waiting for the next ride.

Nudging the door open just far enough, I went inside and sat on the bench where Walter and I had shared a Popsicle, closed my eyes, and prayed for answers. I ran my fingers through my messy strawberry-blonde hair, then grabbed it like I was making a ponytail and lifted it off my neck beading with sweat.

I squeezed my eyes tight as chills ran down my spine. A gentle hand rested on the nape of my neck. The touch grounded me and for a split second, I thought maybe it was my father. Tears welled and I pressed the palms of my hands into my eyes, trying to stop the longing I felt for my dad who'd left me years ago. I saw Chloe perched on John's hip with her arms around his neck in my mind. It seemed like eons since I was *that* little girl in my own father's arms.

Through the tears, I stared at my dusty boots. John ran his fingers up my neck and into my hair. I squeezed my eyes tighter, hoping this wasn't a dream.

John knelt beside me, his hand on my knee, and his finger under my chin. "Saw you leave. Wondered if you were all right?"

I shrugged. Cocoa ran past, and then nestled in the straw at my feet and stretched out, letting her kittens suckle. "No, guess not," I said.

"Anything I can do to help?"

I scooted over on the bench and John sat beside me. "I don't think so." I tucked my hair behind my ears.

"Well I think there is, but I'm going to let you solve your

own dilemma."

I wiped the corners of my eyes and watched the kittens nuzzle up to their momma's belly, safe from the world around them until she went out to hunt. "Probably best." Locking my elbows, I rested my hands on my knees. I liked the feel of worn blue jeans, inside, and out.

"Dinner is almost ready," John said.

Our gazes met. My stomach wasn't the only thing growling. "I don't know if I want dinner. I kind of like it out here." The barn truly was a sanctuary.

"Well, you've got to eat, darlin'." John wrapped his arm around my shoulder and drew me close, his green eyes trying to hide his own disappointments.

I couldn't help but think I was one of them.

"A girl your age can't live on s'mores and beer, 'cause that's what we're having later."

"I beg to differ."

John's breath brushed up against my neck. His lips followed. Tension oozed from my shoulders like dripping wax, my guard giving way to the heat. He whispered in my ear, "Let me love you."

I swallowed the temptation, but it stuck in my throat and lingered at the back of my tongue like bitter sweetness. "I don't know how."

Afraid, I prayed again. From under my lashes, I saw a man earnest and true, his eyes fixed on me yet not demanding, something I wasn't used to. Flecks of passion danced in his irises.

"How the hell do you know what you want?" I asked.

"Because I know," he said.

His strong hands held my face. His thumbs stroked my cheeks like he was settling a skittish filly.

"Let me ask you this, neighbor lady . . ."

"Why do you keep calling that?"

"Does there have to be a reason?" he asked.

"Isn't there a reason for everything?"

"No. Sometimes things just feel right." John kissed me as I took in his words, his breath in sync with mine. My stomach rolled over and I let myself kiss him back as if it were the very first time.

Chapter 21

After dinner, the kids headed to the pond to fish with Winston and Judy. With poles in hand and jokes on their tongues, John and I sat on the porch as they strutted away.

"Chloe seems so content." The crisp air gave me goose bumps. "And so do you." Part of me didn't want him to like it here so much. My chest buckled as I exhaled.

"You seem pretty comfortable yourself." John crossed his legs and picked at the heel of his boot. Dried mud drifted to the floor.

"I'm just trying to fit in, besides it's a whole other way of life. No hustle. No bustle. No driving with your hands clenched to the steering wheel in traffic." My voice trailed off just as the kids' silhouettes disappeared into the backdrop of mountains speckled with pines, their voices faded as John and I rocked in our chairs.

"Yeah, but there are other obstacles," John said.

"I'm sure there are." I closed my sweater to the nip in the air. "Like what?" Fingering the worn spot of denim at his knee, I studied his profile, imagining what he'd look like at Winston's age. And when that time came, Winston and Ida May would be together in the Montana air whispering to John and Chloe. My mom would probably be gone, too. My deep breath cut me. God, Bradley would be my age and Chloe would be Chloe, just all grown up, a woman. I tried imagining myself, but couldn't see myself any differently.

"The hardest obstacle would be not having you here." John uncrossed his legs. His heel made a thud against the porch floor. He rocked his chair back using the balls of his feet and put his hands behind his head. "Chloe's right. It's gonna hurt."

His words stabbed at my heart because I knew he wouldn't be the only one with a monumental ache. I held his hand. "I know."

"Will you come with me?" John asked. "I have something to show you." He stood and hooked his thumbs in his front pockets.

I held his stare. "Yes." The truth was, I wanted to follow him wherever he went. John's mother, Ida May had followed Winston to this place, and maybe it was my turn to follow in the footsteps of a woman I'd never met, but could feel in the air when Winston spoke of her. John took my hand and we went through the living room and into Winston's office. The walls were decorated with horseshoes, tack, and vintage photos of Montana and his family.

John touched a silver horseshoe on Winston's desk that sat on top of a pile of legal documents. He ran his fingers over the shiny metal. "Dad thinks these horseshoes bring him good luck."

"Maybe they do," I said, inspecting the photo hanging behind his leather chair.

John's mom sat in an old pickup truck, behind the wheel with her elbow out the window, her fair hair dancing in the wind, her eyes set on the horizon, gazing into the distance as if she could read the Montana landscape. Her light eyes eerie with premonition, her careworn skin shone diligence from ranching alongside the man she loved.

"These photos are beautiful." I faced John. His eyes resembled his mother's in the photo. "What is it?"

"Coming here wasn't just a yearning. It was a calling so Dad could teach me how to run this place. Someday when he's gone, it'll be mine, and then Chloe's." His fingers tapped the papers under the silver horseshoe.

I tucked my fingers into the pockets of my jeans.

"I'm not going to regret running this place. The only thing I'll regret is not fighting harder." John's T-shirt hugged his chest as he breathed harder. "Chloe doesn't know about this and I'd appreciate it if we kept this to ourselves. She'll find out someday, but if I have my way, not for a while."

"I won't say a word," I said as he stepped closer to me.

"I know you won't," he whispered, touching my lips with his fingers. "I want you to know that someday I'm gonna want to marry you, Maggie Abernathy. I'm not just asking for a long-distance relationship. And if I don't say it now while we're alone, it'll eat me alive."

Raising my eyebrows, I dug my hands deeper into my pockets with balled fists holding on for dear life. I caught my breath. In my wildest dreams, I never imagined *those* words. I pressed my lips together and swallowed the surprise. "What?"

"I'm sorry, Maggie, but you're leaving soon. I'll be back to empty the house, but I didn't want to—" John's voice broke and he glanced toward the floor.

"You didn't want to what?"

His temples twitched as he swallowed. "I didn't want you to leave without me telling you. I know this isn't very romantic, but I couldn't take a chance waiting for the perfect moment. I didn't want to regret not saying anything at all."

I held his stare. "I don't know what to say."

"I don't expect you to say anything, but I want you to know how serious I am."

Chloe burst into the room. She stopped in her tracks at the sight of her father. "Who died?" she asked, the smile fading from her lips.

"No one," I said. "We were just talking."

"Geez, you two look pitiful. Is that the right word, Dad?" Chloe walked over to her dad.

John ruffled her hair. "Yes, I believe so. What's going on?"

"I caught a trout in the pond. Super cool. Judy took a picture with her phone. She said she'd send it to you." Chloe tugged at my hand, her smile beaming.

"That's wonderful. Did either of the boys fall in?" I asked, expecting more sabotage.

Chloe laughed. "No, but almost 'cause they were pushing and shoving, but Grandpa caught them both by the ear and that was the end of that."

Chloe's toothy grin appeared to mature with each passing day. John wanted to marry me, *someday,* and along with him, I'd inherit Chloe, the girl next-door who'd scraped my nerves when we first met, the girl who'd weaseled her way into my life, and into my heart despite her impulsive antics. I replayed John's words in my head as Chloe and he talked about how she reeled in the fish knowing that *she'd been fishing all along.*

"So while Grandpa was helping me net the fish, Harry hooked Walter, but Grandpa said he'd be okay 'cause there was no barb on the hook. Walter had a few tears, but he mostly looked mad."

"Ouch." I winced, but I knew that Harry would be at Walter's mercy for the rest of the trip.

Walter came bounding in with his hand in the air. "Look, Harry hooked me. Chloe caught a fish and Harry caught me. The hook went right in there." Walter held up the back of his hand.

I inspected it closely. It didn't look much like a wound. "Wow, that must have hurt. No Band-Aid?"

Walter shook his curls from side-to-side. "Nope. I wanted Harry to know that I wasn't a baby."

"I would have cried," I said.

Walter wrinkled his forehead at me while Chloe scratched her head.

"I doubt that," Walter said.

John's skeptical expression mimicked Walter's words.

"You didn't cry when I made your head split open," Chloe said. "You're pretty tough, Maggie."

John nodded in agreement.

"Okay, maybe not, but, ouch!" My eyes met John's gaze, still finding it difficult to breathe from his confession. Walter yanked at my hand until I bent down closer to him.

"You should have seen how bad Harry felt. It was great," he whispered.

Walter's breath tickled my ear and his delight captivated me. "I guess this was just a bonus," I said, touching his button nose.

Chloe ran out of the room.

"Yeah," Walter said before following in Chloe's footsteps.

John and I stood side-by-side. The air filled with the electric charge from the youth that surrounded us. My mind raced. Clearing my throat, I scanned Winston's collection of horseshoes, each one a little different in color and shape.

"Maggie, I meant what I said. This isn't some fleeting notion." John closed the space between us.

I leaned against the heavy pine desk with my hip. "Um," I said, the papers beneath the silver horseshoe caught my attention. This was more than a marriage proposal. And I could hear my mother's voice as I dissected the details of John's intentions. "I don't know what to say."

"I told you, I don't want you to say anything. I just want you to know where I stand and what's at stake."

He touched my hand. His eyes spoke the truth.

"I have to check the barn. Want to tag along?"

I nodded. "Sure."

Chapter 22

"Let's leave the window open," Chloe said. "We'll be able to hear the night."

I propped myself up on one elbow as I lay in bed. "Sounds like a nice idea." Moonlight washed across the ceiling as Chloe knelt on her bed, raised the blinds, and cranked open the window. "What do you hear?" I whispered across the room.

Chloe scooted beneath the covers and put her hands behind her head. "I hear peace."

Her eyes fluttered as the sandman dusted her soul with his magic sleeping potion. I watched her as she listened to the creek and serenading crickets while I held my secrets close, coveting John's proposal.

"I liked it when you picked me up today," Chloe said under her breath. "I miss my mom."

"I bet it's hard not having her around." I blinked away the sandman as his spell drifted over me, too.

"Sometimes yes and sometimes no. You know how she is," Chloe said, closing her eyes. She pushed the hair out of her face. "This hair is crazy. I don't know how my mom does it."

Shadows moved across the ceiling as I wondered if Ida May was watching over her granddaughter. "Do you want me to braid it so it's not sticking to your face while you sleep?"

Chloe flipped over on her side. Her eyes glistened in the dark like a cat's. "Really?"

"Really." I kicked the sheet off and patted my mattress. Chloe snatched the hairbrush from the nightstand and sat beside me. I brushed her hair back. "My hair was always a tangled mess when I was your age. Glad would tell me I should cut it so she wouldn't have to get the knots out." Chloe's hair reminded me of Brook, and I wondered how she'd feel if I married John.

"My mom likes long hair. So do I, but my dad doesn't do it very good. He can brush it, but I always have to fix it," Chloe said, rubbing Voodoo's ear. "And, I'm not that good at it."

"I like long hair, too," I said, dividing her tresses into three thick strands. I wove it over and under until I reached the ends. Reaching for a hair tie from the nightstand, Chloe moved her head with me. "Sorry." I looped and twisted the tie at the bottom of her braid. The scent of coconut shampoo tickled my nose. "There, all done." Chloe scooted around until she was sitting knee-to-knee with me.

There was a knock at the door. "Come in," Chloe whispered. John poked his head in. He was still in his jeans and T-shirt. He padded across the wood floor in his socks. Chloe held his gaze while hugging Voodoo. "Hi, Dad."

"Hi," he whispered. "Judy and Walter are asleep. Harry's watching television downstairs. Just thought I'd check on you two."

"Maggie braided my hair so I could sleep better." Chloe fingered her braid then laid it over her shoulder in front of her to play with the ends.

"Yeah, I wouldn't want you to miss out on any good dreams." I set the hairbrush back on the table.

"She's not pestering you, is she?" John asked me.

"No, not at all. It's kind of nice having a roommate." In fact, it reminded me of the times when Bradley used to lay on my bed when he was frightened, and we'd talk into the night. Mostly he'd talk while I prayed to the heavens that he would just fall sleep.

"Well, I just wanted to say goodnight," John said.

Chloe held out her arms to him and he swept her off my bed and into her own bed in one swift movement. John kissed her on the forehead as she wiggled beneath the covers to find the perfect spot just like Bones, and I couldn't blame her because I was the same way. John picked Voodoo up from the floor and tucked the purple cat next to his daughter.

"Night, Dad."

"Night, munchkin. Don't keep Maggie awake."

"I won't," she said.

"Night, Maggie," John said.

"Night, cowboy. We promise we won't stay up too long." But I wasn't so sure I'd ever fall asleep with his words stuck in my head.

Chloe let out a monumental sigh and closed her eyes. With a tiny wave, John shut the door slowly behind him as he left.

"Maggie," Chloe said.

I wiggled under the sheet to find my sweet spot in the bed. "Yeah."

Chloe yawned. "Would it be so bad if you guys decided to really *like* each other?"

It was as if the day had never happened, and Chloe and I had never left our room.

"I'm not sure how that would work," I whispered into the night air that cooled the dark room. I couldn't believe Chloe and I were talking about this. But then again, I couldn't believe most of the things that happened today.

Chloe let out a gentle snore.

I peeked in her direction. "Chloe?"

She didn't answer me.

When I thought she was truly asleep, I quit tossing and turning, and got out of bed. I slipped my feet into my moccasins, grabbed my fleece from the end of the bed, and padded through the hallway and down the stairs quietly. Harry was sacked out on the sofa and the light in Winston's office glowed. I turned the knob of the front door and went outside. Leaning against one of the timber pillars, the Montana night sky sparkled with more stars than the eve before.

"Maggie," John whispered.

He was sitting in the dark on the bench at the end of the porch. I zipped up my fleece and crossed my arms. "What are you doing out here?" I asked.

"Same thing you're doing. Not sleeping." John patted the bench beside him. I shuffled over and sat beside him.

He wrapped his arm around my shoulder. "You know when we were out here earlier, I could see us when we're old. Chloe was walking away and someday, she will, and when she does, I'll be left here," he said with a sigh, "but you've already experienced that with Bradley."

"Yeah, I have." But I imagined it wouldn't be any easier saying goodbye to Chloe whether she was eight, eighteen, or eighty-eight. Saying goodbye never came easy for me. "I wonder what Bradley is doing tonight." John squeezed my shoulder. I snuggled into him and rested my head against his burly chest. He nuzzled his face into my hair and his breath brushed against my cheek. "It's going to be difficult leaving here." The hitch in my throat caught my words.

"It's going to be hard watching you drive away."

I closed my eyes and chastised reality.

John kissed my left temple. "It's the scars that give us character."

I could feel the creases form at the corners of my eyes as I smiled. "I know." I touched the place where Chloe had split open my head last summer like I'd done a thousand times before. My heart spilled over with love, finally admitting she'd ruptured my heart, too. "I wonder what my mom is doing."

"I know you worry about her."

I stared up into John's eyes as we sat in the glow of the moon. "I do," I said, making the confession. "Even if she gets under my skin sometimes."

"I know how you feel."

I nuzzled closer to the cowboy lassoing my heart.

"I think it's a mom thing. My mom made my business her business. And as irritating as it was, I'd give my eye teeth to relive every disagreement, every opinion, just to have her with us."

John's words only reminded me that time eventually stops.

I wrapped my fingers around his hand on my shoulder then kissed them. "I'm sorry." My words drifted off into the night.

"Thanks for being so nice to Chloe."

The stars tugged at the corner of my mouth. "No problem. She keeps me on my toes."

"Me too," he said. "I know you've already raised your son and I know this isn't what you had in mind, a guy with an eight-year-old."

He was right, but I couldn't say it. I'd already lived through grade school, junior high, high school, and college with Bradley. I knew the effort and energy that it took. "It's a lot to think about." The night air filled my lungs. "I told you before, I don't want to hurt her, or you. Never in my wildest dreams did I imagine you saying what you said to me earlier."

"I'm not sorry," John said. "You needed to know, and I needed to say it."

I laid my head against his chest, my heart in his hands, even though I don't think he truly realized it yet.

John lifted my chin with his finger, his eyes focused on mine. "This isn't an easy life, but it sure would be a hell of a lot better with your spunk around."

"You think I have spunk?" I asked.

"Sure as hell do. When you peel away the sarcasm, break down the stubbornness, and ignore the unwarranted insecurity, you sure do. It's in there, Maggie. You just need to let it out more often and not worry about the rest of the world."

"Sarcasm and stubbornness are necessary to keep control," I said. "What you're proposing is a pretty tall order."

"Maybe so, but well worth the effort."

"Is this you fighting harder?"

"No, this is."

John ran his finger down my jawline, over my neck, and across my collarbone. A shiver ran down my spine.

"Close your eyes, Maggie Abernathy."

I shut my eyes and waited for him to kiss me, but he didn't.

"Keep them closed."

John's breath warmed me as he whispered in my ear, "Okay."

A soft moan escaped my lips as his lips grazed my neck.

"Just listen to your heart," he whispered before letting his lips linger behind my ear, "it'll tell you everything you need to know."

Taking it all in, I listened. "Sounds like good advice. I can hear your heart, but I feel like mine is buried."

"So get out your shovel and dig. It's in there." John stroked my hair. "Just have a little faith."

I wrapped my arms around his waist and held on. Apprehension sparked the hallows, and I scorned it for rearing its ugly head at a moment like this, a moment that might never come again. Filling my senses with all that was around me in the wee hours of a perfect Montana night, I held on to the perfect Montana man.

Chapter 23

"How you feeling today, neighbor lady?" John called as he steered his horse around in a loop to ride beside me.

"I'm good. I love this girl." I patted my horse's neck. "She doesn't have that feel that Pippin had, not so skittish. She's nice and calm. I like that." Tullia whinnied as if she agreed with me. "I know, Tullia, you're more than just a pretty face."

John laughed while Tullia snorted.

"She's watching you. She knows all about you and your antics," I said, admiring her sleek white coat that covered her neck, withers, and chest. I peered over my shoulder to inspect her brown-speckled hindquarters. "Where'd the name Tullia come from?"

"It's the best kind of name, Irish, and it means peaceful and quiet. That's why I saddled her up for you today. Thought her Zen might help settle what's brewing inside of you."

"Comedian." I stroked Tullia's hide. "You're a good girl, aren't you?" She stared back at me and I fingered her coarse brown mane.

"Yes, she is," John said. "Couldn't have you bolting off again. You might not come back with all this crazy talk between us."

"You ready to climb girl?" I asked Tullia. She tugged at the reins and snatched a mouthful of grass.

"Give her a little nudge when she does that. Greedy girl," John said.

Breeze stepped carefully over thick tree roots to find her footing. Tullia followed in her footsteps, her hooves clomping against the sunbaked earth. I leaned forward and coaxed her with a clicking tongue as I ducked under low branches, pine needles tickling my shoulder. John checked over his shoulder when Breeze found flatter ground.

"You really do look like a natural," John said, resting his hand on his thigh. "We'll go to the top, look around, and take a break before heading back to the barn. We can stop anywhere to take photos. You got your camera?"

"Yup, in the saddlebag."

Tullia nuzzled close to Breeze at the top of the hill.

"You like Breeze?" I asked her.

"Yeah, they don't like to be separated," John answered. "Dad got them as youngsters and they stick together. When you find one of them, the other is not far behind."

My body swayed in time with Tullia's tempo as I listened to John talk, thinking this could be my last ride before it was time to head home. Judy and I had no definite plans, but had a rough idea when we'd be leaving. John pointed to the left. I peered up the hill to see a group of deer grazing in between the pines. They leered at us then fled, their white tails bobbing up and down.

"See that ridge up there?" John pointed straight ahead.

"Yup."

"We'll stop there."

Tullia's shoulder blades glimmered in the sun. She was hot from the ride and I was grateful for her hard work. "We'll stop in a minute, girl."

"You still talking to that horse back there?"

John's hat shaded his face, but I could see the laugh lines lines at the corners of his eyes as he grinned at me over his shoulder.

"Yup."

John gave Breeze a nudge with the heels of his boots then cantered across the field. Tullia's ears pricked up and I knew we were going, too.

"Let's go girl." I clicked my tongue and she raced to catch up. Hunkering down in the saddle, I hung onto the horn until she slowed to a trot. "Good girl," I whispered into the wind. A chill ran across the nape of my neck like one of John's kisses.

John and Breeze sauntered along the ridge with Tullia and me in tow. Breeze swished her tail and shook her mane free at the view of the valley. John stopped, dismounted, and then tied Breeze to a limb with a view. He guided Tullia next to her buddy and wrapped her reins around the branch. Sniffing the ground, she munched on blooms before shifting her weight, and lowering her eyelids.

I found my camera in the saddlebag while John got the canteen. He handed it to me after taking a long drink.

"Um, do you have cooties?" I asked.

He narrowed his eyes at me, set the canteen on the ground, and then reached out to grab me. I lurched backward, my heart pounding. The game was different up here without an audience.

John came closer with his hands up like he was surrendering. Raising my eyebrows at the glint in his green irises, I backed away at the prospect of being caught. "From where I come from, girls don't like this game on the playground. I think I mentioned this before."

"Well, from where I come from, girls don't like it either unless they're just pretending they don't like it."

I stood knee high in daisies, wild bushes lined the ridge. We were as close to heaven as we could possible get.

"There's nowhere to go, unless you head that way." John pointed to a grove of dense trees. "But I wouldn't do that."

I scrunched my forehead. "Why not?"

"Bears, maybe. Moose, maybe. Bobcats, maybe." John grinned with pleasure as he listed the wildlife that lingered in dark places on the mountaintop. His whiskery chin shimmered in the sunlight.

I snapped a photo of him. "Oh. Not sure which is more dangerous. You or them." I placed my camera on the rock I hid behind then anchored my hands on my hips. John raised an eyebrow at me. He planted his hands on the rock and leaned toward me.

John whispered across the boulder in the middle of the field that resembled an expensive postcard. "Now, you wouldn't have put that camera down if you thought I wasn't going to get you."

I raised an eyebrow. My heart beat faster. Excitement flooded my body, something I craved. Beckett and I never played games like this when we were married. Beckett and I never played games, period.

"You look like you're sweating," John said, holding out a bandana in my direction. "Hot flash?"

"Nice," I said.

He snickered.

"Is this part of your persuasive plan?" I asked, moving to the right as he moved closer.

"Could be, sweetheart. Depends on how hard you kick and scream until you give."

My heart fluttered against my chest walls. "Stop it," I said. "This is silly."

"Come on, this is fun."

"For who?" I squinted in his direction. The sun peeked out from behind a rolling cloud that hung alone in the blue sky. John shushed me and pointed over my shoulder.

"Too bad because it's gonna swoop down and get you."

"Yeah, right." John hooked his thumbs in his back pockets and watched intently over my shoulder.

"Okay, but can't you see the shadow?" John tucked his fingers in his armpits then flapped like a bird. "You want to look, don't you?"

I nodded.

"Go ahead, I won't get you," he said.

I glared at him. "Promise?"

"Promise."

The hawk's shadow flitted across the grass behind me. It let out a piercing shriek then dove to the ground, snatched up a furry critter that waggled in its talons, then flew away over our heads.

"Told ya."

"What did it catch?" I shaded my eyes and watched it fly off.

"Probably a mouse. Pretty cool, huh?"

"Food chain."

"Natural selection. Aren't you big on that?" John asked.

I smiled. "Yeah."

"Good, me too."

John grabbed me around the waist and reeled me in. The brims of our hats touching.

"Um, I thought we called a truce." My lips grazed his neck.

The heat between us was sultrier than his mischievous grin.

"When you see a chance, you gotta take it, neighbor lady, and I don't know if I'm gonna get you alone again before you leave."

Smiling, I flicked the Stetson back from his brow and kissed him. Beads of sweat trickled down my back as the sun beat down. John sat on the rock then drew me in. I rested my arms on his shoulders while he cradled me between his thighs.

"Pretty sneaky," I said. "Not sure how you got me to kiss you like that."

"See, you wanted to be caught." John took his Stetson off and set it down beside him, next to my camera. Then he took off my cowboy hat, laid it atop his, and ran his fingers down my cheek.

He unbuttoned my shirt, and I closed my eyes.

"Open your eyes, Maggie."

His fingers grazed my neck. Heat washed through me as he ran them down my chest to the little black tattoo between my breasts. I watched his gaze as it followed the path of his hand. He exposed my collarbone, then touched the little black tattoo on my shoulder. When the shirt slid from my shoulders, I pointed to the two black specks on my side. He kissed each mark left from radiation then kissed the one between my breasts, again. My heart raced.

"You could turn those little black dots into something."

"Not sure I could. Those four pokes sent me to the moon."

John unbuttoned his shirt and let it fall to the ground. Crossing his arms in front of him, he tugged upward on the hem of his undershirt, then pulled it over his head.

"I'd say you messed up your hair, but you really don't have any." I ran my fingers through the short stubble on the sides of his head. A tiny smirk crossed my lips, and John smiled back at me. I flinched as he ran his fingers across my belly.

"Pippin's not the only skittish one around here. Maybe that's why she took off, because of you," he said.

I covered his hand with mine as he rested it on my belly. John leaned forward and kissed the skin between my breasts just above my lacy bra band, then rested his head against my chest. His shoulders fell forward. I kissed the top of his smooth head then traced the horseshoe tattoo on his left shoulder.

John's eyes sparkled like gemstones, his pupils clear enough to see my own reflection. I caressed his cheek. The stubble tickled. My dreams caught in my chest, my words lost in the breeze.

"You okay?" John asked.

"I don't want to go home, but I have to." My mind flashed back to my kitchen when Chloe and I sat on the floor, crying about having to say goodbye before they left, her letter on my night table, her words in my heart.

"It doesn't have to be forever. You have a home here."

Gravity tugged at my mouth. "What about Mom? What about—" I caught my breath. "I can't leave her. And I have—"

John interrupted. "You have a job that is sucking the life out of you. You give yourself to everyone. You deserve to have what you want. Times are changing. I see it with Chloe. What ever happened to animal crackers and milk, learning cursive, playing Four Square, and playing period, because that's how we learned to live our lives?"

John raised me onto his lap. I wrapped my arms around his neck and gazed deep into his eyes for the answer.

"I don't know how Glad would feel if you up and left, but I have a sneaking suspicion that she'd want you to be happy. I think she'd even help you pack your bags."

"You really like her, don't you?" I knew I didn't have to ask, but I needed to hear his answer.

"Yeah, I do. She can be a handful like you, but yeah."

I kissed his cheek, thinking about how she'd pestered me to have a *fling* with John, the man who was holding me on his lap at the top of a mountain, the man who said he'd want to marry me someday. "Well, I have to get it from somewhere."

"Yeah, ya do, just like Chloe. Apples don't fall from the tree. That's what Dad used to tell me and it took me all these years to believe him."

John held me close.

The breeze kicked up, making our hats tumble to the ground and we held on to each other like we'd been together all our lives.

Chapter 24

John was right. Scars gave us personality.

All roads led home, and John said I had a home here in Montana. I lifted my chin to the sun and closed my eyes as Tullia navigated the path back to the ranch where a young girl played with Walter and Harry, the boys from Michigan who wore Speedos at the beach and resembled Mark Spitz with their curly dark hair, and learned about life from a litter of kittens, a crow named Frankie, horses, cattle, fly-fishing, Winston, and most importantly John, who wasn't afraid to follow his heart. My skin tingled as I imagined his kisses and how he held me like I'd never been held before. That familiar sorrow surfaced as I thought about packing for home.

"I like my bracelet," I said, playing with the braided strands of grass around my wrist.

"Yeah, I hear women like that sort of thing."

"We do. In fact, I still have Chloe's macaroni necklace."

"When we make our way down, remember to let Tullia find her path."

Tullia stared back at me with dark eyes as I ran my fingers through her mane. She stumbled then caught herself. I held steady as she jerked the reins from my hands. "Easy, girl," I said. "You're okay." She shook her head like a wet dog then carefully stepped over the rocks and tree roots in her way.

"You talking to your girl again?" Johns said, looking over his shoulder.

"Yup."

Tullia snorted then exhaled.

"See, she likes it."

John's laugh drifted in the air. Breeze whinnied. "Okay, girl, I'll talk to you, too."

I patted Tullia's taut shoulder. Breeze's bright gaze watched me. "Us girls have to stick together. Right, Breeze?"

Breeze swished her tail and trotted into the open field as we descended from the ridge. Tullia followed on her heels.

Justin met us at the barn. "Was Tullia a good girl for you?" he asked with a wink.

"Perfect."

Justin tied Tullia to the hitching post so I could dismount. I noticed my knees fared a wee better than the last ride. "She's always a good girl," Justin said between his teeth as he patted her nose.

I ran my hand over her wither then down her front leg. She felt warm and so did I with my shirt stuck to my back. "I think we both need a drink."

"You'll probably need a different kind of drink than your lady friend here with the hooves." Justin laughed at his own joke.

"Yeah, a beer does sound good. It's hot this afternoon."

"You're not kidding." John yanked up on Breeze's girth and unhooked her saddle. With one clean jerk, she was bare backed, the sun glistening on her sweaty coat.

Chloe poked her head out of the barn door. "Hi, Maggie." She fingered her braid and beamed beneath the brim of her Stetson. "Look, I didn't mess it up today."

Trying to cool off, I rolled up my sleeves. "Even if you did, that's an easy fix. How are those kitties?"

"Little and furry. Their eyes are still shut. They're waiting for their mom to come back, wherever she is. I'm just keeping them company."

"Probably out huntin'," Justin said, walking past with my saddle and tack.

"Thanks, Justin."

He nodded. "Anything for you. It's nice to have a lady around. We don't get that much." His boot heels clunked across the barn floor.

"Hey, what about me?" Ashley leered at Justin as she appeared from behind the stall by the door.

Justin laughed his sinister laugh. "Just checking to see if you were listening."

"Yeah, right." She poked him as he strode by. "Don't you have some fences to mend somewhere?"

"Gonna take more than that to hurt this cowboy," he said, puffing out his chest. "And no. I finished the fences early. That's why I'm hanging around here."

Chloe scooted back into the stall and sat on the bale of hay. Ashley and Justin continued bickering as John groomed Breeze. "How about you help Justin brush down Tullia? Chloe can you hear me?"

"In a minute. I want to see the kitties."

"Good thing they aren't purple like Voodoo," John said.

Chloe laughed. "Yeah, good thing," she said, resting her chin on bent knees.

"I'm really thirsty. You want me to get you something to drink from the house?" I leaned against the doorjamb, taking in John from head-to-toe. Feeling his bare skin next to mine only made me want him more.

John mopped his brow with a blue bandana from his back pocket. He grazed my shoulder as he strode past, igniting the smoldering heat I'd carried down the mountain. His wink stirred my insides with giddy butterflies that bounced around like drunk flies stuck between the kitchen windowpanes.

"I'll finish up here, you fetch the cold drinks, and I'll meet you under that tree." He nodded to the willow in the pasture.

"Can I come, too?" Chloe asked.

"Of course you can," I answered. Her toothy grin made me smile, too. She'd be a welcome distraction.

"That's why I like you, Maggie. You don't ever leave me out."

"See you in a few minutes." I strolled to the house where Walter sat outside eating Oreos while perusing a Spiderman comic book. "Hey there, little man," I said, breezing past.

"Hey." He gave a little wave, but kept his eyes focused on his favorite superhero.

Judy was inside on the phone with Pink, giving him a rundown of everything she'd been doing while I rummaged through the cupboards and fridge for snacks and drinks. I loaded the cooler with beer, water bottles, a can of orange soda for Chloe, cheese and crackers, and a chocolate bar. Judy gave me a wave as she told her husband she loved him. Goosebumps covered my arms, thinking maybe I could have that, too. She told him goodbye and that she'd call him later with more details.

Judy leaned against the counter her fists under her chin. "What's going on?"

The glint in her eye left a puddle of hope within me. "Getting some snacks and drinks. Gonna meet Chloe and John under the old tree in the pasture. Wanna come?"

Judy sighed and leaned a closer. "So what's the skinny?"

"What skinny?" I questioned, organizing the cooler.

"You seem different. You look happier. What's going on?"

Closing the lid to the cooler, I rolled my eyes at her. "If I tell you, can we please keep it between us? I've been holding it hostage and you know me."

"Yes, I promise," Judy said. "And you have to quit holding details hostage."

"Cross your heart, hope to die, stick a needle in your eye?"

Judy frowned. "Gross, but okay." She stuck out her pinkie and we shook on it.

"John said he wanted to marry me," I whispered. "Can you believe it?"

Judy hopped around, clapping her hands. "Oh, my, God!" Her eyes brimmed with tears.

"Stop it. You're acting crazy."

Judy pointed her finger at me and grabbed an apple out of the bowl on the counter with her other hand. "Hey, there's nothing wrong with a little excitement, and this is huge."

I shushed her. "Chloe can't know anything about this."

Judy narrowed her eyes. "Why? What did you do?"

"What did I do? Are you kidding me? I just don't want her to get her hopes up. I still don't know if or how I can have this relationship long distance. There are a lot of details to work out, especially back home."

I watched Judy intently as she closed in. She pinched me in the arm as hard as she could.

"Ow," I howled. "What did you do that for?"

"Because you're crazy. It's going to hurt a lot more *not* being with that man," she said. "What did you tell him?"

"I didn't say anything. There's nothing to say yet." I took the apple out of her hand and bit off a juicy hunk.

"What exactly did he say? I want details."

I handed her Granny Smith back. My cheeks puckered with the tart aftertaste. "He said, 'I'm gonna want to marry you someday.'" I chewed. "He also told me that I'd always have a home here." Goose bumps covered my arms. "Do you want to come to the tree with us?"

"Oh my God! You act like nothing even happened. This is epic."

"Nothing has happened yet and it might not ever happen. Let's not count the chickens before the eggs hatch, sister." I took her apple again and took another bite. "But it is exciting, isn't it?" I wiped the apple juice from my chin.

"This is great. Wait until Glad finds out."

I shook my finger in her face as soon as her eyes flashed wildly. "And that is exactly why I want you to keep this on the down low." I paused. "Please."

Judy pretended to lock her pursed lips and throw away the imaginary key.

"Thank you." Fanning myself, I took the cooler and headed outside. I peeked back at her. "You coming or not?"

"I'll be down in a while," she said.

"Remember, mum's the word."

I laid out the blanket under the shade tree. Chloe bounded across the field. Sunny stopped grazing and trotted over to meet her. Ray shook her head and meandered in the opposite direction. "Hey, girlie-girl," I said.

"Hey, Mags!" Chloe's crazy canter slowed to a skip.

"Mags? That's different." I squinted in Chloe's direction.

"Yeah, I figured we knew each other well enough that I could call you Mags." Chloe patted Sunny's nose then dug out a couple sugar cubes from her jean pocket. After Sunny licked the palm of her hand, she turned toward me. "Is that okay?"

"I guess. It could be worse, but let's not use it too much." It felt good to stretch out in the shade.

Chloe scrunched up her face. "What do you mean?" she asked. "Cool, a Hersey Bar. Can I have some?" She licked her lips.

I nodded. "It just means that I could have worse names, you know, like mean names." I brushed away the bumblebee buzzing near my face.

"Who would call you mean names?"

"Ah, let's not go there." I thought about seeing Jenny McBride in the oncologist's office during Judy's last appointment. Jenny appeared so sullen and gaunt. I said a prayer and focused back on Chloe.

"Okay," she said. "How was the mountain?"

Peering down, I sought out a beer from the cooler to hide my delighted spirits about spending alone time with John. I opened the bottle and took a long draw. The cold ale slid right down, quenching my thirst. "This tastes so good." Sighing, I took in the scenery like I took in John's body. "It's hot this afternoon." I wondered if the Montana midday sun would leave its mark on my bare skin. My chest hadn't seen the sun in a long time, thanks to my treatment last summer. I inspected my freckled arms and tanned hands. I twisted the lid off of Chloe's orange soda then handed it to her. "There ya go."

"Walter says that you guys have to go home soon." She took a swig of soda then took her hat off and laid it next to her. Sunny galloped away to meet her momma on the other side of the pond.

"I guess so." The sharp tug at my heart persisted. "We have to figure that out. Judy spoke to Walter's dad earlier."

"I don't want you guys to leave." Chloe scooted over and settled in next to me.

"Yeah, I know. But I bet I could visit again. And you'll be back to help your dad pack," I said, hoping we could work something out.

Chloe's shoulders slumped forward. "Maybe, but then, you know."

"What?" I popped a piece of cheese into my mouth then handed her one.

"People always say that they'll visit, kind of like my mom, then it usually doesn't happen." She took the cheese and nibbled at the edge of the cube like a frail mouse.

My insides crumbled. I loved her so much. Scanning the field, I sipped my beer. "You once told me that you could always count on me. Do you remember that?"

Chloe's eyes dimmed as she nodded.

"Well, I have to say that you moving here will not be the end of our friendship. I promise."

Chloe scrunched up her nose. "Stick a needle in your eye?"

I held out my pinkie. "Yes." Chloe wrapped her pinkie around mine and we shook on it. Her soft hand touched my cheek after we were done. I knew what she was doing because I found myself doing the same thing earlier. She was remembering me just in case things didn't work out. Chloe touched the braided grass tied around my wrist. "Will you make me one of these?"

I set my beer down, searched the grass for three perfect strands, plucked, one, two, three, and began to braid while she held the ends.

"Did you make that one you're wearing?"

"No," I whispered, thinking about John's arms wrapped around me.

"Who made it?"

"Your dad." The taste of his skin still on my lips.

The slightest of smiles formed between her innocent lips. "He's nice that way." Chloe shifted her weight forward to get a better look at my grass jewelry.

"He sure is," I said. "There, that should do it. Hold out your wrist." I tied the grass creation on her wrist and broke off the extra length with my nails. "Perfect."

"Thanks, Maggie."

Chloe leaned against me and gave me a hug. My Stetson fell off the back of my head as her words brushed against my ear. "You're right. I won't worry about not seeing you anymore because I know I can always count on you. Even if you're not here, you'll always be in my heart."

Chapter 25

"Okay, so how is this going to work?" I asked as John unrolled Chloe's tent across the side yard between the house and the stream.

"Chloe, Walter, and Harry are going to sleep in this tent." John assembled the poles bound together with a bungee. "Remember, you and Chloe did this at your house."

"Yeah, but we were inside. There was a fireplace and I could sleep on the sofa after she sacked out. And you were nowhere around."

John knelt close to the ground and yanked at the corner of the tent to get the wrinkles out. "See that tent over there?" He pointed to another small gray dome tent that was already assembled. "Chloe wants you to sleep out here, too. We can sleep in that tent."

I raised an eyebrow at him. "Sounds like *your* plan," I said, crossing my arms in front of me. "You and me in the same tent?"

"Well, you could sleep with the kids. I hear that Walter talks in his sleep and passes gas."

Chloe crossed the stream and sauntered over, snuggling Voodoo in her arms. "Hi, Mags, did Dad tell you that we're sleeping outside tonight?"

Judy touched my arm. "Yeah, it's going to be nice not having to share a room with the boys."

Her sweet smile filled me with guilt.

"Come on, Maggie, it will be fun." Chloe stuck out her bottom lip.

John and Judy shot me a look. John finished assembling Chloe's tent while Judy marveled at the neoprene shelters. "Come on. The kids will love it. Do it for Chloe."

"You are evil," I whispered between clenched teeth and crossed my arms. Being outside all day was one thing, but sleeping in a tent was a whole other gamut. I loved my bed.

John echoed her. "Come on, do it for Chloe. I'll make sure nothing gets you."

"It's not the critters I'm worried about."

Chloe grabbed my hand. "Come on. We might never get to do this again. Please." She tilted her head to the side, her eyes filled with something, not sure what, but it made my gut twist with obligation.

"Let me think about it." I tapped my chin. "I need to come to this on my own terms."

"Please," Chloe whined. "Oh, come on, it'll be fun. You can have snacks in your tent and stay up all night."

I rolled my eyes as John bumped into my shoulder, knocking me off balance.

"Fine." I blew a loose strand of hair from my face in defeat.

"Woo-hoo," Chloe gave her dad a fist bump. "This is gonna be fun."

"What else can we do to wear them out after dinner?" I asked Judy.

"I'm not sure, but if you think of something, let me know." Judy draped her arm around my shoulders, and then gave me a squeeze. "You're a good egg, Maggie. And don't you forget it."

"Yeah, yeah, yeah," I said. "We're gonna make s'mores again tonight, right? 'Cause I'm gonna need a few."

John patted me on the back. "I think it's about time for dinner, don't you?"

Winston came around the corner of the house with Justin. "Looks like a party back here. Gonna do a little camping?"

Chloe scooted over and gave her grandfather a hug. "Yup. Dad and Maggie are going to sleep outside with us tonight. I can't wait."

Winston rubbed his chin. "I bet there won't be much sleeping going on."

"I hope there is," I said.

John laughed. "That's my girl," he whispered in my ear as he strolled past, giving me a hearty pat on the back.

Judy's gaze followed John's path. "You are so not gonna sleep."

After giving her the stink-eye, I went inside to check on dinner. John was milling around in the kitchen. He peeked out the kitchen window, and then pinned me up against the counter. "It's just a tent."

"A tent with you in it," I said. "Isn't that weird? It's like shacking up."

"No, it's not, and nobody else thinks it's weird. I'll have my sleeping bag and you'll have yours. No shenanigans."

"Fine."

"Unless you want to fool around. I'm sure we can arrange some secret meeting somewhere else."

My eyes held his stare. "I'll get back to you on that," I said, trying to get a grip on the situation. John's carefree attitude was charming nonetheless, but for me, it was serious. God, I hated being like that.

John ran his hand across my belly. "You worry too much. I'm just yanking your chain. It'll be fine. The kids will end up coming inside anyway, then you can have a tent and I can have a tent and it'll be fair."

"You're so funny." I tried to wiggle away but couldn't.

"You're a squirmy little thing."

Judy came through the kitchen and her eyes lit up when she saw John holding me. "Hey, hey, not in front of the kids."

John laughed and kissed my cheek. "I'm just giving Maggie a hard time. Don't mind me."

"Pesky boys." She leaned in my direction. "I'd think twice about that one. He's kind of cute."

I tried not to smile, but couldn't help it. "You two are terrible." Their sheepish expressions embarrassed me. "Oh brother," I said, shooing them away, but secretly thanked them for showing me how fun life could be.

Harry strolled in from the living room. "When's dinner? I'm hungry." He shoved his hands in his pockets and stood by the island, picking at the fruit salad.

"In a few minutes." Harry's hair was smashed down on one side of his head.

"Were you sleeping?" When he yawned, I could see his molars. "Tired?"

He nodded.

"Anything new?"

He shrugged.

"Cool," I said, remembering similar conversations with Bradley.

"Will you call me when dinner's on?" Harry carefully took a handful of chips from the bag then left.

"Sure." I shook my head and wondered how they roped him into sleeping in the tent with Walter and Chloe. Chloe's vivacious personality with sketchy boundaries seemed so different than Harry who wore an invisible suit and tie with matching wing-tipped *My Three Sons* shoes.

Walter skipped in from outside, singing a Katy Perry tune.

"Want to help me set the table?" I asked, trying to keep a straight face.

He nodded and took the fruit salad to the table.

"You have all gone bonkers," I said to myself.

"Whatcha mumbling about?" Chloe stepped on my toe. "Sorry." She stepped backward and inspected my foot.

"Everyone is being silly." I handed her the napkins. "Can you put these on the table, please?"

"Sure." She laughed as Walter came back to the counter, singing into a fork.

I handed him the chips and sent him on his way.

Judy came in with a platter of burgers and John was on her heels like a teenage boy. Harry appeared moments later, looking just as sleepy as before. And by the time I got to the table, Winston, Trout, and Justin were all seated waiting like hungry boys, chomping at the bit to be fed. The rest of us made our way to the empty seats. Winston waited for a lull in the action before he spoke. He cleared his voice as if he were going to address the nation. Chloe and Walter hunched their shoulders forward to see him better.

"Well, I have something to say," Winston started. "When I invited you all here, I wasn't sure what I was getting myself into, but I want to thank you for being part of this ranch." His moustache twitched, his eyes scanning the cast of characters. "And tonight, I'd like to say grace." He looked over to Judy, who smiled, nodded, then rested her hands in her lap then gave the boys a nod.

I rested my hands in my lap while Chloe clasped her hands on the table in front of her as if she were kneeling beside her bed. I closed my eyes and listened to Winston's words.

When Winston finished, John lifted his water glass. "Now, it's time for a toast. To good friends, fun, laughter, and the future."

My cheeks grew hot as his gaze met mine.

"Cheers," Judy said, clinking Walter's glass. "And a very fun campout tonight." She clinked John's glass, twice.

"Yeah, you enjoy your cushy bed in your quiet room. There'll be paybacks," I told her.

Holding my marshmallow over the red embers, I rotated it ever so slowly to get the perfect crusty brown exterior.

I inspected my work, and then decided it needed a smidge more time over the fire. "Almost done."

"That's not how dad does it," Chloe said.

"I know. He likes to light them on fire." I cringed. "Gross."

"I like them both ways," Chloe said, smiling at her dad.

"Not me," Walter said. "I like Maggie's way." He patted my shoulder with a wild grin.

"I'm working on it," Judy told him. "It'll be done in a minute."

Winston strummed his guitar while Judy and I made plans for the trip back to Michigan.

John listened intently while Chloe licked chocolate from her fingers. "I still can't believe you guys didn't fly out here."

"I don't mind driving and with Maggie, it's all good." Judy's marshmallow fell off the skewer and burst into flames.

"I liked that rock with all the presidents' faces," Walter said, handing his mom another marshmallow. "That was neat. I still can't figure out how they did that."

"You mean Mt. Rushmore," Harry said.

"That's what I said. The rock with the presidents' faces on it, geez. Why do you have to correct me all the time?"

Judy cleared her throat and made a face at the boys.

"The horse stalls could use some extra elbow grease," John said.

Walter and Harry sat up a little straighter, and Walter pretended to button his lip.

"So we'll leave day after tomorrow?" I asked with an ache in my chest. Judy nodded. "I'll call Mom tomorrow and give her the itinerary so she knows when to expect us."

Bones' mug popped into my mind. I wondered what he was doing and if he was driving my mom crazy, or if she was driving him crazy.

"Can I play with Bones when we get there?" Walter

shoved a hunk of s'more in his mouth, a glob of marshmallow stuck to his chin.

"Sure can," I said. "He'll be excited to see you."

Chloe's eyes dimmed, so I nudged her. "You'll get to see him, too, when you and your dad head back." I glanced over to John. "Anything new on the house?"

"As a matter of fact, I accepted an offer yesterday." He blew out another burning marshmallow at the end of his skewer. "We'll be heading that way soon."

"I hate this part." Chloe grumbled as she took half her dad's s'more. She nibbled at the corner.

"I'm sorry, kiddo." He wrapped his arm around Chloe and squeezed her shoulder.

"Hopefully, this will be the last time we move."

Winston stopped playing his guitar. "Better be, 'cause I'm not letting you go, short stuff. We need you around here." He clicked his tongue at her and winked in her direction.

Chloe wiggled out of her dad's arms and climbed into Winston's lap. John took Winston's guitar and set it in the chair beside him.

"Yeah, my family moved a lot when I was a kid. I went to four different elementary schools," Judy told Chloe. "I got to meet lots of people that way."

"Maybe, but you guys will be so far away."

Judy glanced over at Winston. "Well, if it's okay with your grandpa, I'd like to visit again. I bet Walter and Harry would like to come back, and maybe next time their dad can come."

"Really?" A spark passed between Chloe and Judy.

"We can see each other through the computer. Maybe Maggie could come over and you could see us all at once. That would be fun." Judy leaned back in her chair. Walter crawled into her lap and snuggled into her chest.

"You have some awfully nice friends," John said.

"But let's not focus on that. We have a camp out to get to," I said, trying to lighten the moment.

Walter wiggled out of his mom's lap then sat next to Harry.

Chloe wrapped her arms around Winston's neck then pressed her cheek against his. John's eyes gleamed in the firelight as he watched the exchange between his dad and Chloe. Chloe was lucky to have two great men in her life. Chloe kissed his cheek. "Tent time," she told him. "See you tomorrow, Grandpa."

"See you tomorrow, squirt," he said, swatting her bottom as she hopped off his lap.

"Come on, you guys." Chloe gestured for Harry and Walter to follow her.

"First brush your teeth. I laid some sweatpants and a T-shirt out on your bed," John said. "Grab a fleece from the mudroom on your way back."

"All right," Chloe said. "If I have to."

Harry's and Walter's faces glowed in the dying firelight with anticipation. Their messy black curls danced in the sauntering breeze. I closed my jacket and crossed my arms over my chest as I watched the interaction around the fire. The ease of human kindness waltzed amongst us. And the fact that I'd be saying goodbye the day after tomorrow made the ache exponential.

Chapter 26

The kids giggled and their shadows wiggled across the tent walls. Chloe said goodnight and zipped up the fabric door.

Angst slithered through my veins and into my mind, knowing that John waited for me in the other tent. I rolled my eyes at myself for worrying and poked my head inside. He was on his sleeping bag in sweats and T-shirt with his hands behind his head.

"Come on in."

I hunched over to fit in the door and held his gaze. "Where'd you find that?" I pointed to the pad under my sleeping bag.

"Dad had it tucked away."

My skin tingled as John watched me get situated.

"Nice sleeping pants. Like the Michigan State sweatshirt. Nice touch," John commented with a wink.

I fluffed my pillow. "Thanks, Bradley gave it to me a long time ago when he was a freshman. I wear it when I miss him."

"I suppose when your kids grow up and move away, it's hard. I think there just might be a part of me that'll be happy for the solitude. Chloe can be a handful."

"You wouldn't miss her?" I crisscrossed my legs pretzel style and wondered what was in the cooler.

"Yeah, I'll miss her, but it's not like Brook is around to help out."

"Yeah, at least I had Beckett." I peeked into the cooler, my curiosity got the best of me, and then noticed John's expression. "Sorry."

"Brought a couple of beers for me and a piece of chocolate for you." John's face brightened. "Thanks. And don't be sorry. I don't ever want anyone to feel sorry for me. It is what it is." He crossed his ankles. "Besides, if Brook was here, I wouldn't know you."

"Guess you're right. I was thinking about that earlier. If I'd stayed with Beckett, I wouldn't know you either."

"You'd probably know me, but just not like you do." He cleared his throat. "This is going to sound selfish, but I'm glad Beckett's not around."

I smirked. "Wouldn't be much of a marriage. That's for sure."

John and I smiled at each other when the kids' voices ruptured into a burst of laughter.

"They sure do like each other," I said, lying down on my back, mimicking John's pose. A black lantern hung in the center of the tent.

"They're not the only ones."

"I know. But what are we going to do?" I asked. A multitude of possibilities lay dormant at the back of my mind. "I'd like to finish my career."

"I know."

"This long-distance thing seems crazy, not to mention that *other thing* you mentioned." I closed my eyes and pictured myself traipsing back and forth with luggage as a credit card bill dangled in the background. I knew the long stints of absence would prove difficult, too.

"I can go back and forth, too," he said. "And that *other thing* will work its way out in time."

I turned on my side and propped my head up with my hand to see John's face. "What about Chloe?"

"She doesn't always have to tag along. We have plenty of hands here if that's what you're thinking." John rolled over on his side to face me.

"What would we tell her?" I asked. "This seems so foreign to me. I don't think I'm equipped to handle this."

"The truth," he answered. "People do it all the time. We have a good relationship with her. Don't you think she would want us to be happy?"

"Yes," I said.

"I hate to say this, but she has a better relationship with you than she has with Brook. I know that's hard for you, but it's true."

John's intense gaze settled my nerves. "Yeah, I never thought I'd be with anyone again, let alone a cowboy with a child."

John moved the cooler and motioned for me to come closer as he put out his arm and lay back. I wiggled over and nestled in beside him.

"You worry too much."

"I can't help it. That's how I roll."

The chatter in the neighboring tent faded. I wondered how fast I could roll over to my side of the tent if one of the kids unzipped our tent door.

"I see that look in your eye. We're not doing anything bad. You're dressed. I'm dressed. We're just talking," he said. "You can go back over there if you want."

I sat up then moved back over to my sleeping bag when I heard the zipper on Chloe's tent, and then we waited for our visitor as feet shuffled outside the tent. John put his finger over his lip and reached up to turn off the lantern. Wisps of flashlights flickered about. Sitting still, I watched the nonsensical paths of light as they circled our tent. It suddenly went dark and the zipper to their tent echoed into the night.

John switched on his flashlight. His eyes glowed in the dark.

"What are they doing?" I whispered.

He slipped on his boots, unzipped our tent, and went to investigate.

I snuggled in my sleeping bag. *We could go back and forth, or at least try.* I was beginning to believe that voice inside my head. I wanted to trust myself with all my heart. I wasn't sure I'd even done that before.

Walter's giggle drifted into the tent as John spoke to Chloe.

"What are you guys doing?" he asked her.

"We were just checking things out. We thought we heard a something."

"All the more reason to stay in the tent," he told her. "Bobcat, skunk."

"Okay," she said.

"I told you," Harry said. "Bear." He growled.

I grinned at his animated tone.

"What are you and Maggie doing?" she asked.

"We're just talking," he told her. "Listening to you knuckleheads."

"Hey," Walter chimed in, "I'm not sure I've ever heard that word before, but it doesn't sound like a compliment."

"It's not," Harry informed him. "Can we just get back to the ghost story now?"

I raised my eyebrows, wondering what kind of ghost story they were telling.

"If you have to get up," John said, "use the walkie-talkie I gave you. Harry knows how to use it if you don't. I'll check things out."

"Okay, Dad. Tell Maggie I said goodnight."

I smiled and waited for John to return. He zipped up the tent, took off his boots, and plopped back down on his sleeping bag. "Uh, yeah, I'll miss her, but—" John rolled his eyes. "She said goodnight."

"I know, I heard."

Situating himself, John set his walkie-talkie on the cooler. A ghostly howl made by a youngster penetrated the tent walls. John held the flashlight beneath his chin and made silly faces.

"We're not getting any shuteye tonight," I whispered with a huff.

"Would that be so bad?"

One corner of my mouth went up. "I really like my sleep."

"Me, too, but you're leaving soon."

A hint of sadness rimmed his late night eyes. The intermittent sounds of crickets rubbing their legs together sounded in the distance. "When are you coming back to Michigan?"

"I'm not sure of the exact date, but it'll be the week after next sometime."

"If you need something, let me know. I'll be around."

"I do need something."

I propped my head up to see him better. "What?"

"I need you in Montana, with us."

I scooted off my sleeping bag and over to his. I rested my hand on the side of his face. His temple twitched like it usually did when he was unsettled. I kissed his forehead. "I know." He nuzzled me closer and I rested my head on his chest. "How could I not?"

"I'm glad. Now maybe I'll be able to get some shuteye," John said. "I've been worrying about this since you got here. I was preparing to say goodbye, forever."

I reached up, touched his chin, and then pushed myself up from his strong chest. "I made a promise to Chloe."

"You're not saying we can try this just because of her, are you?" A shadow crossed his eyes.

"No. This is me fighting harder, even if it doesn't seem like it."

John ran his fingers down my cheek and across my neck. "What did you promise?"

"I promised her that no matter what happened when you moved, we'd keep in touch. It wasn't just for her, you know."

John ran his fingers over my lips. "When you guys moved in," I said, playing with his shirt, "I thought she was going to drive me batty and you, I thought you were just some guy with an attitude."

"Thanks," he said. "That's very nice."

"Oh, get over yourself," I said, swatting him. "Cancer really sucked, my mom was driving me crazy, and Chloe lurked around with you in tow. And I just wanted to be by myself."

John rested his hand on the small of my back, his warm touch under my sweatshirt against my bare skin. "Do you want to be by yourself, Maggie? If you do, I'll understand. You can keep your promise to Chloe. I won't stand in your way."

"No, I want to be with both of you. I think I've been standing in my own way for long enough." I inched closer, knowing that somehow in the invisible rhythm of time we'd grown together. I kissed his lips as he held my face. The walkie-talkie static broke the moment, and then Chloe's voice echoed through the night air.

John pressed the button on the side of the walkie-talkie. "What do you need, Chloe?"

"I have to go to the bathroom," she whispered.

"Okay," he said, "I'll be right there. Anyone else have to go?"

"All of us," she answered.

John sat up, put on his boots, and scooted out of the tent. I slipped my feet into my moccasins.

"What are you doing?" he asked.

"I might as well go, too."

"Come on, neighbor lady." He reached for my hand, helping me up. "There's never a dull moment."

I zipped up our tent to keep out the critters and small children. Walter flitted over and held my hand. His eyes studied the twinkling stars above. "It's like Never-Neverland."

"Sure is," John whispered.

Chapter 27

The soles of my boots scuffled across the dusty ground on the path next to the creek. With my hands in my pockets and my head down, my camera bumped against my chest. My Stetson blocked the view as it hung over my brow, but the Montana landscape was etched in my mind and this trip would long be remembered. I breathed in with a heavy heart, knowing I was leaving and the thought of driving back weighed me down.

John and I had exchanged words, but people do that when they know something has to end. Part of me kept that in check when I thought about him saying he wanted to marry me, and that I always had a home here. The creek roared louder today over its pebbly basin.

Vibrant blooms supported by slender green stems poked their heads into the air proudly. I took the cap from the lens, stuffed it into my back pocket, and knelt beside them. The shutter clicked as I focused on nature, trying to get the mountains behind the split rail fence into the frame as I told myself everything had boundaries, and for that, I wasn't sure I had the gumption to leave my own backyard to explore another one.

I listened to my heart as it thumped against my chest walls, trying to get out. Extraordinary vastness surrounded me, grounded me, suffocated the world back home. Lifting my chin to the sky, the sun warmed me and I wondered how I could betray a lifetime of memories for a whim that presented itself in the lush mountain pastures, wild creatures that I trusted when I rode, a man, his father, and an eight-year-old girl named Chloe.

Their love called out like the gray wolf tipping its nose to the Montana moon howling into the night. Its echo ricocheted and I heard nothing else. As the ranch faded into the distance, my footsteps grew heavier.

I sat down in the long grass with my spine against the trunk of an ancient shade tree, the creek my company. The rough bark snagged my hair when I leaned back after laying my cowboy hat on the ground. Holding the viewfinder to my eye, I clicked then turned to see who was coming as the sound of horse hooves grew louder. Even with his face shaded by the sun that hit his back, Winston Ludlow McIntyre's silhouette was undeniably recognizable.

"Hey, girl. I thought that was you."

I started to get up to greet him, and he motioned for me to stay put.

With a groan, he dismounted and tied his black beauty to the tree. "It's been a long morning. How about if I join you?"

I nodded, held my camera in my lap, and felt my jeans stick to the back of my legs. "Anything wrong?"

"No, got three little ones that like to stray."

"Is one of them named Chloe?" I asked jokingly.

"Not this time. I'm talking about cattle, but I could see how that would happen." Winston knelt, took off his hat, mopped his brow with his bandana, and then sat down beside me.

His rugged profile softened as he settled in next to me. My words got tangled in my throat like hard-knotted thread, and my brow beaded with sweat. His aged green eyes searched my face.

"Suppose you have a lot on your mind," he said softly.

Not sure what he knew, I nodded. "Thanks for letting me ride with you while I was here."

"It's hard work, Maggie. Takes a hearty soul to make a go of it."

"Nothing worth having is easy. I guess that's where the phrase labor of love comes from." And love was labor to me. It poked, prodded, and twisted in my gut just waiting for me to yell *uncle*.

Damn.

Winston's sigh drifted off in the air as the drooping willow branches swayed in the breeze.

"I sure will be sorry to see you go." He drew in a long breath then rubbed his temples with his right forefinger and thumb. His thick hand practically covered his whole face.

"Yeah, me too," I said under my breath.

Winston's gaze connected with mine. "You still have that ticket I left for you?"

"Yeah." I fidgeted with my camera.

"It's good any time," he said, drawing one knee up to his chest.

"Thanks."

"You're a woman of few words. Never knew a girl who didn't like to talk." Winston tucked the bandana in his right shirt pocket, and then he dug in the left shirt pocket for a cigarette and a light. "Don't tell my son you saw me smoke. I've been trying to quit, but it's like trying to stop breathing."

"No worries," I said, with a grin.

Winston touched the lighter to the end of his cigarette then took a drag. His eyes narrowed as a stream of white smoke billowed out from his nostrils. "Chloe sure does think the world of you."

"I *really* like her, too." My heart swelled.

"She has the same look in her eye that her daddy does, even though he tries hard to cover it up. He never was very good at hiding his feelings." Winston took another drag of his smoke then he proceeded to talk. "Since you don't feel like talking, I got plenty to say. Just let be whatever will be."

I soaked up his words and wished to God this would all work out.

"It's that simple. Life is too short, Maggie." Winston flicked the ashes from the end of his cigarette. "Sometimes when you get it, you throw it away or it leaves before you realize what you have and you just can't get it back, no matter how hard you try."

Studying his profile, I listened harder than I'd ever listened before.

"Maggie, I'm not gonna be able to do this forever. I go out there—" He waved his cigarette out in front of him. "—knowing I'd better live for today 'cause tomorrow might not come."

The knot loosened at the back of my throat, but what was there to say to that? I focused on breathing then scanned the horizon through the wispy branches that almost touched the stream.

"I don't mean to be harsh, but it's the truth. Sometimes people go too long without hearing it, and sometimes it takes a stranger to deliver it."

"You don't feel like a stranger to me," I said.

"Maggie, you know a little bit about me. You're so busy looking around for the speeding train to run you over that you're missing what's right in front of you," he said in a low, even tone. His temple twitched like John's. "Girl, there aren't any speeding trains in Montana, just some cowboys trying to make sense of the day upon the backs of their horses. And that includes Chloe."

The silence between us seemed infinite.

"Am I making you uncomfortable?"

I dug my fingers into the back of my neck. He waited for me to answer. I blinked, swallowed, and stared into his eyes.

"Good," he said, "just wanted to see if you were present."

Sweet Jesus, what had I gotten myself into? Winston meant business. His unwavering tone, even keel, not intimidating, just matter-of-fact. I bit my lower lip to keep it from quivering. Winston puffed on his cigarette in a cool manner. His eyes flickered when the breeze picked up. Wisps of wavy hair brushed against my cheeks like a mother's touch. The willow rustled overhead and the nettle that brewed beneath my skin subsided. He was doing nothing more than protecting his own and that was something I understood.

Winston finished his cigarette then snubbed it out, got up, stepped closer to the stream, bent down and soaked the butt, and then put it back in his pocket.

"Did I do something to upset you?" I asked.

Winston shook his head at me as I stood up. Flecks of sunlight floated across his cowboy hat like confetti under a disco ball. Winston bent down, grabbed my hat, and held it out to me as I tucked my hair behind my ears.

"Quite the opposite, darlin'. Quite the opposite." When the right side of his mouth curled up, an innocent dimple eased the intensity of our conversation.

The urge to bolt slithered through my veins.

"I've seen that look before," Winston said. "Had a wild pony once, always ready to run, but over time she settled in once she realized she was home." His horse neighed and shuffled her feet. "Meet that little horse. Not so little any more. Big heart, one of the best girl's I ever had."

"What's her name?" I asked, stroking her hide.

"Sage." Winston checked her girth. "You're a good girl, aren't you?"

Sage shifted her weight. Her knee cracked and her hooves clunked against the ground with restless intent.

She showed me her teeth and batted her long lashes. "I like her one white sock."

"Me too. It's a good reminder that not all things are black or white."

I ran my fingers through Sage's black mane and down

her shoulder. Her muscle twitched as a dragonfly hovered above my hand.

Winston rested his hand on the saddle horn, looking as if he was going to mount her and ride away, but he didn't. "Sage isn't just a plant."

I fingered her wavy mane.

"It means wise through experience and reflection."

"I like that."

Winston's tanned skin seemed inviting, and something inside nudged me to reach out. He held my stare as I wrapped my fingers around his and held on just for a moment, hoping to feel my father's presence, but I didn't.

Winston squeezed my hand back. "You hang on to that ticket."

I nodded as he let go of my hand. With one swift movement, he was up, over, and settled in the saddle.

"John's a good man. And you're a good woman," he said. "You just keep thinking. Your mind will catch up to your heart, if you let it."

Chapter 28

Thinking about tomorrow when Judy and I would pack up the Suburban and head back to Michigan, Chloe and I hunched over the bale of hay next to Cocoa's kittens. Their fur was fluffier and they had grown since the last time I'd seen them.

"Where's their momma?" I asked.

Chloe shrugged. "Not sure. Probably out hunting." She stroked the gray fur of the kitten closest to her with her pointer finger. "Not sure what we're going to do with all these cats. Maybe we should find them homes."

Chloe's eyes flashed in my direction. I leaned over on my knees, surprised I could still bend over and be crunched up like my eight-year-old friend after all that riding. I couldn't take my eyes off her. My heart melted, and not from the button noses that sniffed around and mewed for their momma.

"Maybe Dad will let me keep one." She held her breath and her eyes flickered with thought. "Or maybe two now that we live on a ranch. What ranch doesn't need cats to keep the mice away?"

I raised my eyebrows. "Maybe he will. Who knows?" I took a deep breath, pondering which one I'd keep. "Which one would you keep?"

Chloe leaned closer to the brood of kittens. "I like this gray one. I like his white feet and pink nose. Wait is it a him or a her?"

"Not sure. I guess someone can check that out for you." I was reluctant to touch the fuzzy gray kitten that was curled up next to its wiggly brothers and sisters. "It sure is quiet compared to the others."

"Yeah, that's part of the reason I like that one best. I like her, maybe his, manners." Chloe grinned.

I speculated that John would have no problem letting Chloe keep a couple of kittens. It could run with the other barn cats and be right at home. "She, maybe he, seems awfully sweet. What would you name it?"

"Hmm." Chloe tapped her fingers against her chin as she thought. "Misty Pearl. The fur looks like fog when it covers the ground in the morning and the white toes remind me of the pearls my mom wears."

"What if it's a boy?"

"Not sure." Chloe tapped her fingers against her chin. "Maybe Peter, cause I like that Peter Pan guy, or maybe Crush cause I got a crush on him." Chloe stroked the kitten's head softly as she whispered, trying her best not to disturb him.

"I like Crush. That's a good one." I leaned back against the stall wall and tucked my knees to my chest. "You're really good at naming these guys and you're really good at helping with the horses. Not to mention our friend, Bones, back home."

"I do love animals." Chloe patted her chest.

"I know. I think it's a gift," I told her as she wrinkled her nose at me. "You know, a gift, something that God gave you that other people might not have. Not everyone is good with animals," I explained.

"I'm glad I'm good at something, 'cause some days I think I can't do anything right."

"I know the feeling. I think we all feel that way sometimes."

Chloe sat back against the stall wall and rested her knees to her chest like me. She stared into my eyes as she wiggled into place beside me. "I like it when you braid my hair." She brushed her cheek with the tassel of hair at the end of her braid.

"Me, too."

"It feels good when we get to talk when no one else is around." Her chest puffed out and she let out a rush of air through pursed lips.

My smile grew and my heart ballooned.

"I don't know anyone like you," she said, touching my hand. "I think you're a gift."

I let out a giggle. "You're funny," I said, noticing that the corners of her smile began to droop.

"Do you like me, Maggie?"

"That's a silly question. Of course I like you." *I love you.*

Chloe's gaze searched my face.

"I more than like you," I continued, caressing the side of her face.

Chloe's smile warmed my heart, and I imagined it was melting like chocolate on a hot day.

"Thanks for coming to Montana this summer," she whispered under her breath.

"You're welcome. Thanks for inviting me. This has been the best trip ever," I answered, picking at the hole in the knee of my Levis.

A shadow passed over Chloe's expression.

"What's the matter?" I asked.

"Well, you know when we talked about what Harry said about you and my dad liking each other?" she said, pushing out the extra air at the end of her sentence. "Well, I think he's right. I think you two do like each other more than you think."

I sat quietly, not willing to validate her inquiry because I wanted this to be between John and me and no one else. We had to figure this out on our own.

"It's okay that you like him."

I stayed silent, not quite knowing what to say.

"Aren't you gonna say anything. Get mad or—" She rolled her hands in front of her like an Italian grandmother as she spoke. "Nothing?"

I smiled.

Chloe smacked her forehead with the palm of her hand. "I wish I knew what was going on." She drew out every word.

"Me, too."

"Grown-ups are weird."

"Yeah, we are, and you know something?"

"What?" Chloe said.

"So are kids sometimes. We all have our moments."

Chloe rolled her eyes. "I really was hoping to get something out of you. Geez."

Laughing, I patted her shoulder. "Sorry." But I wasn't. I really didn't know what was going to happen and I wasn't about to hold my breath, but I was willing to try something new, something I hadn't done in a very long time, and it scared the hell out of me. I sat up and hung my legs over the edge of the bale of hay.

Chloe scooted to the edge and I rested my hands on her shoulders. "What do you say we see what the others are doing?"

"Sure."

Chloe held my hand and we strolled out of the barn together like two lazy cowboys at the end of a long day. She shaded her eyes and inspected the sky overhead as a loud caw echoed through the air. A black shadow hovered overhead. I studied the flapping wings as it dove closer to the ground.

"It's Frankie," Chloe said with a squeal.

The blackbird swooped across the field and flew over the pasture. "I bet it is."

"I'm glad he can fly now. I'd be sad if he couldn't?"

"Yeah, really sad. He'd probably end up as someone's dinner."

"Without you, he might not have survived."

"'Cause I got a gift." She beamed with pride. Chloe touched the Tiffany heart necklace hanging around her neck. "Mom's gift is being pretty. Dad can do just about anything. He has lots of gifts except cooking. I'm good with animals and you—" She looked into my eyes and scratched her chin like she did when she was naming the gray kitten. "You, you're good at making other people feel better."

I squeezed her hand. "Thanks." I didn't always feel that way, and Chloe had no idea the sacrifices. I was pretty sure I didn't make Daniel McNabb feel better when I sent him to the principal's office after throwing a book at my head because I wouldn't let him skip the math assignment.

"Maggie, are you really going to keep your promise about keeping in touch with me?"

"Of course." How would John and I ever break it to her that we were going to try and be a couple? Would she turn into one of those children who resented me, or would we keep on doing what we were doing? Beginnings were exciting, and in this case a bit nerve-wracking. I'd never want to come between her and John. I'd never want to make waves between her and Brook either. Lord knew Brook was capable of making enough waves on her own. I swallowed away worry at the back of my throat and smiled at Chloe as she rambled on about how Harry's gift was being smart in school, Walter's gift was burping the alphabet, Judy's gift was being patient with the boys, and Winston's gift was his way with the cattle.

"And Ashley is good to kids, and Justin is strong and can fix anything, and Trout, well Trout is good at everything, too, now that I think about it. Maybe that's why Grandpa likes him so much, and he's nice, like you Maggie, he's just nice." Chloe stopped rambling and studied my face. "Maybe that's why Dad likes you so much, 'cause you're nice. You have a good heart."

I hadn't always considered myself as "nice." What did that mean anyway? Did it mean that I was complacent, cheerfully stepped on as my high school English teacher would say to us girls in the front row as she sipped her coffee from a Styrofoam cup, her nails stained with nicotine, and her voice rough with cynicism that made me slump in my seat as she told the class that she would bring us out of our shyness? Chloe's voice faded with the daydream.

"Why do you look like that, Maggie?"

"Sorry, I was just thinking about when I was in school."

"Harry says that sometimes people were meant for each other, like his mom and his dad."

Her eyes flickered as she held my attention. A thread of suspicion snagged my conscience like nails on a chalkboard as Chloe spoke of Harry. It seemed like Harry was doing a lot of talking. Sunnyside Up galloped over to the fence and I was glad for the interruption. I leaned against the railing as Chloe wiggled her way through the cracks to greet her friend. She took a couple of sugar cubes from her pocket, and then let Sunnyside Up nibble from her open palm as she petted the crown of her head.

"Really, Maggie, would it be so bad if you and my dad decided to get together?"

I choked on the moment. *Yeah, thanks Harry.* I'd avoided this conversation before with her, but damn she was savvier than ever, not to mention persistent. Chalk that up for the "gift" column. Beads of sweat ran down my back and the hot flash smoldering in my torso burst into flames. Chloe went back to coddling the horse as I floundered for a comeback.

Chapter 29

Winston strummed his guitar as we huddled around the fire for the last time. The sun rode low on the horizon behind the mountains. I scanned the faces as Harry and Chloe discussed going back to school in the fall. John had driven Chloe by her new school down the road, but hadn't visited yet. Walter picked pebbles from the dirt and stacked them neatly in a pile near Judy's chair. Justin and John discussed ditches and the cattle. I crossed my arms in front of me, leaned back in my sturdy Adirondack chair, and listened to the conversations until Winston's stare caught my attention. He gave a discrete nod as if he were telling me not to let go. Raising the camera to my eye, I snapped some pictures, knowing I didn't need a photo to remember this place or these people.

"Dad, can you take a picture of me and Maggie?" Chloe asked.

I handed her the camera and she passed it to John.

"Your hair is getting lighter with all this sunshine." I fingered her messy braid.

She crawled into my lap like Bradley used to do when he was her age, and I wrapped my arms around her waist and rested my chin on her shoulder. John clicked away as she snuggled into place.

"Cheese," he said.

We smiled at each other then turned toward the camera.

"Good one," John said, snapping a few more frames. "Modern technology is the best. Remember when your parents wouldn't let you near the camera because it was expensive to develop the film. Now you can take as many as you want."

The intensity in John's emerald eyes matched the weight in my heart. I leaned back and took Chloe with me. She rested her cheek against mine. Winston's glance was an *I told you so*. John focused the camera on us and snapped another photo. I peered into the fire, pretending not to see Judy's stare as she bent over in her chair to play with Walter.

"I can feel your heart beating," Chloe whispered.

Petrified to let her go, I nuzzled closer. She smelled of lavender and hay. My heart pounded.

"Your hair tickles," Chloe said as she turned to look at me.

"I haven't seen you this up close in a long time. You've gotten a lot of freckles this summer." Her pink lips perfectly innocent.

"Mom doesn't like freckles."

"I do," I whispered. "They look perfect on you."

She touched my face with her pointer finger as if she were playing a delicate game of hopscotch. "You have a lot of freckles, too."

"So does Glad," I said. "I bet Bones is lonely without us." I missed him and Mom, too. I felt like a tug-o-war rope being yanked at opposite ends. I longed to stay with John and Chloe, but I longed to be home, too.

"Wonder if he's wrecked her garden," Chloe said.

I laughed. "Remember last summer when he bit into all my tomatoes?"

Chloe chuckled. "Boy, were you mad."

"Yeah, I was, but not anymore."

"Yeah, it's hard to stay mad at that guy. I sure will miss him."

"He'll miss you, too," I said as she snuggled back into

my lap with her cheek against mine, two peas in a pod staring into the fire. John's expression tugged at my heartstrings.

"Can we have s'mores tonight?" Walter asked.

"I've never eaten so many s'mores in my life," Judy said, ruffling his hair.

"Please?" Chloe said with sad eyes.

"I guess so," John said, "but when your friends head home tomorrow, we're gonna lay off the s'mores for a bit."

"Okay, Dad." Chloe wiggled out of my lap. "Come on, Harry, let's go get the stuff."

Harry followed on her heels as she skipped toward the house and Walter scuffled behind them.

An idea popped into my head, and I tucked it away for safekeeping. I rested my feet on the log in front of me. The sun went down and Winston's tune of mountain living burrowed into my subconscious.

Winston leaned his guitar against his chair and excused himself. "I'll be back in a bit. Going inside to check something."

Judy stood and stretched while I sat like a bump on a log with a list of questions in my head.

"You two all ready for your trip back home?" John asked.

"I think so," Judy said. "We're going to try and make it to the Badlands."

"I'll be back in Michigan next week to close on the house. I'm going to fly in. I'm meeting with the realtor and packing up a truckload."

"Is Chloe coming with?" Judy asked.

"Yeah, she'll be there with bells on. She's anxious to see Glad and some of her friends." John crossed his legs and leaned back in his chair.

"I'm going to see what the kids are up to. You guys want anything?" Judy asked, stuffing her hands in her pockets.

My insides screamed with a wish list. I didn't want to leave. I didn't want a commitment back home. I wanted to stay in Montana with John and Chloe. "Can you bring me one last Beltian beer from the fridge?"

"Sure. What about you, cowboy?" she asked John.

John nodded. "I'll take one of those, too."

When Judy left, John stood up and gestured for me to follow him.

"We're gonna take a stroll to the barn. Be right back," he called after Judy, who gave a little wave of her hand over her shoulder as she walked away.

"What's in the barn?" I asked, tripping over a rock.

John squeezed my hand as he caught me. He didn't answer, but led the way with long strides.

"What's the hurry?"

He patted the pocket of his jacket. "Nothing, really. Just need you to see something without the kids."

Falling in step with John, I hustled to catch up. Sun Ray and her mother meandered in the field, the air was still, and our boot heels plunked against the hard ground. John's temple twitched as he slid the barn door open. He turned on a small lamp I'd seen Ashley use when she read her phone. Our steps echoed in the empty stalls.

John peeked through the open door then shut it slowly behind him. `

My stomach rolled over and the hair stood up on the nape of my neck. "I—"

John tapped his finger on my lips with a quiet shush. His eyes flickered with purpose and before I knew it, his hands were on my waist drawing me close to him. "I-" I stuttered. His fingers caressed my cheek, ran down my chin, and over my neck.

"I can't believe you're going tomorrow."

"I—"

John touched my lips with his fingers. His eyes held my attention. I couldn't turn away if I wanted to.

"You're ripping my heart out."

"This isn't easy for me either," I said.

"I have something I want to show you."

"Okay." I made a wish when his lips grazed mine.

"Please don't go all *Maggie* on me when I show you," he whispered, rummaging through his pocket.

"I'll do my best. Let's have it, cowboy."

John's fingers lifted my chin. "Remember when we were in Dad's office and I said that someday I wanted to marry you?"

I nodded my head. "Yeah." I blinked away the hazy stuffiness of the barn. "How could I forget?"

"I meant it. I've never felt this way about anyone." John's words trailed off into the air between us.

"Not even Chloe's mom?" I asked with a knot in my stomach.

He shook his head. "No, not even Chloe's mom."

His warm lips kissed my forehead. I rested my hands on his forearms as I shut my eyes. When I opened them, John held a wooden box in his hand. The carved scroll pattern on the top was elegant.

He loosened the lid. "This was my mom's ring. I've had it tucked away." John took a deep breath as he peered into the box then into my eyes. "When I was younger, Dad told me it was mine to give to the person I loved with all my heart."

My breath caught in my throat.

"And that's you, Maggie."

Sucking in a breath of air, I covered my mouth in awe. "What is happening here?"

"You promised you wouldn't go all *Maggie* on me." John tilted his head to the side. "Nothing, because I know you need to take baby steps. I just wanted to share this with you. I just wanted you know I *am* for real."

I touched the antique setting that held a square diamond. Chills ran down my spine and cooled the heat between us. "It's beautiful, but shouldn't Chloe have it?" I asked, fingering the design.

"That's just like you, thinking about someone else."

I stroked his cheek and held on to the moment, not believing I was living it.

"We can discuss that later." John put the lid back on the treasure, his past, his memories, and his love for his mother. "I love you, Maggie."

His lips brushed up against mine, and I saw a glimpse of my future in his eyes just before he closed them to kiss me.

John took my hands in his and held my stare. "Thanks for not going all *Maggie* on me."

I chuckled under my breath. "You're welcome." Leaning against the split-rail fence next to him, we watched Sunnyside Up snuggle up to her momma. The sun hung lower in the sky and dusk lurked on the wings of the birds that circled overhead. I rested my chin on the rail. "When Chloe was in my lap earlier, I didn't want to let her go." Tears welled at the back of my eyes.

"I know, I saw it," John said, wrapping his arm around my shoulder. "I think you fell in love with her before you even considered me."

He was right, and I held out admitting it to myself because I wasn't sure if I could see one more baby fly the coop. It'd been so damn hard when Bradley grew up, got a place of his own, only to remind me that I was growing old, and Beckett knew he didn't want to grow old with me some years back. My breath caught in my chest. How could I possibly be thinking of doing it all again?

"I'll be the best man I know how to be, Maggie." He held me close. "And we don't have to say anything to anyone until you're ready."

"I can't believe you're saying all this," I said. "Now you're the one making it all too damn hard." I patted his chest. Sleeping wouldn't be easy tonight, nor the trip home now that John's words swirled inside of me like a summer storm.

John rested his head against clasped hands on the top rail of the fence. "I'm fighting harder."

I studied his profile. "Apparently."

"You Abernathy women may be stubborn, but us McIntyre men are relentless," he said with a wink.

Chloe's and Walter's cackles erupted in the dusky night as they ran toward us. Walter bumped into me and Chloe wiggled in between the rails with ease like she'd been doing it all her life. Sunny craned her neck when she heard Chloe's voice. Chloe clicked her tongue and dug in her pocket. Sunny stayed close to her momma.

"Darn, I thought she'd want a treat," Chloe said with a frown.

"She just might want her momma," John said, watching Walter wiggle in between us.

"What are they doing out there?" Walter asked.

"Getting ready to settle down for the night." John ruffled Walter's messy hair.

"Me too, but not without a treat," Walter said. "You guys coming over to make s'mores with us?"

I ruffled his hair. "You bet." Then I patted my belly.

"Me, too," Chloe said, holding out her hand in Sunnyside Up's direction. She shifted her weight, clicked her teeth, and waited. "It's all right, girl." She tucked her free hand in her front pocket, "I'll save it for tomorrow."

Sunnyside Up swished her tail and bowed her head as her momma nudged her. Walter nudged me, too. "Come on, Maggie. Will you help me roast the perfect marshmallow?"

"What, you don't want me to help you?" John pretended his feelings were crushed.

"No way, you'll just burn it and that's gross," Walter said.

Chloe bent over and plucked a yellow flower from the

ground. She handed it to me as she wiggled back through the split-rail fence.

"Turn around," I said to her.

Chloe spun on a heel and I wove Montana's gift into her braid. "There."

Walter showed me all his teeth like a pony begging for a treat.

John knelt and Chloe mounted his back. She wrapped her arms around his neck as he slapped his thighs. He moaned when he stood up to jiggle Chloe into perfect riding position. "You're getting heavy, girl."

"Wow," Walter said, "you guys look like pros at that."

"We've been practicing," John said. "Almost got it down."

"Can I try?" Walter said.

"I'll tell you what, let's have a s'more then you can have a turn."

"Promise?" Walter asked, wiping his forehead with the back of his hand.

"Promise," John said.

"Pinky-swear him, Dad. That way he'll know you mean it."

John stuck out his pinky and Walter hooked his sweet pinky with John's. Walter smiled and skipped ahead. John faced me, Chloe on his back. "If the girl speaks the truth then I reckon I owe you one too, neighbor lady."

I raised an eyebrow in his direction, knowing he wanted me to wear his ring. Holding out my hand, I hooked my pinky with his, his warm touch filled with electricity, his eyes filled with patience.

"You guys are weird," Chloe said. "What would you have to pinky-swear about, anyway?" she asked, wrinkling her nose at me.

"I just didn't want Maggie to feel left out," John said. "Now how about that s'more?"

"Yum." Chloe kissed her dad's cheek.

Her braid bounced off her back, as John carried his daughter down the dirt road back to the fire pit.

Together.

Chapter 30

Judy and I rehashed our game plan for the long haul home as we sat by the fire and the kids told ghost stories. Sparks flew from the flames, leaving red specks of heat trailing to the heavens. Walter rubbed his eyes and Harry yawned.

"I think they just may sleep all the way home," I said.

"It's been great," Judy said, zipping up her fleece. "Thanks again for having us in your home."

Winston rubbed his chin. "You're welcome here anytime. Your boys are good men."

"Did you hear that, Harry? Winston thinks I'm a man." Walter puffed out his chest.

"Yeah, yeah, yeah," Harry said.

Judy shot him a look.

"Yeah, you're a good man, even if you're little," he said, throwing up his hands. "Is that better, Mom?"

Judy approved. "Much."

"Well, you two wranglers can come work for me anytime." John winked in Harry and Walter's direction.

The fire reflected in Harry's eyes. "You going to own this place someday?"

"Harry," Judy said. "I'm sorry, John."

Winston cleared his throat. "It's all right. Not for a long time if I have anything to say about it." Winston reached over and mussed Harry's curly hair.

Chloe snuggled up to John. "Dad says we're not moving again after this. I'm glad. I just want to stay in one spot."

Chloe's gaze met mine. Something subsided within me knowing she was okay with the transition.

"Dad even said I could keep a kitten or two, right, Dad?"

"This is news to me," he said.

"Please."

"We'll talk about that later," he said. "I was thinking you might like a dog instead."

"What?"

"Grandpa and I were talking and we thought we could use a herding dog, thought you might like to help pick it out and train it since you got the four-one-one on Bones."

"Cool, a dog that runs with cows." Walter tugged at his mom's hand.

"A herding dog," Harry said, rolling his eyes. "You are such a dork."

Walter leaned over and punched him in the arm.

Harry rubbed his bicep. "Whatever."

I couldn't hide my grin. Judy laughed and I knew the trip home would be an adventure. Mom's absence tugged at my heart. I didn't know how to tell her about John's proposal, my second thoughts about completing my career, and the dream of a new life that would be miles away from her. The school year was about to begin and my heart that had been dedicated for years now waned and longed for something different.

Judy nestled Walter into her lap. She smoothed his curly mop top away from his eyes and kissed his forehead. "I think it's about time for bed," she whispered in his ear.

"I don't want to go to bed. If I go to sleep that means it will be morning and I don't want to leave this place."

I raised my beer in Walter's direction. "Me, neither."

Judy's dark eyes sparkled. "We all want to stay, but we have to go home sometime. Come on, sleepy boy, let's get you ready for bed." Judy wiggled forward out of her chair and hoisted herself up with her youngest in her arms.

"Wow, you're a beast to lift such a big kid," I said.

Harry laughed. "She called you a beast, Mom. I like that."

Judy narrowed her gaze at Harry. "Thanks, Maggie. I'm sure we won't be hearing *that* on the way home."

"Sorry, but I do have some other lingo that I'm sure you'd like even less."

Harry's dark eyes sparkled with curiosity as the flames licked the singed logs. "Cool, will you tell me what they are?" he asked.

I raised an eyebrow and weighed the consequences. "Better not, maybe when you're a little older."

Harry grimaced with disappointment.

Judy brushed past me as Walter's limbs dangled from her arms like a rag doll. "Thanks. I owe ya."

The glow of the firelight highlighted her defined cheekbones. Her curly hair fell around her face and she looked beautiful. "You're welcome."

Harry scooted over into his mom's chair when she was out of earshot. "Will you tell me later?"

I sipped the last of my beer. "I'll make you a deal, if we make it back to Michigan without any major issues between you and Walter, I'll tell you some, but your mother must never know that they came from me." I narrowed my gaze and leaned in Harry's direction. "*Capiche*?" Harry wrinkled his nose like Chloe when she didn't understand something. "That's Italian for, understand," I said, watching his dark eyes process what I was saying.

"*Capiche*," he said.

"Well then, let's consider that the first installment before we even pack the car." I tipped my beer can up to savor the last swallow.

Harry rested his feet on the log in front of him and leaned back. His stare connected with John's. "Thanks for letting us come here. I had a blast."

Chloe's admiration for Harry shone in the dying firelight. Ashen logs tumbled down saying their last goodnight.

John nodded. "Thanks for being such a good friend to Chloe."

Chloe's eyes were half-mast as the night settled in. "I think we should get you two to bed, too. We have an early morning."

"I don't want to go," Harry said.

"Oh, so the truth comes out. You do have something in common with Walter," I teased.

Harry rolled his soon-to-be fifth-grade eyes at me and frowned.

John nudged Chloe, and her eyes popped open. "I'm awake," she said. "I'm awake."

"I beg to differ, darlin'. It's time for bed."

"Maggie, will you put me to bed?" Chloe asked, her voice sleepy.

Harry stretched, then yawned. "What fourth grader needs someone to put them to bed?"

"Me," she said. "Cause Maggie's leaving and I want to remember her face just before she turns out the light."

"I guess I can't argue with that," Harry said. "She is kind of pretty."

Studying Harry's face, I poked him in the shoulder. "I get it from your mom."

"Not sure about that." Harry trudged down the path ahead of me. He seemed taller, his thin frame and skinny shoulders holding up his curly head of hair that bobbed in the moonlight. John and Chloe chatted as they strolled behind me. My heart skipped a beat as I realized how much my family loved me.

Harry held the back door open for us. His eyes followed the bugs flitting around the light fixture. "Civil Rustic Moths."

"What?" Chloe asked.

Harry pointed to the jittery insects jutting back and forth. "Rustic moths. The larvae like to eat alfalfa, dock, hawkweed, and sow thistle," he said like a textbook on audio.

"Sometimes I just don't get you," Chloe said, shaking her head. "They look like just plain old bugs to me."

John set Chloe down and she stepped inside. She stared at Harry until he came in behind John and me, and then shut the door.

"Whatever." Harry said.

"She's all yours." John put Chloe's hand in mine.

"Night, Dad." Chloe reached up and hugged John, and then kissed his cheek. "You're scratchy," she said, touching his chin.

"Night. And Maggie, after she's settled, could you come back down?"

Harry glanced over his shoulder, a direct hit into my well of secrets. I ignored the question in his eyes. "Sure." I looked down at Chloe who was trying to rub the sandman's spell free from her eyes. "Come on, let's get you in bed."

Harry waited by the staircase for us. His eyes focused on me, a question on his lips. Chloe's hand slid up the wood banister as she moseyed up the stairs with heavy feet.

"What?" I asked with caution.

Harry's eyes flashed with savvy. "Never mind."

Chloe's feet shuffled onto the landing at the top of the stairs.

"What?" I asked again, wanting to clear the air.

"If I say what I am thinking, will you still tell me your secrets when we get back home?" His left eyebrow arched like a sneaky cat ready to pounce.

"Go ahead, press your luck," I said, running my fingers through my hair. His eyes challenged me. I nodded and waved my hands toward him, urging him to get there faster.

"I know what you've been telling Chloe. And don't be mad at her. I'm sure she didn't tell me everything you've been saying, she likes you too much."

"Remember that." Harry fidgeted with the railing.

I waited.

The corner of his mouth curled upward.

"I guess I don't need to ask you because I can see it in your face," he said, squinting his eyes. "I guess I was right."

I narrowed my gaze at the young man before me, not afraid to play with the master, but maybe I wasn't the master anymore now that he'd called my bluff. Harry grabbed the end of the banister and swung his left foot around to the first step without taking his eyes off me. A spark flew between us. He trotted up the first few stairs and I followed in his footsteps, poking him along the way.

Chapter 31

Chloe and I kicked off our boots and peeled off our socks in unison as we sat on the bedroom floor across from each other. She'd thrown her clothes in a messy pile at the end of her bed, slipped on her pajamas, and stumbled to the bathroom to brush her teeth before climbing into bed. She sat with her back to me. "Will you brush my hair before you turn off the light?"

"You want a ponytail for bed?"

"No, a braid please." Chloe yawned.

I sectioned off her hair into three even strands then wove her hair into a lose braid. "Does that feel okay?"

She patted the back of her head inspecting my work. "Perfect." She burrowed beneath the covers and tucked the sheet under her chin.

"Night, kiddo," I said, touching her nose. Chloe stared at me with solemn intent. I brushed her cheek with the back of my hand. "Don't worry."

"That's what grown-ups say when something bad is about to happen and they think you don't know." Chloe rubbed her eyes.

"Okay, how about this?" I took a deep breath. "Don't look so sad, little girl. I will see you again. Distance won't be between us forever."

"That doesn't make me feel any better," Chloe said, her knuckles taut from gripping the seam of the sheet she scrunched up with her thumbs.

"Okay, how about this. It sucks that I have to go home." The corner of my mouth tugged toward the ceiling fan that blew cool waves of air against my neck. A thread of happiness pulled at the corner of Chloe's mouth.

"Better. I know I'll get to see you next week, but then what? When can you come back?" Her eyes filled with angst. "Mom always says she'll come back and she doesn't."

Chloe's words were a dagger in my heart. I reached out and rubbed her hands with mine, trying to free her grip from the bedding. "I know. That sucks, too, but try to remember the times that made you smile when you could see her. Like the time she gave you this necklace." Chloe's eyes searched mine, her expression flat. "You know there are times that Glad makes me sad, too."

"Really?"

I remembered Chloe muttering in her sleep when I first got here. Her words implied that I could be her mom. My heart knew I couldn't take Brook's place, but my head nagged me that maybe I could fill in the cracks of time in between the sparse visits. "Yeah, moms aren't perfect. Just ask Bradley."

Chloe grinned.

"Sorry, little girl, life isn't always the bees knees like it has been these past few days that we've together with Harry, Walter, and Judy."

"Sounds like something Glad would say." Chloe reached for Voodoo at the end of the bed. She sat up and cuddled with her purple scrappy stuffed toy with one eye as she studied my face.

"It is. I'm just repeating it because it reminds me of her."

"You remind me of her," Chloe said, stroking Voodoo's head. "You're a lot alike."

I never thought Mom and I were a lot alike. I raised my eyebrow at Chloe and touched Voodoo's black winking eye, the one Mom had sewn on last summer.

"She's funny like you. She loves me and I think you do

too." Chloe's words tapered off into the night as the crickets sang outside her bedroom window.

My breath caught in my chest. "I do," I whispered. "That's what makes this suck even more." I put my pointer finger in the dimple below her right cheek just before she fell into my arms like a child who hasn't seen her momma all day long. Chloe muttered something into my chest. I lifted her chin so I could see her eyes. "What?"

She pressed her lips together.

"What?" I said, lowering my voice. My shoulders fell forward as a shadow passed over her green eyes rimmed with sleep.

"Don't not like my dad because of me," she said then buried her head in my chest.

"What?" I said, lifting her chin. I remember my conversation with Harry at the bottom of the stairs and wondered if this was his doing. "What did Harry say to you?"

"Nothing. This is me," she said softly, playing with the hem on my T-shirt.

"You know that would never be the case." *Damn it*. This was exactly what I was trying to avoid. Worry washed over Chloe's expression. Thinking about John and how drawn I was to him, I tucked stray strands of blonde hair behind Chloe's ears. "I'm not leaving you. I told you before, we'll always have each other no matter where we live."

Chloe tilted Voodoo's face toward hers as she listened.

"Believe me," I said.

Chloe lifted her eyes.

"Trust me." I held out my pinky and hoped like hell I could trust myself to keep my promise. She was the last person who deserved a broken heart. Chloe contemplated the gesture then hooked her pinky finger with mine. Tears stuck at the back of my throat like a wet lint ball. "I need you, too," I said solemnly, hoping, yet knowing she could sense my the apprehension I carried day-in and day-out.

"Okay."

She caressed my cheek with her soft touch. I kissed her forehead.

You look like Glad, too."

Mom's face flashed in my mind. She'd stuck with me through Bradley's childhood, Dad's death, Beckett's astounding secret that provoked divorce, my battle with cancer, and normal everyday crap. "She'll be glad to see you next week."

"I know, but I don't want to say goodbye." Chloe played with the end of her braid. A tear dripped down her cheek. She wiped it away with the back of her hand.

"She loves you very much, maybe even more than me," I said.

"This really does suck."

"It won't suck forever."

"Yeah, but it still sucks."

I raised an eyebrow at her. "Are we square?" She scrunched up her nose at me. "Are we all set? Do you think you can go to sleep now?"

Chloe let out a sigh and covered her mouth as she yawned. "I guess so. Are we having special breakfast in the morning?"

"I think so. French Toast and bacon."

"Yum." She lowered her head, her downy pillow cradling her sweet head.

"That's not going to suck," I said, pulling the comforter up to her chin as she closed her eyes. "Is it okay if I turn off the light?"

Chloe opened her eyelids a smidgeon. "Yes."

She reached out to me and I hugged her. Turning off the lamp, I said a prayer. Light from the hallway crept between the bottom of the door and the floor showing me the way. I picked up Chloe's clothes and thought about all the times I picked up after Bradley and the students in my classroom. I peeked over my shoulder as she whispered my name.

"I trust you," she said into the darkness.

"I know." I turned toward the door, threw her clothes down the laundry chute in the bathroom, and padded down the stairs in my bare feet.

Judy was on the sofa with her feet up on the leather ottoman large enough to sleep four. I plopped down beside her, drained from the day of emotion. "What a day." She handed me a map with a highlighted route.

"Glad you got this covered." I yawned, thinking about the long haul ahead.

Judy closed her eyes. "John told me to tell you he's on the porch."

I handed her the map and scooted closer. "Thanks for being such a great friend and coming all the way out here with me."

She peeked at me through tiny slits. "Are you kidding? This has been great."

"I know. I told Chloe we'd have French toast and bacon for breakfast. Gotta feed those boys, too." I rested my feet up on the ottoman and smoothed my hair back from my face. "God, I remember taking Bradley in the car on long trips and he'd be hungry before we even left the driveway."

"Gotta love 'em," Judy took her feet off the leather footrest. She straightened her pile of maps and travel books. "I can't wait to see Pink."

"I'd be glad to take the boys so you two can have date night. They can even stay over if you want. I could even come to your house. I don't mind sleeping on the sofa, besides I kind of owe you."

"You don't owe me anything and you wouldn't have to sleep on the sofa. I wouldn't have missed this for the world."

Judy's eyebrows lifted. "But, we just might take you up on that." She took in the grand room. "This sure is a different way of life," she said, fingering her curls.

"Way different, but I could get used to it pretty easily, I think." I crossed my arms in front of me. "Imagine, just picking up and moving out here."

"Wouldn't that be something?" Judy closed her eyes and yawned. "I better get to bed."

"Night." I closed my eyes and rested my head against the leather sofa.

"Don't let me forget this in the morning. Oh, and John put a present in the back of the Suburban for you."

"What is it?" I asked, opening one eye.

"Montana's finest beer."

"Well that's not a kick in the pants. Yum!"

"Night, girl."

"Night, sister."

Judy touched my arm. "Um, don't forget, there's a handsome man on the porch waiting for you."

"I know. I won't forget." How could I forget? God, he showed me his mother's wedding ring, said he wanted it to be mine. "Night. See you in the morning." Judy left and I was alone. Thoughts sprouted in-between heavy breaths, dangerous thoughts, tempting thoughts, life-changing thoughts.

I forced myself off the sofa then headed for the porch. John sat in the dark. He eased me down into his lap. I wrapped my arms around his neck and hung my feet over the side of the chair. "Why are you sitting in the dark?"

"I like sitting in the dark."

I rested my head against his shoulder. He smelled like hay and sweet Montana air. "I like the way you smell."

"I like the way you feel." His hand slid up my thigh and around my bottom.

I ran my hand over his rough chin of whiskers. "I've never seen you this unshaven."

"Do you like it?"

His breath warmed my neck and his lips nibbled at my ear. "Yeah," I said. "I don't want to go home."

"Good, this fighting harder stuff is working."

John tugged the back of my shirt free from my jeans and ran his hand up my spine. My mind flooded with tempting thoughts.

"You know, you really should have your shoes on," John whispered.

"Why?" I asked, letting out a soft moan.

"If you had your shoes on, I'd take you out to the barn and make love to you."

My hand crept across his cheekbone and down his jawline, the connection between us strong, harmonious. I wiggled my toes as they cooled in the refreshing night breeze. I swung my feet over off the arm of the chair and stood without breaking the spark between us. Our stares focused on each other, neither one of us willing to abandon the moment. Anticipation trickled through my veins. In the quietest of voices, I spoke. "Let me get my shoes."

"Just seeing if you were willing," John said through narrow lips. He held me close, his hand on the small of my back.

I stood on his boots as he lifted my chin. "I think we've already established that, cowboy." The moon pulled at the corner of my subtle grin as I reminisced about our ride to the top of the mountain. My stomach twitched with excitement and my heart yearned for his touch, just once more before our morning goodbye.

"Now we're getting somewhere, darlin'."

John swept me off my feet, then cradled me in his arms like a sack of sugar, only I had arms and I wasn't risking letting them slip from his strong shoulders. "Are we really heading to the barn?" The butterflies knocked against my ribcage like thumping drums at his attentive midnight gaze.

"Heard you slept with a pediatrician back home. Thought you might like a cowboy better."

His deep tone spurred my heart. "There's only one way to find out." My words grazing his cheek along with my lips.

John's green eyes twinkled in the moonlight as he carried me down the steps. We stopped just outside the barn that was illuminated with ivory haze. John's mouth covered mine. I grasped the back of his neck and drew him closer, drove him deeper into the kiss. He let out a groan as he reached around with one hand to slide the barn door open. He kissed my forehead before letting my feet touch the ground.

"Wait here." He stepped softly on the wooden floor, and then stopped at the desk in the corner and clicked on a lantern. He grabbed a stack of blankets from the bench then walked to the far stall filled with hay.

I watched intently as he came back with the glowing lamp in hand. The aroma of wood ignited my senses. I wrapped my arms around his neck as he swept me up into his arms again. His breath tickled my neck as he kissed me lightly, and then he slowly let his mouth wander until his lips met mine. Three little words paraded through my head. John eased me down on a bale of hay, unbuttoned his shirt, and then stepped closer. I rested my head against his stomach while my fingers undid his button-fly jeans. I stood up as the last button popped out of its buttonhole. John's fingers strummed my cheek like a feather.

I scooted closer, running my fingers down his chest, and let my hands rest on his waist. This was the perfect way to say goodbye.

Chapter 32

Gentle fingers touched my forehead as I started to wake. It took great effort to open just an eye. "What is it, Chloe?" I asked.

"They're running the horses this morning. You didn't get to see it, and I don't want you to leave without seeing it."

I propped myself up on my elbows then gazed out the window into the hazy early morning sky.

"Come on. You don't even have to get dressed. We'll just throw on a sweatshirt and our boots and go out. You have to see it, Maggie."

My chest heaved as I took a deep breath. "Does it really mean that much to you?"

"Yes, the horses are so beautiful when they run together. It reminds me of when they open the school doors and we all run out trying to get free from the teachers, only the horses are prettier. And it's loud like thunder," Chloe said. "Come on or we'll miss it."

I threw back the comforter and the sheet, and then swung my legs over the side of the bed. "Okay, let's go." My socks and boots were in a pile right where I'd left them last night. Chloe sat on the floor and pushed her bare feet into her cowboy boots. She popped up like a Jack-in-the-box and wiggled into her fleece. I yanked my hair-tie from my messy ponytail, ran my fingers through my hair, and then redid my ponytail. Chloe stood beside me, inspecting my face as I dodged morning's call. "Okay, let's go."

Chloe took my hand.

We tiptoed down the hallway to the stairs. Walter peeked out of the bathroom. "Where you guys going? It's still kind of dark out. You running away?"

My insides warmed at his innocence. "No, we're not running away. We're going to see the horses run," I said, trying not to wake everyone.

Judy stuck her head into the hallway. "What are you guys doing?" She yawned.

Chloe tugged at my hand. "Come on, Maggie, you can't miss this."

"Can I come?" Walter's eyes bulged with excitement.

"Judy, do you and Harry want to tag along?" I asked.

She yawned and covered her mouth. "I'd like to see them, but my bed is calling. Harry is sawing logs."

"I want to go." Walter pulled at his mom's hand.

Judy disappeared back into her bedroom then reappeared with a sweatshirt in her hand. "You really don't mind?"

"No." Tugging the sweatshirt over Walter's dark curly mop-top was a challenge. I picked him up and carried him down the stairs. He wasn't as heavy as he looked. Chloe opened the front door and we followed her out to the road down by the creek. We crept through the morning fog as the sun shone its first light. Walter sat on my hip as he wrapped his arms around my neck and sniffed my hair.

"You smell like hay," he whispered. "I like that smell. We don't have that back home."

Chloe beckoned for us to hurry. "Stand here by the creek. The horses will come from behind those trees, across the field and the road over there." She pointed to the pasture by the barn where Sunnyside Up and Sun Ray spent much of their time. "Just listen. You'll hear them."

Walter pressed his lips together, his forehead creased like a little old man's. He explored my face with his fingertips and an elfin grin, then shifted his weight on my hip.

Chloe shoved her hands into her fleece, her eyes focused on the horizon. When the corner of her mouth curled up, goose bumps covered my skin. Walter's eyes popped open at the sound of hooves trampling the ground. The rumbling of running horses grew louder as they galloped free in a traveling herd. I couldn't take my eyes off them, their muscles flexed and twitched in the early light, their manes bounced and thrashed, cutting the morning dew as their breaths billowed through the chill in the air. Their whinnies muted beneath pounding strides. Breeze and Tullia led the way.

"Look, Maggie. It's Tullia. You rode her to the top of the mountain."

"I know. She's fast," I said, remembering the sweet girl that she was with her white chest and dark speckled hindquarters. "And Breeze is there, too."

Chloe grinned and buried her hands further into her pockets. "I think they like each other."

"Me, too," I said. "Me, too."

Walter uncovered his ears as the thunder of horses diminished into the morning glow. "That was cool."

A shiver crept down my spine at the magnificent sight of horses galloping full speed. Chloe's bright eyes stared through me with barbs of elation and I knew what she was doing bringing me out here to see the beautiful creatures. John wasn't the only one fighting harder. Winston rode behind the traveling herd on his black mare with one white sock. Trout, his right-hand man alongside, pressing his spurs into the sides of his cream-colored beauty with a black mane and fire in her eyes. Winston glanced in our direction as he trotted behind Huckleberry, the young horse whose black spots appeared dark purple when the sun washed over on her.

Loose strands of Chloe's hair stuck to her cheeks.

Walter rested his head on my shoulder. "I gotta come back to this place," he said as his fingers rubbed my neck.

"That you do, darlin' boy, that you do." I felt his smile against my collarbone.

Judy packed the back of the Suburban while I made French toast and bacon for the troops, including Ashley and Justin who joined us for breakfast.

Chloe sat with her chin on the counter. "You gonna be home when we come to Grosse Pointe next week?"

"Yup. Glad, too. I talked to her yesterday and she can't wait to see you."

"Good. Will you help me pack?"

I handed Ashley the spatula and she took over the cooking that filled the air with the aroma of cinnamon and love. "I'll help with whatever you need. I'll be home all week."

"This is going to stink. Harry and Walter will be gone. You and Judy will be gone. And I'll just be here."

"With me," Ashley said. "We can ride Huckleberry all you want."

"I do like Huckleberry a lot!" Chloe said. "Her spots remind me of my favorite color, Voodoo, and the hat that Glad knit for me last summer."

Taking the platter of French toast from Ashley, I smiled, letting her know I appreciated her efforts in taking care of my girl. "You want to go get the boys and tell Judy breakfast is ready?"

John came through the kitchen, sniffing the air. My stomach rolled over with excitement thinking about being in his arms, relishing the moment he'd swept me off my feet, and carried me to a secret place where he'd made love to me. My cheeks warmed as he brushed past me, and I supposed my grin was a bit bigger than it had been in quite some time.

Harry, Walter, and Chloe ran into the dining room like a herd of cattle.

Chloe skidded into a chair and bumped the table. "Sorry, Dad. Just a little excited to eat. It smells delish."

John and I sat next to each other after getting Chloe situated, our knees touching like school kids. The connection of the innocent touch make my heart race. Winston joined us and sat at the head of the table while the kids dished up.

"Thought you had business this morning," John said.

"I do, and it's the people around this table. Smells mighty good in here," he said, winking at Chloe. "I wouldn't miss this for the world. Trout can hold down the fort while I say goodbye to my new friends." Winston's emerald eyes twinkled as he scanned the table. "You ladies all packed?"

"Yup." Judy sipped her coffee. Her dark eyes shone with anticipation for the long drive home.

The hair on the nape of my neck bristled when Winston's gaze met mine. His eyes sent a message, a tender message disguised by his rough exterior. John's hand covered mine under the table. Disappointed about leaving such a beautiful place filled with beautiful people, I held on to John's warm hand, masquerading my true feelings with a happy face.

I sat between a father and his daughter, realizing I had a place in both their lives. We fit together like missing pieces, and it made sense. The twinge of panic trickled through my veins. There had to be a way to work our situation out.

John's hand left mine as he reached up to fill his plate with homemade goodness.

Chloe's gaze met mine. Freckles on the bridge of her nose stood out like a path of stars at midnight leading to heaven in the Montana sky, just like the ones I'd wished upon last night as John and I held each other. I hated the murky glow of uncertainty and I wanted desperately to quit doubting the tide in my heart that toyed with the thoughts in my mind. Chloe smiled, and I smiled back. I reminded myself that things have a way of working out for the best, but I desperately wanted the gods to sway my destiny in her direction.

Judy studied us from across the table, cradling her coffee mug in her hands. I hoped like hell no one else at the table saw me flinch when I began planning how to get myself back to Montana as soon as possible. Getting anyone's hopes up unnecessarily wouldn't be fair, and that included mine.

Chapter 33

I reviewed the pictures on my camera as Judy crossed the Michigan state line. Mom was three hours away, Montana was two and a half days behind us, but imbedded memories were fresh in my mind. Judy glanced over to me, then checked her mirrors, and changed lanes. She eyed the boys snoozing in the back seat through the rearview mirror, and then looked over to me again as I pressed the button on my camera to replay the trip one more time.

"You look a little homesick already," Judy said, adjusting her visor. "You're one pitiful woman."

"Yeah, I miss Mom." I fiddled with the grass bracelet that John made me. The sticky texture was now smooth and the strands of grass supple to the touch. It made me happy that Chloe was still wearing hers when I said goodbye.

"That's not what I meant," Judy said. "Your mom is just up ahead. I meant Montana."

"Montana's not my home," I whispered, staring out the window as the flat fields whizzed past.

"I beg to differ. You belong there. You're not kidding anybody." Judy checked her mirrors then changed lanes again.

A picture of John and me lit the camera screen. "Shit. How am I going to do this?"

"You're gonna do what you always do. Figure it out and get your butt back there to your *family*."

I choked out words. "My family is here."

She scoffed in my direction. "You belong with John and Chloe." Judy sighed and gripped the wheel tighter. "They're family, too, new family."

I swallowed away the tears. My eyes burned and my heart ached. "What about my mom?"

"She's been antsy to see you move on, too. She wants you to be happy." Judy tossed me a packet of tissue from her armrest. "I can't believe you haven't cried before now."

I swiped the corners of my eyes with my fingers. "Sorry to disappoint you." I could barely say the words.

"On the contrary. It's just another hurdle. You'll figure out how to get over it."

Tears flooded from my eyes even though my lips curled upward. "This is so stupid," I said, blotting the streams running down my cheeks.

"It's not stupid. You three belong together. Anybody in their right mind can see it."

There was a rustle behind my seat. "I knew it." Harry stuck his face between the front seats.

I glared back at him. His goofy grin made me smile harder.

"I knew it. I knew it. I knew it. I told Chloe you and John *loved* each other. I am the man."

Reaching back, I pinched him. Judy grinned, and Walter stretched his arms over his head with a yawn. "Are we home yet?" he asked.

"Almost," Judy said.

Harry rested his hands behind his head and leaned back in his seat. "Does this mean we get to go back to Montana?"

"We'll see," Judy said. "See, Maggie, if he can figure it out, so can the rest of us. Get on board, girl."

"Hey, I'm the smart one in the bunch."

"Apparently." I stared out the window at the passing cars.

"Can we stop to go to the bathroom?" Walter asked. "And what are you guys talking about?"

"Yes, we can stop," Judy said. "And nothing."

"I thought Harry said we're going back to Montana." Walter yanked at his seatbelt.

"He didn't mean today. Harry, will ya' knock it off?" Judy veered onto the off ramp. MacDonald's was just off the highway.

Giving Harry the stink-eye, I stared back again between the seats. "Who wants fries and a drink?" Judy asked, parking the truck.

"I do," Walter and Harry said in unison.

"Me, too. Can I have a double?" I asked, unbuckling my seatbelt.

Judy chuckled. "Whatever it takes, 'cause it's time to shove you out of the nest."

"It's time to fly, sister, just like Frankie." Harry's voice carried through the parking lot. A gray-haired woman with a walker scowled at his boisterous antics.

Harry closed the door then I shut mine. We stood nose-to-nose. "You know, last summer you were a lot shorter and a lot less nosey."

"Chloe's taught me a lot," he said.

"Yeah, me too."

Harry squinted as the sun hit his face. "You're not going to tell me any more of your secrets, are you, or smart-aleck comebacks as my mom calls them?"

"Nope, you'll figure them out on your own."

Harry's grin flat-lined. He stared at me, his dark brown eyes flickering. "It's okay," he said. "'Cause I knew it all along. And so did Chloe. Maggie and John sitting in a tree—"

Judy interrupted. "That's enough, Harry. We want her to. Leave. The. Nest."

Walter narrowed his gaze at me. "Now you know how I feel. My brother is annoying!"

"I guess so." I held Walter's hand in mine.

Judy draped her arm around Harry's shoulder. Her voice was low and menacing. "I swear I'll make your life a living hell if you press this any further."

Walter smiled at me. "And she means it," he said, jumping up onto the curb. "I'm gonna get an orange soda. What are you getting?" he asked, tugging at my hand.

"I'll have what you're having," I answered.

"Can we get it to go, Mom? I want to get home," Harry said, holding the door for us. "I've got people to see."

"Sounds like a plan. You guys want a hamburger?"

"Chicken nuggets," Walter said.

"Hamburger for me," Harry said, leaning on his mom's shoulder.

I was glad that Harry suggested we get takeout because I wanted to get home just as much as he did. Mom and Bones were waiting, and I missed them terribly.

Judy parked the Suburban in my driveway. Mom sat on the front porch, head down, and her hands working the knitting needles. Judy honked, and Mom's expression warmed my heart. I had so much to tell her. Before Judy could put the truck in park, I unbuckled my seatbelt. Mom greeted us with open arms. Bones barked at the front door and pawed at the screen. He nudged the door open with his front paws and ran to my feet. His stocky legs landed in my hands as I caught him, his weight against my thighs. Judy opened the back of the truck, then sifted through the contents to get to my stuff. I set Bones down and went to help her while Mom went to the window of the truck to talk to the boys.

Judy two-fisted one of my bags. "Here ya go. Geez this is heavy." Then she handed me the other bag. "Oh, and don't forget your beer."

"Thanks," I said as she closed the back of the Suburban.

Her hands covered mine. "Don't go getting all weird on me. You have something great going. If I know you, you've already begun planning. If you need me, you know where to find me."

"Thanks for going on this adventure," I said, setting the case of beer next to my bags. "It feels like I've known you forever. You're a great friend."

"Are you kidding me? This was fabulous. I can't wait to go back."

"Are you sure you'll go back?" I asked, holding her stare.

"Positive." Judy patted my hand. "Thanks for inviting us and thanks for putting up with the boys."

"No problem. They're wonderfully wacky." I said my goodbyes.

Walter jumped out of the truck, then wrapped his arms around my waist. "Bye, Maggie."

Walter squeezed me tight, and I moaned as he squished me. "Wow, that's a bear hug." I lifted his chin with my finger to get a better look at his sweet face.

"Thanks for letting us go with you to Montana," he said. "Chloe's gonna be really lucky someday."

"What are you talking about, short stuff?" I cradled his face in my hands, smudges of dried ketchup dotting his cheek.

Walter beckoned me to kneel down to his height. He cupped his hands around my ear. "Harry says you're going to marry John. If you do, that means Chloe gets to have you as her new mom, and that's really cool."

Mom's forehead wrinkled with curiosity and I was glad that she couldn't hear Walter. "Let's just keep that between us. And Harry's just talking." I touched the end of Walter's button nose with my finger. "Shh." I put my pointer finger to my lips.

Judy reached out, and I hugged her. Walter climbed back into the truck and I poked my head inside the window. "Thanks for the great trip, boys. I'm sure I'll be seeing you soon." Harry beamed, and I felt my cheeks glow. My heart danced as I contemplated a new beginning.

"I know your secret." Harry boasted while climbing into the front seat.

I leaned into the window further to whisper. "Yeah, you and I will chat later."

Harry laughed out loud and slugged Walter in the arm. "Pee-wee."

Walter leaned over and slugged him back. "Jerk," he said under his breath. "Mom, can we get this bus moving? I have to go to the bathroom."

Judy hopped in the driver's seat and started the oversized Suburban's engine. She hung her elbow out the window. "Did you really mean what you said about watching the boys?"

"Yup. Just let me know when. Maybe next week when Chloe is here I can take all of them for one last hurrah."

Walter stuck his head out the window. "Cool." He gave me a thumbs-up.

Harry laughed and waved to me.

Judy checked her mirrors and backed out of the driveway.

Mom and I waved goodbye, and then I picked up one of my bags and carried it to the porch. I went back for the second bag and my Montana beer while Mom settled back into the swing on the porch. She yanked at her ball of yarn and peered over the rim of her glasses at her knitting project.

"Walter's pretty smitten with you."

"He's great. Harry's a pill, but I like him, too."

"You're lucky to have such great friends. How is Chloe? Was she sad when you left?"

Sitting down beside Mom, I held the ball of pink yarn in my hands. "She was okay, I guess." My smile faded as I unwound yarn and fed it to Mom as she worked her steel knitting needles. "It was so gorgeous there. The air was so sweet. The weather was great. We did so much," I said quietly, thinking about John's touch and Chloe's face when she stared in to my eyes as Winston and Trout ran the horses.

"And how was John?"

"He's good. He seems happy and Winston was so kind. Did you know he plays the guitar?"

Mom beamed as I unwound more yarn for her. "Sounds like you really had a great time. I bet it was hard coming home." She lowered her gaze and stopped knitting. "Actually, I'm surprised you came home."

"Why would I not come home? This is where I live and this is where you live. This is my home." I blew a loose strand of hair from my eyes as I tucked my foot under my leg.

"For now," Mom said then stopped. "I can see it in your eyes. I saw it before you left."

"What are you talking about?"

"You were running toward something this time, not away." Mom tucked her needles in her knitting bag and took the ball of yarn from me. Bones ran up the stairs and bounded into my lap. I grunted as his four paws pounced on me. He was too hefty to be jumping in my lap.

"You shouldn't roll your eyes at me. I'm your mother," Mom said, patting Bones's head. "He was a perfect angel while you were gone."

"Of course he was." I scratched his ears while his hind leg twitched feverishly. "I missed you." I held Bones's head up, and his brown eyes reciprocated my inner joy. Drool dripped from his jowls while Mom's knowing eyes focused on me.

"What's next?"

"What do you mean, 'what's next'?" Why was it so hard to talk to her? She was my mother for God's sake. Why did I feel the need to be secretive? The only judge here . . . was me. I had to get over it. She knew how I felt about my career, Chloe, and John. Nothing was a secret. Mom rolled her eyes at me as she took off her silver reading glasses and hooked them on her collar.

"Oh, for Pete's sake, Marjorie Jean. What about John?" Mom lowered her gaze. "And Chloe? What happened out there? That's why you went, wasn't it?"

I caressed Bones's wrinkly neck. He moaned then shut his eyes. His husky back leg twitched. "A lot, actually." I paused, waiting for my mother's reaction. Her gaze remained steady as I finally swallowed hesitation to share. "I want to go back."

"Okay," she said, caressing Bones's hindquarters.

"I want to go back and not come home," I said, speculating what it would mean to give up my life in Michigan. The corner of Mom's mouth crept up. Her eyes gleamed. Embarrassment crept over me, but I wasn't sure why.

"Then I think you should go."

"What about my job? I've worked this long toward a pension. I don't have enough years in."

"I'm sure you'll figure it out, Marjorie Jean."

I ran my fingers through my hair and covered my face. "Why can't anything be easy?"

Mom's touch was soft as she pried my fingers away from my face to see me better. "I don't think life was meant to be easy. If this is what you want, just do it. You gave your youth to Beckett. You raised a terrific son. Now it's your time."

Her words were tender as she caressed my hand. Her skin was supple and the wrinkles of time framed her youthful disposition. "I don't want to leave you."

Mom chuckled at my words. "That's just like you. Always worried about the other guy. I'll be fine."

Emotion stuck in my throat. "What about my house, my things?"

"Sell the house, take the things you want. You'll always have a home in me."

My chest heaved at her sensitive words. "Thanks, Mom." Bones lifted his head and opened his eyes. "I just want you to be okay. Montana is a long way away."

"Maybe, darling girl, but so is heaven, and I've managed to keep your father with me every day since he died." She blew a kiss into the air.

Tears burned behind my eyes. I looked to the sky, and then blinked away the puddles. "Who am I going to have to bug me? I don't think I can function without you around."

Mom's laugh made me smile harder. "Oh, you'll have Chloe. And you'll have me. I'm gonna visit. You couldn't keep me away if you tried."

Mom patted my knee, and I covered her hand with mine.

"Good," I said. "Chloe would be disappointed if you didn't visit."

"What are you going to do about work?" Mom asked.

"I have an idea, but I have to check into the logistics."

Chapter 34

The pit in my stomach seemed like a black hole. The last days of summer depressed me. John and Chloe would be here in seventy-two hours, but I focused on the start of school. I opened my laptop and typed in the school website then opened my e-mail. The list of unread items covered the screen. I deleted junk mail then scanned the rest, expecting to see birth announcements with the occasional death.

The last announcement caught my attention. My eyes burned and my hands shook as tears streamed down my cheeks. Jenny McBride was not announcing the birth of a grandchild. In fact, she wasn't announcing anything. I leaned closer to the screen and reread the words over and over, not believing the news. She had passed away.

The image of her at the cancer center plagued me. A pang of loss constricted my chest. I'd told Jenny to call me, and I knew she wouldn't. Our friendship tainted by ambition. Details didn't matter, the fact remained the same, Jenny McBride former friend, and colleague had passed away from cancer. She'd seized her dream of becoming principal while I wallowed in rejection, not knowing what fate had in store for me. With the beat of time, my future was upon me, and I now understood the "big picture."

I sat back in my chair, closed my eyes, and then said a prayer for Jenny and her family. I said a prayer my own family. Bones trotted in, his jowls flapping, his stout bulldog body bobbing and weaving with each step. He sat at my feet.

"This is a sign." I dabbed my cheeks with tissue. He

tilted his head in my direction. "I know you don't get it, but it's a sign, God rest her soul."

Bones grunted then wobbled over to his bed, circled it three times, and plopped down.

I read the e-mail one more time. Her funeral had been three days ago. While I was riding shotgun, reminiscing my vacation, she'd lost her battle with disease, closed her eyes, and said goodbye to the world. Guilt brewed as I caught my breath. It just didn't seem possible.

My phone buzzed. It was John. My eyes blurred with emotion as I read the screen. I tapped out a reply. *Yes, I'm here. Mom is great. Can't wait to see you. xo*

Setting down the phone, I scanned the e-mail for an address to send my condolences. I scrolled down to the last unopened e-mail, a job posting. My heart bound by sadness, I opened it, perused the details, and closed it just as quickly, not giving me time to mull over the proposition before me.

In the top drawer of my desk, I dug for the book that held my username and password to the state retirement website. The gray-haired couple on the front held each other in jubilee. I imagined how free they felt. My phone buzzed again. I looked at the screen. It was John again. I read the message. A smile crept across my lips. I tapped out another message. *I'm sure Glad will watch Chloe when you are here.* My stomach rolled over at the thought of being in his arms again.

I read the first page of the schoolteacher's retirement book, and then typed my information into the login box of the website to double-check my years of service. Highlighted blue font on the left side of the screen caught my attention. I squinted to read the tab again. I clicked on the words, *buying years.* I read the explanation, then reread it, thinking I missed something. Since when did the state re-instate the privilege of purchasing years? I'd given up the hope a few years back as we were told that wasn't an option any more. I could've sworn I read it on paper.

I reread the passage in disbelief just as I'd read Jenny's obituary. What was the catch? Was this a trick? I read the formula and gulped at the amount of money it would cost me to buy my way out.

Leaning back in my chair, I closed my eyes. Jenny's face haunted me. She was gone at such a young age. She was dead and I was here in my cozy house large enough for a good Irish-Catholic family, pondering my own dilemma, which really wasn't a dilemma in retrospect. Tears ran down my cheeks and my chest heaved. At one time we'd been so close. How could we have let enterprise unravel the threads of our friendship like one of Mom's knitting projects when she yanked at the yarn to start over?

I bowed my head and my body convulsed with remorse. "Goddamn it." The lump in my throat constricted my voice. I swiped at the tears. The computer screen blurred in front of me and my brain throbbed against my skull. My phone vibrated against my desk.

"Goddamn it," I cried, letting it all out.

The screen of my phone flickered as I opened the photo. It was from Chloe. She was perched on Huckleberry. I swiped my fingers over the screen to make the photo bigger. Huckleberry's spots glistened in the sun, the intensity matching the expression on Chloe's face. I read the text. *Hi Maggie, I got to ride Huckleberry today. I just wanted to send you a picture so you wouldn't forget me.*

I dabbed my swollen eyes. *God, how could she think I would forget her?* "Shit." I tapped out a message back. *I could never forget you!*

Recalculating the retirement formula again, I reviewed my years of service, then started plugging in numbers. I swallowed at the total cost. How was it even possible? Who could afford five digits, teetering on six digits, one more snack cake, and the scales would tip. The total number of snack cakes consumed in a twenty-seven-year career probably cost just as much. Who knew? I should have put the money in a secret bank. Even with Bradley on his own, it seemed impossible. I shut the computer down in disgust. My phone sat quiet while I dreamed of being with Chloe and John at the ranch.

A knock at the door jarred my train of thought. Bones jumped from his place and ran to the door. I followed as he skidded around the corner. Mom stood at the screen door. "How come you just didn't come in?"

"I figured I'd better start knocking," Mom said. "Never know what I might interrupt."

My cheeks simmered. "Ha. Ha. You're funny. Nobody here but me." I joined her on the porch.

"Why the long face?" she asked, sitting beside me on the swing.

"I don't think I can afford a buy out."

"What do you mean, sweetheart?"

"I can buy the years I need to qualify for my pension, but it's seems too expensive. It's based on your highest years of salary, not current rate."

Mom made a face.

"What?"

"I'm not sure you want me to butt in, Maggie."

"Seriously, you're going to disappoint me now? This sucks."

Mom frowned at me.

"What?"

"How much do you owe on this house?"

"Not really sure of the exact number, but we've, excuse me . . ." A bitter note of Beckett lingered at the back of my throat. God, why was I so angry with him today? I hadn't spoken or seen him in months. I tucked my foot under my thigh and rested my arm on the back of the swing.

"So what do you owe?" she asked.

I shrugged. "Well we had a thirty-year mortgage and I've been here for at least twenty-five years, maybe, I don't know," I said. "I can't count anymore."

Mom took her glasses off and leaned close to me. "Sell the house, dear. The market has gone up."

My eyes scanned the porch then peered through the screen door to the inside that sat dormant most of the time. My breath caught in my chest.

"What's the problem? What in God's name could cause you to look like that?" Mom nibbled at the end of the arm of her glasses.

"Jenny McBride died. Do you remember her?"

"How could I forget? She's all I heard about for the longest time."

"Sorry," I said. Tears didn't come. I glanced up into my mother's eyes and held her hand. "I don't think I was a very good friend."

"You tried." Mom took a deep breath. "It takes two."

"Maybe, but she died of cancer, Mom. And I'm still here."

"Thank God for that. And I do every day, sweet girl."

A lump formed in my throat as Mom's glossy eyes stared at me. I inhaled, held my breath, and then let it out along with the sting of tears.

Mom wiped my eyes. "I'm sorry, Maggie. I know you two used to be close. It's a shame how work interfered with your relationship."

I pictured Jenny lying in a coffin, gaunt, not the blonde-haired, blue-eyed woman who seemed vibrant not so long ago. A wave of nausea rushed through my belly, and I covered my mouth then swallowed hard.

Mom's forehead creased with worry.

"Sorry." My chin quivered.

"Oh, Maggie."

I pressed my lips together gathering my scattered thoughts. "I was off in Montana having the time of my life and she was here dying and I didn't even know it. Judy and I saw her a few months ago. I had no idea."

Mom sighed. "You can't feel guilty for living your life."

I picked at the hem of my T-shirt. "What?"

"You can't feel guilty," Mom said, again. "If things had been turned around, she would've been doing the same thing and rightfully so."

Bones plopped down on the porch floor and let out a deep sigh.

Mom stroked his back with her toe. "He gets it. Why can't you?"

"I don't know."

"Sell the house and move on," Mom said.

"I'd have to talk to Beckett." I nibbled at my thumbnail. The prospect of selling made my stomach churn. This was Bradley's childhood home.

"Fine, talk to Beckett, but I see that as just one more reason for you to hang on to it. You let him dictate your life for all those years. You really want to go there?"

"No." Mom was right, but I didn't have the nerve to look her in the eyes. *Damn it, she was right.* "Maybe Bradley would want it."

Mom pressed her lips together in disgust. "You are impossible. You worry about everyone but yourself. You've been like this forever. Why can't you just focus on you?" She laid her glasses on the bench between us.

"I don't know." Truth was I did know. Truth was, it was less painful to focus outward. There was something prickly inside me. It nicked my heart. It rang in my head. I didn't know myself the way I should have. I was afraid to know myself.

"I think you do know," Mom said. "It's time to face the music."

"It's just so scary. The thought of moving, the thought of a new life. What if it doesn't work out?"

"And if you don't go, you'll always wonder. What will hurt more?"

Mom's blunt words made me cringe, a direct hit as if we were playing Battleship and she just torpedoed my last ship. I bit my lip as it trembled. Chloe's image danced in my mind. John's touch lingered in my memory. I knew I couldn't live without them.

Chapter 35

Beckett's hair was shorter than usual and a tinge grayer, too. I sat with my hands under my chin thinking about what I saw in him. With a tilt of my head and a blink of my eyes, he was nothing to me. He rambled on about teaching art history, the new Japanese restaurant downtown, and the thought of dying his gray.

I nodded along for a while until I couldn't listen anymore. "So, I'm thinking about selling the house."

Beckett frowned. "Sell the house? Why would you do that?"

A million reasons crossed my mind, but I couldn't bring myself to tell him just yet about John and Chloe. He didn't even know I went to Montana, and I liked it that way. "I'm just one person and it's getting harder to keep up," I said. That part was true. Beckett's eyes dimmed as hurt creased in his brow. "I just wondered if you wanted to buy it."

"I thought you'd live here forever. It's the home you love and are comfortable in."

"That's one of the problems. I guess, if I've learned anything since our divorce, comfort doesn't necessarily equate to need." Beckett's eyes darkened and his forehead furrowed. I knew I wasn't getting my point across. "I think it's time to pass it on to another family."

"Does Bradley know you're thinking about selling it?" Shoulders drooping, Beckett played with the keys to his Prius.

"Um, no. I thought I'd talk to you first. Thought you might be interested in buying it?"

Beckett shook his head in disbelief. "I can't believe you want to move. We put so much into this house."

"Yeah, but I'm getting to the end of my career and this house is a lot for one person."

Beckett didn't get it. The hint of anger sparked within me. Once again, Beckett wanted me to keep something that I didn't want. He wanted me to hold it close for him. God, what was he going to do when I told him I wanted to buy out my last few years and move away from the suburbs of Detroit that he still treasured? It was fine for him to transition into a new life, but not me.

"I thought you wanted the house. We agreed you'd take the house when we divorced." His Adam's apple bulged as he grew more irritated.

I played with the grass bracelet on my wrist. John's touch alive and fresh. "Um, we did. You also told me that you wanted to live closer to the university. It wasn't an issue then." Not much was an issue between us at that point. Beckett had come out and he did everything he could to make me comfortable, too comfortable, sometimes suffocating me with kindness. If he wanted the house, he should've said something. My patience wore thin.

Beckett leaned back in his chair, his peeved expression personified.

Folding my arms across my chest, I leaned back into my chair, preparing for a showdown.

"This is just like you," he said.

I shook my head. "What?" Mom's words flooded back. The electricity in the air warned me to tread lightly.

"I gave you everything you wanted, needed. And now you don't want to live here."

"Why are you trying your best to make me feel shitty about this? Yes, you've given me more than I think many ex-husbands would give their exes, but sometimes . . ." I stopped. I didn't want to fight and thought we were past this petty behavior.

"What, Maggie? For God's sake, just say it. You could never just say what you really wanted. It was like a guessing game half the time."

I pressed my lips shut and avoided his disgusted gaze, trying to maintain control, but then again, I thought maybe I should speak my mind. *Lose control. It might do me good.* "Okay." I stifled the nerves that menaced my self-confidence and pushed my shoulders back. "You know what, Beckett?" I pointed my finger at him as his lips parted. "You gave me all those things because you felt so damn guilty about your part in all of this. Jesus, you hired an interior decorator last summer and wanted me to date him. You can't just give away things in hopes that it'll Band-Aid the wounds that you helped create." I challenged Beckett with my stare.

"What the hell are you talking about?"

"Let's try this again. Listen," I said. "All your generous gifts were a coping mechanism, for you." My tone was strong and certain. "Sometimes people have to hurt. Sometimes people have to figure out life by themselves."

"Why are you pushing me away, Maggie?"

I stared at Beckett, long and hard. "You thought that if you gave me the house, helped with the decorating—" My hands flailed in front of me as I stumbled over my words. "You thought that I wouldn't hate you."

His expression softened. His tense jaw flexed.

"Am I right? You did it so I wouldn't hate you. You were afraid there wouldn't be anyone else who truly cared about you after you came out." Oh, my God, did he really feel that isolated and alone? How could he possible think I'd be that shallow?

Beckett sat frozen, his eyes glazed over, and his fingers stopped working his keys.

"Am I right?" I looked around at the kitchen he'd picked out, letting him think it was a compromise because that's what married couples do. My chest heaved with exasperation. I was as much to blame as he was. We pacified each other, and not in a good way. "Well, am I?"

He said nothing.

I glared at him.

"Fuck, Maggie. I gave you the better part of my life."

"You didn't have to." My teeth ground together as I seethed. "So you stayed with me out of pity?"

"You're making this worse than it has to be, Maggie."

"No, I am making it real. If you stayed for pity, shame on you. You wasted your time and mine." Shouting at Beckett felt great.

Beckett cleared his throat. "I stayed because I thought my son would hate me, more than I hated my own dad."

I smoothed my hair away from my face. "Oh, Beckett." I wiped the corners of my eyes. "How the hell could you think your own son wouldn't forgive you?" He'd sold Bradley short. He'd sold me short. He'd sold himself short.

"Why didn't you tell me?" I hissed. "Now you're the one not being fair to Bradley. Has he ever made you feel less than all the things that you are?"

Beckett lowered his gaze. "No."

"What?"

Beckett's eyes glistened with tears as the stern words left my mouth. "I love him too much. I just didn't want to lose him. It was bad enough that I had to split with you."

My hands shook. "We could never raise a human being to be so hateful." What was Beckett even thinking?

"Don't hate me, Maggie."

"The only thing that's going to make me hate you is this condescending attitude that you're displaying. What the hell? I know I'm not perfect." I stopped myself from going any further. "Do you want the house or not?"

"I don't know." Beckett rubbed his temples. "I really like my place downtown. I just don't know."

"Fine, then think about it and get back to me." Pushing back my chair, I left the table. It wasn't Beckett's hard stare that unnerved me, it was his reminiscing. I opened the refrigerator door and peered inside for a magic wand to fix what I stirred up, or better yet, a baseball bat to beat him with. I hoped like hell this conversation would go better with Bradley. I snagged a bottle of water and rolled it across my forehead. The glass bottles rattled as I slammed the refrigerator door. Beckett stood then paced back and forth with his hand on his chin. I rolled my eyes. *God, what made me sleep with him all those years ago?* He irritated the hell out of me.

"Is it really that important that you have to sell the house now?"

Shit. Screwing the cap back on the water bottle, I wanted to throw it at his head. "You know what, let me just put this on hold like all the other things in my life and maybe it'll pass me by. Will that make you happy?"

Beckett stopped in his tracks and glared at me.

Everything felt so familiar even though we hadn't lived together for more than two years, legally.

An alarm went off in my head. What if John and I ended up like this? I extinguished the absurdity and slammed that tiny door shut at the back of my brain. Or so I thought. I couldn't do this again with another person.

"Maggie, I really like my place downtown. I really don't want to give it up."

"Then don't," I said, trying to derail my temper. "Letting go doesn't mean you don't care." I picked at the label on the water bottle. It ripped. I twisted the cap off and took a long swig. My face burned from the uncontrollable heat my body couldn't control any more than this conversation, Beckett, or what was to come in the future.

"I just hate to see you sell it then have regrets."

"Oh, for the love of God, Beckett. Enough!" Something inside snapped. "I'll talk to Bradley then I'll get back to you. This is stupid. It shouldn't be this hard."

"No, it shouldn't," he said, stuffing his hands in his pockets and stepping closer to the island in the kitchen.

I made a face at him. "Fine, we're even, but I'm thinking bickering isn't the issue here." I wasn't going to let him win. Leaning back against the counter, I was thankful for the cold ugly tile beneath my sweaty feet.

My thoughts must have shown because Beckett said, "You always did hate that tile, didn't you?"

"Yup," I said. "Still do. Thought it would grow on me, but that never happened."

"I see the house next door is for sale. Are John and Chloe moving?"

"Yeah, they're pretty much gone." I clammed up, wanting to keep them to myself.

"You're going to miss them, I suppose."

He didn't know the half of it. I nodded, staring at him through tiny slits.

"Maggie, I'm not stupid. What are you doing?"

"Why does it matter? Bradley is grown and gone. It's my time. I was the dutiful wife. I worked at a career to help with this house, but those days are gone."

"Must be something pretty important to get you all worked up like this."

I shook my head from side-to-side. John and Chloe were locked away, my treasure. "Maybe this was a mistake. I shouldn't have asked you come over to talk about the house."

Beckett rubbed his perfect chin and leaned against the refrigerator. "Just think about it, Maggie. You got a good thing here."

I have an even better thing in Montana. "Sure, Beckett."

Beckett strolled back over to the table and picked up his keys. His thin, tall, lanky frame, leaner than usual. I wondered if he was dating. I knew he didn't want to live here with a partner. He was too worried about what the neighbors would think. The keys jingled as he snatched them up. It was fine for me to stay, though. I guess he thought it'd be easier for me.

"Stupid," I said as I had a conversation with myself.

"What's stupid?" Beckett faced me.

I squashed my emotion. There would be no John to cuddle up with tonight. There would never be a John to snuggle with if I didn't grab the golden ring this time around. I pictured myself on a jeweled horse, leaning over so far I teetered on the brink of falling. I reached, feeling the strain in my shoulder and the bitter taste of disappointment. With my tongue sticking out of my mouth like a second grader guiding his scissors around a hairpin turn of dotted lines, I saw my life without Chloe and John. "You know I could never completely cut you out."

"I know."

"Bradley couldn't either," I said.

"I know."

"Then why in God's name are you giving me all this shit?"

"Because you got a fire in you, Maggie. I haven't seen it in a long time. Why won't you tell me what's going on? Are you sick again? Do you need money?"

"No, Beckett." I messaged my throbbing temples. "I need a life. It's that simple." I stared through him. "When it's time for you to know, I'll tell you, but that time is not now."

The front door slammed, making my nerves prickle, and Mom waltzed in like Queen Elizabeth at a cotillion. Her eyes darted back and forth between Beckett and me. "Figured you two could use someone to mediate. The neighbors are forming a crowd out there." She put her purse down on the counter. "Just kidding. Anything I can help with?" Her eyes said, *told you so* in secret Mom language.

"No," I said.

"Hi, Glad," Beckett said politely. "I should be going."

"Probably a good idea." I could feel the sarcasm in my forced grin.

"You're looking well, Glad."

She held his stare. "Thanks. I'm in a walking club and I joined a travel club."

My eyebrow arched toward the ceiling. *Oh, please keep your mouth zipped.* The plastic of the water bottle crinkled in my grip.

"Seriously, I joined a travel club. My friend Lois has been asking me to join for months. I think it's time to get out there and see the world before I can't move around anymore."

I peered at her over the edge of the bottle as I drank the rest of the water, and then tossed the empty bottle in the sink and wiped my mouth with the back of my hand. "That's great, Mom. We can talk about that after Beckett leaves." I headed for the foyer.

"I can take a hint," Beckett said. "I'd like to hear about it someday, Glad."

Beckett's words trailed off as he followed me to the front door.

"Bye, Beckett." Mom's voice trailed into the foyer.

"I'll get back with you after I speak to Bradley." I crossed my arms across my stomach. The humid breeze whisked in on the cusp of darkness. Beckett's lame smile wasn't appeasing. "Bye, Beckett."

Beckett played with his keys again. "Bye, Maggie."

Chapter 36

I went into the living room and plopped down on the sofa. Shadows fell across the khaki-colored walls like movie reels of past memories.

Mom came in and sat with me as night set in. "It's peaceful in the dark."

"I shouldn't have asked him if he wanted the house." The words caught in my throat.

"You did the right thing." Mom smoothed the hair back from her face and let out a sigh.

"Thanks, but it doesn't make me feel any better. How much did you hear?"

"Almost all of it. I came in, but you didn't hear the door so I panicked and stood there like a dope, then went back out and waited. Figured you needed an interruption."

"I don't care what you heard, and thanks." I reached under the lampshade and switched on the table lamp. "Did you really join those clubs?"

Mom grinned, and I couldn't help but mimic her expression.

"Yeah, I did. You kind of inspired me. I'm not getting any younger."

Scooting closer to her, I laid my head on her shoulder, wanting her to stay alive forever. "Don't remind me."

Mom stroked my hair as she spoke. "You're a strong girl, Maggie. Just because someone ruffles your feathers doesn't mean you're doing the wrong thing. More often than not, you've done the right thing and they just can't stand it."

Mom smelled like vanilla and coffee, her blouse soft beneath my cheek like a pillow. My nerves settled. "It's just so stupid."

"It's not stupid to him. You're his security blanket whether he wants to admit it or not."

"He really thought Bradley would hate him for being gay."

"I don't buy that for a minute," Mom said.

Staring at Mom, I wondered if I'd look like her after twenty years or so on the ranch. "Thanks for not telling him about Montana or John."

"Never. That is up to you, dear girl."

"What?" I said, lowering my gaze.

Mom touched my cheek. "Although Beckett gave you the most wonderful son, I like John better. You belong together."

"You're not just saying that to get rid of me?" I yelped when Mom pinched my arm. "Geez, Mom. I bruise like a peach."

She scowled. "Chloe was put on this earth for a reason. And it was to get you two knuckleheads together. The roads may not always be clearly marked. Detours and potholes happen."

"No wonder Chloe likes you so much." Mom's caring touch made me feel better. Her caress was something that didn't age or change with time.

"Now what are you going to do?"

I laid my head back on her shoulder. "I looked up the balance on the mortgage. It's not that bad. I'd have a chunk of change left over. I just worry about having enough for the future."

"We all do, darling girl, but if you spend all your time fretting, you're going to miss out on some pretty important stuff, including the future. Besides, I have some money tucked away."

I sat up. "I don't want your money, Mom. I don't want John's either. I want to make my own way."

"You already have." Mom drew me close. "When your dad died, there was a life insurance policy. He didn't just leave it to me. He left it for both of us."

I felt my eyes grow wide. "I helped you with all the legal stuff. The beneficiary was you."

Mom's mischievous agenda emerged. "Your father and I talked about that policy many times and what we should do with the money God forbid he should leave us. I invested it. He wanted to make sure you had what you needed. He told me to take care of you. I made a promise and I never go back on a promise."

"I still don't want it."

"I know, and you don't need it. It's not millions, but someday it might help." Mom beamed. "Well actually, it'll do more than help."

"I can't believe you didn't tell me." She grinned as I touched her hand. "On second thought, I can."

"For God's sakes, child, you've been through enough. Do whatever it is that's going to make you happy. You've done your thing here and we both know that the next chapter in your life is elsewhere."

My mother amazed me. "Yeah." My eyes scanned the room. The feeling of home diminished slowly. This felt like my home, but not really like my home. "This is going to be weird."

Mom's green eyes flickered. The hair on my arms bristled, Mom's smile reminiscent of my father's.

"I know," she said.

"I'll put the house on the market then make an appointment with the retirement office to get the paperwork started." I couldn't help but smile. I had set myself free.

"You're doing the right thing. Bradley has the kindest

heart of anyone I know. He'll be fine. He's making his mark on the world in his own way."

"I know." I picked at my thumb.

"Beckett may never be happy about it, but it's not up to him."

"Promise you'll visit?" I said, holding her hand.

Mom laughed. "Are you kidding? You won't be able to get rid of me."

My mouth curved toward the ceiling. Her wicked cackle caused me to shake my head. "You are so quirky."

"I know. You get it from me," she said proudly.

"John and I already talked about going back and forth."

"So you've already planned this."

"Um, kind of, but this selling my house and moving to Montana . . ." I took a deep breath. ". . . he knows nothing about."

Mom's eyes lit up. "I love a good secret. When is he getting here?"

"Next week."

"When are you going to tell him?" Mom picked a piece of lint from my sweater.

I shrugged. "I don't know." Goose bumps covered my arms. My life was about to change. Forever. "This is huge."

"Yeah, it sure is," Mom said, tucking my hair behind my ear. "And you deserve it."

"Thanks, Mom."

"Oh, my goodness. Chloe is going to be out of her mind." Mom beamed with excitement.

"I hope so, because I am. This will change everything for her, for all of us. God, what if she really doesn't really want me around?"

"Oh hell, you sound as bad as Beckett. No way is that going to happen."

She was right, as usual. "I can't wait until they get here next week."

Mom rubbed her hands together in anticipation. Her pearly whites gleamed. "I'm happy for you," she said. "It's about freakin' time."

I pinched the skin on the back of my left hand. Time had graced me with an age spot and a few more laugh lines. "This is the scariest thing I've ever done."

"My girl's finally leaving the nest. I'm so proud of you."

Gray strands streaked Mom's strawberry-blonde hair. Mom hadn't said she was proud of me in ages. I made a mental note to tell Bradley how proud I was of him when I called next. "Hey, why did you stop by?"

"Same old, same old, to get in your hair." Mom propped her feet on the table and crossed her ankles.

I pictured the living room empty and I felt okay with that. Of course I'd take my grandmother's clock and few pieces of antique furniture. Anything from my marriage, I'd give to Bradley or Beckett. Once again, it was time for new memories. A little over a year ago, I cleaned out. The designer encouraged me to fill the space, but I said no. I wanted new memories to fill my world and now I was going to get not only new memories, but a whole new world, too. "Figures."

"You know you like it when I just show up."

"I didn't used to," I said, giving her a sideways glance, "but now, I think I do." I teetered as Mom pretended to slug me in the shoulder like a best friend. "Thanks for putting up with my crap," I said.

Mom's grin made her appear more youthful than ever. "No problem. I'm sure I've given you some angst here and there."

"I'll say." I rolled my eyes when Mom glared at me with her feisty green gaze. Taking a deep breath, I played with the hem of my shirt. "Thanks for saying you were proud of me."

"You're welcome. Thank you for being my daughter."

She nudged me with her shoulder. "Now, maybe we should order a pizza. I'm hungry."

I picked up my phone from the table. There was a text from Judy. *Next week can you watch the boys? Maybe Friday?*

I grinned, and then typed out a reply. *Sure.*

Chapter 37

My heart pounded against my ribs. They'd be here any moment. John had texted me from the airport when their flight had arrived. Sleep hadn't come easy with my decision. Judy recommended a friend of hers who sold real estate and we'd set up a meeting for next week. I held my breath as the porch swing swayed. Soon, it would belong to another family. I'd rocked Bradley on this swing, read to him, taught him to read, and cuddled with him when he was sad.

Wetness formed at the corners of my eyes and I smiled, knowing I had a good life here, not only in this house but in Grosse Pointe with my mom and my dad. The humid breeze swept across me like a prairie fire, but I couldn't leave my perch as I watched for them to come home. It was going to be a busy week of packing, and at some point I needed to tell John about my decision to leave Michigan.

The image of his mother's diamond ring flashed in my mind. I didn't think there'd be anyone in my life after Beckett and I'd prepared to live alone. The idea of getting married gave me goose bumps.

The street was quiet today for most of my neighbors had fled for northern Michigan and their second homes or boats that waited for them. Bones lay by my feet with his head on his front paws, snoring. His back leg twitched as his eyelids fluttered. I'd give anything to know what he dreamed of. I hoped he dreamed of chasing butterflies, eating bits of pizza, and a vigorous belly rub. A car slowed in front of my house and turned into John's driveway. I got up. The tags on Bones's collar jingled as he sat up.

"Sorry, boy," I said.

The black sedan parked, the door flew open, and Chloe appeared. My heart swelled as she sprinted over to greet me. I skipped down the stairs, choking back tears knowing that someday I'd be her step-mom. I wanted us to be a family as much as John did.

Chloe sped full throttle, grabbed my waist, and squeezed.

"Oh, my goodness," I said. "It hasn't been that long."

"It's been long enough," she said.

With her cheek pressed against my belly, we fit together like a lock and key. Chloe wasn't the pesky neighbor anymore, she was so much more, and she had no idea.

"Boy, do we have a lot to do this week."

She stared up at me and my breath caught in my chest as I tucked lose strands from her blonde tresses behind her ears.

"Yeah, Dad's been telling me everything we have to get done. Oh brother."

"Well, tomorrow I'm watching Walter and Harry. Maybe you can take time out from packing and join us. Might even have a sleepover depending on what Judy says."

Chloe let go of my waist and dropped to the ground.

Bones stood at the top of the stairs wagging his tail.

"Come on, boy." She encouraged him to come with a clap of her hands. Bones leaped from the step and scampered over to her. He jumped in her lap and licked her face, his tail wagging fiercely. Chloe's belly laugh filled the yard.

John peered at me over the roof of the car. I gave him a little wave. My insides flipped over like a teenager harboring a mad crush. He shut the car door and joined us. I preferred his jeans and T-shirt to the pediatrician garb, way sexier.

Chloe rolled around on the grass with Bones, oblivious to the connection her father and I were making. I saw our tryst in the barn as the moon peeked out from behind the clouds and the flicker in his green eyes when we touched.

"Hi there, how was the trip?" I folded my arms over my stomach.

"Not too bad. Pretty good landing. No snafus," he said. "Glad we made it."

"Me, too." Chloe popped up from the ground and Bones circled her like a herding dog.

"Can I take him for a walk?" she asked, hopping up the steps to my house.

"I guess, if it's okay with your dad."

"Go ahead, but I'll have a to-do list for you when you get back."

Slamming the screen door, Chloe ignored John's words and went inside like she always did.

"Same old, same old," I said with a smile.

John rolled his eyes, and I stood there staring at him, fantasizing about the days ahead.

"Let me know what I can do to help you two get ready for the move." My voice wavered, knowing I'd be packing my bags at some point, too.

"Thanks. We're going to need it," John said, stuffing his hands into his pockets.

Chloe held the front door for Bones. His leash dangled from her fingers. "Come on, Bones," she said, giving her thigh a slap. She bounced down the stairs. Bones's nails clicked on the cement as he followed her, his hindquarters waggling. "We'll be back in a while." Chloe bent down and snapped the hook on Bones's collar.

John and I watched her skip away.

"Can you come in and look something for me?" John asked.

"Sure." I meandered over to the side door of his house with him. He unlocked the deadbolt with a silver key ring from his pocket and I followed him through the kitchen to the dining room. His keys clunked against the wooden table when he tossed them down. In one swift movement, his hand was on my waist drawing me close. Our gazes connected by an invisible force.

"God, I haven't stopped thinking about you since you left," he whispered.

A slow grin drifted across my lips. He leaned closer and nuzzled his cheek close to mine. His breath on my neck sent tremors down my spine.

"Well, I have to say, I've been a little sidetracked myself. Couldn't wait to see you guys." I wrapped my arms around John's neck. His hand pressed against my lower back. I smiled, fancying the secret I kept that warmed me like his kiss.

"When is date night?" he asked.

"Don't know," I said. "We've got a lot to do."

John grunted. "I sure do."

"I said I'd help."

"I'm not sure how having you this close is a help. Lots of stuff never got unpacked from the last move so that's a no brainer."

"Where are you going to put your things when you get back to the ranch?" I asked, thinking about Winston's furnished home.

"I'm going to store some of it in Trout's house and some of it can go in one of the barns up in the rafters. Gonna try to sell most of the furniture."

I thought about what John was saying and wondered how my stuff would fit in. How would it work when I got there? What about Winston? Maybe he wouldn't want me in the same house. I bit my lip. In my mind, I'd actually solidified a move. What if I had to get my own place? What was near the ranch? John's lips grazed my cheek. My eyes drifted shut, the uncertainties gnawed at me.

"Why do you look so worried?" John's brow furrowed.

"You know me," I whispered as my fingers caressed the back of his neck. John and I were nose-to-nose. "I love how green your eyes are. Magical." My voice trailed off. I closed my eyes as his lips covered mine. I held on tight and kissed him hard just to make sure he was the one I wanted.

John cradled my face in his strong hands. "What's this all about?" He wiped the tear away from the corner of my eye.

"I don't know." But I did know. And I wasn't ready to tell him yet. I wanted to keep my secret to myself just a little bit longer in true "Maggie" fashion. "I just wish you could stay." That familiar pang speared my belly. Leaving my house, my home, and everything behind seemed impossible not so long ago and following through with the plan I'd set in motion was gaining speed. John kissed my cheek. My eyes brimmed with tears.

Chloe came ripping around the corner. "What are you two doing? Why are you hugging Maggie?" She lowered her gaze. "Did my dad make you cry?"

"No, your dad didn't make me cry." I sniffled. "I'm just being dumb."

Chloe tiptoed closer and put her arms around us both. "I don't want to go to Montana. I want to stay here. Please, Dad?"

Her warm breath penetrated my shirt, her face pressed up against me. John's gaze searched mine. It was something we all wanted. I remembered how blue the Montana sky was, the rides across the fields and into the mountains, the sweet air scented with sage and beautiful flowers, my nights with John, the campfires and the kittens that Chloe nursed along. My breath caught in my chest. John wrapped his arm around his daughter as she peered up into our faces, not prying about why we were cuddled together.

"Maggie is going to visit," John said.

I smiled and tussled Chloe's messy hair. "I will." God, I was planning to do so much more.

Chloe stepped back. She wiped her forehead with the back of her hand. "When? Can Bones come this time?"

"I'm not sure," I said, planning on cashing in the plane ticket that Winston gave me, wondering if Bones would be considered a carry on.

"Give her some time. She'll figure it out," John said. "She just got back and I'm sure she's really busy thinking about school."

My stomach rolled over. School would be here before I knew it. Mom's words surfaced in my memory. I told myself not to be a chicken. "Yeah, it's a little crazy right now, but when I figure it out, you'll be the first one to know. I promise."

"Okay." Chloe let out a huffy sigh. "When do we have to start all this packing? I kind of liked this place. What do we have for a snack?"

John went into the kitchen, opened the fridge, closed it, and then peeked inside the cupboards. "Nothing. Sorry, kiddo."

Chloe faced me, her green eyes searching my face.

"I have snacks," I said. "You can come over to my house if you want."

"Can I, Dad?" she asked.

"Sure. I guess we'd better think about dinner, too."

Tucking my hands in my pockets, I sauntered toward the door. "Don't worry about dinner. Glad and I will whip something up."

Chloe jiggled with excitement. "Just like old times."

"Yeah, just like old times." A chill ran down my spine. The future was standing before me. She was taller, lankier, and spunky as ever. My stare connected with John's and his eyes sparked with hope as Chloe tugged at my hand.

I admired John's clear-cut vision for the future. He was a good man, a great man. He was bighearted and loving. He was a cowboy at heart and I liked that he knew his true self and could reckon with invisible forces, especially mine.

Chapter 38

John, Chloe, and Mom had gone home. Bones slept on his bed beneath my desk. I hadn't expected to receive an offer on the house so soon. I hadn't even put up a sign, but when the realtor called she said someone had had their eye on my property for several years. Beckett hadn't gotten back to me, and I could feel this place empty.

I dialed Bradley's number. He picked up on the third ring.

"Hi, honey," I said.

"Hi, Mom. What's going on?"

I nibbled at my thumbnail as I leaned back in my chair. "Plenty," I said. "Um." I thought about how to break the news. The knot of raw emotion at the back of my throat made it difficult to swallow. I didn't know if I had it in me to tell him I wanted to sell the house he'd grown up in. "Um, I've been thinking."

Bradley cut in. "So, it's true?"

"Is what true?"

"Dad called me and said you were thinking about selling the house. He said you asked him if he wanted it."

Rubbing my temple, I sighed. That was just like Beckett to be one step ahead of me. "Apparently, your father wasted no time. I kind of wanted to tell you myself."

"Why?"

There was the million-dollar question. And was I ready to tell him the truth? "You really want to hear the truth?" I asked, sucking in my breath.

"Yeah. Why wouldn't I want to hear the truth? You're not sick again, are you?"

I thought about Jenny. "Oh my God. No."

"You'd tell me if the cancer came back. Wouldn't you?" Bradley asked.

His voice was laced with concern, and the last thing I wanted was for him to worry about that. "No, Bradley. I promise. I've gotten a clean bill of health. I'm perfectly okay. I'm thinking about a move. The house is too big and I just don't know if I can keep it up any more."

"Move where?"

"Well, that's the kicker. Your dad doesn't know anything about this, and if I tell you, could you please not say anything until I have everything set?" I waited as he breathed into the phone.

"I guess," Bradley said, sounding reluctant.

"I want to move to Montana."

"Really?" Bradley's voice squeaked.

"Really," I said. "There's more." I paused, wishing I could see his face. "I wish I could tell you in person. This sucks talking to you long distance."

"Let me have it. I think I can handle it. If I can handle Dad being gay, I can handle anything you've got for me so lay it on me."

That was my boy. "I miss you so much." I fingered the picture that I took last summer of John and Chloe walking on the beach.

"I know. I miss you, too. What gives?"

"John asked me to marry him." I breathed in the truth. "I don't know when, and I don't even know if it'll ever happen, but I want to go to Montana and be with him and Chloe."

"Are you serious?"

"Yes," I said, playing with a lock of hair. "Am I crazy?"

"Maybe, but that's fabulous. What about your job?"

"I'm thinking if I sell the house, I can buy my last few

years and be done. What do you really think? Be honest. This is really hard."

Bones' ears perked up. He grunted then laid his head back down.

"You want my honest opinion?" Bradley asked.

"Um, no, lie to me," I said with my usual sarcastic bite.

"Nice. Now that's the mother I love, right there." Bradley chuckled. "I think you should go if that's what you want to do."

"I want to go," I whispered. "Will you visit?" Tears dripped from the corners of my eyes.

"Hell yeah. I've always wanted to go to Montana. Doesn't Harrison Ford live there?"

A tiny grin crossed my lips. I wiped the corner of my right eye then my left with the back of my hand. "I don't know. Will you be mad if I sell the house?"

"No."

"Will you be upset if I remarry?" I asked, touching John's horseshoe tattoo on the photograph.

"No. Will you quit worrying about me? It's about time you took care of yourself."

"I can't help it. You're my son and I wouldn't do anything if it was going to hurt you. You've been through enough."

Bradley sighed. "The only thing that would hurt me is if you stayed there and you really wanted to be somewhere else. You only live once. That's what you'd tell me."

Remembering that bittersweet day Bradley'd left for Boston, my eyes watered with happy tears. He'd driven away with a dream in his pocket and the willingness to risk change. God, my heart had been heavy, but I was filled with excitement. I'd told him dreams were for following, not just for brooding over. "Yeah, I guess I did."

"Really, Mom, you should go. When will this all go down?"

"I'm not sure. Someone is already interested in the house and I haven't even put up a sign. John and Chloe don't know either. I wanted to talk to you first." I shut my eyes, the Montana landscape ingrained in my memory. "I haven't told your dad either. He just thinks I want to sell the house."

"Um, Mom, I hate to break it to you, but he knows you're plotting."

I held my breath. "Can we please keep the particulars between us until I tell him?" Why did Beckett matter so much? "I'll tell him. I promise. That's if Grandma doesn't let it slip first."

"You people are funny. Sure, I can keep it to myself." Bradley cleared his throat. "Mom . . ."

"Yeah." I stretched my legs out in front of me.

"I really like John. He's a good man. Just thought you should know."

"Thanks, sweetheart. That means a lot." A shiver ran across the nape of my neck. The sun had gone down and I was sitting in the dark. My chair squeaked as I leaned over and switched on the lamp. Bones didn't flinch. "You're not just saying that, are you?"

"Um, no. If I thought he was a jerk, I'd tell you. You deserve to be happy. Chloe's a wee bit crazy, but she's still little. Kind of kooky, but funny."

"Yes, she is, and she's intrigued by you." Bradley's belly laugh tickled me.

"Sure, I could never have a dog, but fifteen years later you're getting me a sister. Figures."

"Sorry about that. I know how much you wanted a dog."

"Yeah, I really did. Maybe when I have a place of my own."

I rubbed my left temple. Bradley was an adult. He was going to get a place of his own. He was going to find someone to share it with, have the dog he always wanted, and maybe even have children. We were all *growing up*. The lines in my hands seemed more defined than I remembered. Listening to Bradley speak, I wondered when I'd aged. Mom explained this phenomenon years ago, but I'd never really grasped the concept until now. It had taken a divorce, a pesky eight-year-old girl, her sexy father, a bout with cancer, a trip to Montana, and the death of a colleague to put life in perspective.

Experience embedded truth.

"Mom," Bradley said.

"Yeah?"

"I love you."

I laid my hand on my heart. "I love you, too. I am so proud of everything you are, dear boy. What would I do without you?"

"I don't know. What would I do without you?"

"I wish you were here. I always wish you were here, but I know you have to live your own life. Thanks for being so great."

"It's time. You know that, right?" Bradley said.

"I know," I whispered into the phone.

"How about I call you in a few days and you give me an update?"

"Sure." I picked up a pen and doodled on a scrap piece of paper. "I'll let you know when I know something."

"Cool. Bye, Mom."

"Bye, Bradley." I wished like hell he was here so I could hug him and hold onto just a little bit longer. He'd always be my baby. Apparently, Beckett and I'd done something right. I ended the call, set the phone down on the desk, and scribbled down some numbers.

My phone buzzed with a text. It was Bradley. I opened his message. *It really is time. Stop worrying.* I tapped out a message back. *I love you, Bradley with all my heart, xoxo.* I stood, stretched, went to the kitchen for an icy Beltian beer I'd brought home from Montana, and then meandered out to the patio with a throw. Squinting into the darkness, I spied pint-sized feet dangling off the end of the chaise lounge.

Chloe lay flat on her back with closed eyes. As I neared her, she stiffened.

"I can see you, you know?"

Chloe covered her eyes with her arm. Sitting next to her, I covered my legs with the throw hoping to keep the mosquitoes at bay. I sipped my beer, its frosty smooth taste slid down easily.

"I know." There was something weighing in her sigh.

"What are you doing over here?"

Chloe grunted and turned her head in my direction. "I had to get out of there. Dad's on a mission and I'm not sure I'm really helping." She scrunched up her nose at me.

I peered at her over the rim of my glass as I drank my beer.

"If I wasn't around, would you be with my dad?"

I swallowed. "What?"

"You heard me." Her voice was faint.

"Why would you say that? I thought we've already discussed this."

Chloe sat up and slapped her hands against her knees. "'Cause I just don't think I'm helping anyone. I know you two like each other. I don't need some dumb boy like Harry to point that out. Dad hasn't stopped talking about you since you left. If I went to live with my mom, would you two get together?"

"You have nothing to do with it. Sometimes grown-ups need time to work things out. You shouldn't worry about your dad and me." My heart thumped against my chest walls. "I love you, Chloe."

Chloe swung her legs over the side of the lounge chair. "I love you, too, that's what makes this suck even more. What if I could convince my dad to send me back here every once in a while so we could be together?" She blew her hair away from her face and sparkled with ingenuity.

"I'm not sure about that."

"Why?" she asked.

"Because I don't know how much longer I'll be living here." I set my beer down on the table next to my chair and then leaned closer to her. The moon glistened overhead. Its power drifted down around me as I spoke to Chloe. I touched her cheek, her soft skin warming my touch.

"Where are you going?" she asked.

The gate latch clicked in the night. I glanced over to see John shuffling across the yard in the night air, his hands buried deep within his pockets. His voice was clear as he said, *"Where are you going, Maggie?"*

I couldn't contain my secret. "I was thinking I'd come live in Montana if it's okay with you two." Chloe scooted over, and John sat at the end of the chaise with her. I'd never felt this comfortable in all my life. "I've been doing some thinking and I'm working on selling my house."

"Really?" Chloe said, her jaw dropping open.

"Really." Staring into her emerald eyes, the prospect of Montana life filled me up. "I think I'd miss you too much if I didn't, and besides, Bradley thinks it's a good idea, too."

Chloe beamed and her shoulders slumped forward as she leaned into her dad.

"Well, what do you think?" I asked.

Chloe stood, our noses touching. She hugged me tight with a mighty squeeze. "You're not yanking my chain, are you?" she asked, her breath brushing against my ear.

I held her close. "No, I'm not yanking your chain, Chloe. I really want to come live with you." John's teary stare moved me. His warm touch confirmed that we belonged together. "Well, what do you think, J.P. McIntyre?"

"I think our lives just got made."

"Mine, too. Then it's settled," I said.

Chapter 39

John and I waved goodbye as Mom and Chloe got situated in Mom's convertible.

"Be good," John said as Mom backed slowly down the driveway.

"I will," Chloe called, sliding her oversized sunglasses up to the bridge of her nose. She adjusted the scarf tied around her head.

"She will call me if I need to come get you," John said firmly. "Seriously, Glad, call me if you need to."

Mom stopped the car then lowered her sunglasses and peered over the top of them. "Please. I'm sure we'll be fine. We're just going out for ice cream then over to my house. We'll have fun."

"Maggie and I will be home, if you need us," he said.

"I got it, but we won't be calling. No offense," Mom said with a nod.

John and I stood in the front yard and watched them drive away. "They really are two peas in a pod," I said, walking toward the house.

We sauntered up the stairs and went inside. John closed the front door, then locked it. A fierce grin crossed his lips as he stepped closer.

I raised my eyebrows at him. "They just left. What if they come back?"

"You heard her, she's not coming back."

"Yeah, but I wasn't ready to come to Montana and look what happened there," I said, stepping backward down the foyer.

John's devious expression made my stomach flutter with excitement. A squeal escaped my lips as I ran into the kitchen.

He caught me, then stepped into me, my back against the wall. "Are you going to kiss me?" I whispered.

"I'm going to do more than that." John ran his finger down my cheek, over my collarbone, and then he unbuttoned my blouse. He fingered the cottony fabric and kissed my skin.

My body craved him as his mouth grazed my skin. Leaning forward, I held his face in my hands. I peered into his smiling eyes. "Really, we should wait until they've been gone a few minutes."

John groaned. "Fine."

The doorbell rang. Bones's toenails clicked along the hard floor as he raced to the front door.

"Told you," I said, buttoning up my shirt.

Unlocking the deadbolt, I turned the doorknob. Beckett raked his fingers through his hair when he saw me.

"What are you doing here?" I glanced over my shoulder at John then I looked back to Beckett.

"Oh, I didn't know you had company," he said, peering over my shoulder.

"It's okay," John said, "I was just on my way home."

I made a face at him, and then opened the screen door and walked outside. Beckett paced back and forth. "I'll see you in a few minutes," I told John, kneading my shoulders with my fingers. "What's going on?"

Beckett leaned against the half wall of the porch and crossed his arms. "I ran into Glad at the market and she said I should talk to you as soon as possible." He shoved his hands in his pockets and jingled his keys.

I rolled my eyes. *Thanks, Mom.* "As you can see there's a 'For Sale' sign in the front yard. I've had an offer already."

Beckett glared at me. "Where are you going?"

"Why does it matter?" I asked. "You have your life, and now I have mine."

Beckett took off his sunglasses and hung them on the collar of his tangerine-orange Lacoste button-down. He rubbed his right temple, softening his hard stare. "Where are you going?"

"Um." I took a deep breath. "I'm moving to Montana."

"What?"

The corner of my mouth lifted as I heard my own words. Beckett's face drooped. I cheered for myself. "Yeah, it's time to move on. I'm heading west."

"What?" Beckett caught his breath with a gasp.

I spoke slowly as if he was hard of hearing. "I. Am. Moving. To. Montana." My heart fluttered, the anticipation making me giddy.

"So this is what Bradley wasn't telling me."

"Yup," I said proudly, knowing that Bradley kept his promise. Good boy.

"Well, I'll be dipped." Beckett ran his slender fingers through his perfect hair. "Now get to the rest of it."

I narrowed my gaze at his words.

"Sorry." Beckett fidgeted with the blooms cascading over the clay pot beside him.

"There wasn't anything I could do when you walked away. I buried my feelings knowing I couldn't change anything. I don't expect you to understand or even be happy for me, but it's my time. I'm going to Montana to be with John and Chloe."

"The guy next door?"

Beckett moved closer to me. I held his stare as he processed the information.

"This is a lot to take in," he said.

"Suppose so." I remembered how I felt as Beckett delivered his life-changing news a little over three years ago. His sucker punch left me broken, and I resented him for it, but we stayed together, feeling obligated to live the charade. Time hadn't healed all wounds, but fate had slipped between the cracks and shown me the way. Montana called to me in a different way than it had called to Winston, John, and Chloe, but it called just the same and I answered. "Have you thought about the house? I have to decide what to do about the offer."

Beckett rubbed his forehead. He looked out over the front yard. "Remember when Bradley used to leave skid marks on the driveway? You'd get so mad."

"I remember," I said.

Beckett faced me, not masking the sadness behind his eyes. "I suppose it's time to move on." His sigh, monumental.

"I thought you already had." I sat down on the swing, nudging my foot against the porch floor to get the sway going.

"I thought I had, too. I just thought you'd always be here." Beckett stopped speaking, his brow wrinkled with thought. "I guess there was some comfort in that."

"Guess so."

"I don't think I could live here. It'd be too sad." A shadow washed over Beckett's gaze.

I grimaced. "It would make you sad?" Did this place really hold that many negative memories for him?

"Yeah." Beckett sat at the other end of the swing. "I think so. It would remind me of you and what I put you through."

With a hard swallow, I crossed my arms over my stomach. "You're forgetting, there was a time I didn't want to be married any more either. It wasn't just you." My heart ached for both of us. Beckett hadn't caused the demise all by himself.

"I know," he said.

My chest rose and fell with the breeze that swept by. It rustled the bushes and left just as quickly as it came, sending a message to both of us.

"Then I'll accept the offer." My heart raced.

Beckett forced a smile. "You deserve to be happy after putting up with me."

Reaching over, I patted his hand. For as many times as I'd held his hand before, it felt strange now. He'd given me Bradley, and for that I was thankful. "I'll let you know when the deal goes through."

"What about your job? You were always manic about getting your teaching years in."

"I got it covered. I'll have my years in. I finished what I started, and that's all that matters. It's not about how you cross the finish line, it's the fact that you finished the race."

"I guess that's good, then."

"Yeah, it's good." Pride filled me up. The paperwork was being processed and I'd soon be on my way. If all went according to plan, I'd be in Montana by Christmas.

Beckett put his sunglasses on. "Well, I guess I better get going. I'm meeting some friends for dinner."

"That sounds like fun." The sun streamed onto the porch and warmed my face. I shaded my eyes to see Beckett.

He started down the stairs then turned as if he had something to say.

I leaned against the railing and waited. "What?"

"There's something different about you. In a good way."

"Thanks," I said, knowing he was right.

Beckett sauntered down the sidewalk and over to his Prius. He was thin like he'd always been, his manicured hair didn't give way to the gentle wind, and I wondered what other secrets he concealed, but knew they were for someone else to discover.

Knocking on John's door, I digested Beckett's departure.

"Everything okay?" he asked, inviting me in.

"Yeah." An unexpected sadness washed over me.

John shut the door behind me then drew me close. "Glad just called."

"Are they coming home?"

John laughed. "They're not. They're fine. She just wanted to let us know that they were settled. I think it was code for get your groove on."

I raised an eyebrow at him, then he kissed me. Melting into his arms, I fiddled with the collar of his shirt. "Did you talk to Winston?"

John smiled. "It's all good. He said he was glad that his ticket would come in handy after all. I'm not sure what that means, but by the smile on your face you do."

I kissed his lips. He held me close and it felt like we'd been together forever. "I love you, John McIntyre."

"I love you, too, Maggie Abernathy."

"Damn you're a lucky man."

"I sure as hell am, neighbor lady."

Dear Readers,

Thank you for joining me on the *Montana Bound* journey. When Maggie Abernathy and Chloe McIntyre called to me, I knew I had to listen. This series was inspired by my own bout with cancer and navigating Maggie's journey made it possible for me to connect with so many others who have had or know someone who has dealt with this disease. I hope Maggie and Chloe have touched your heart in the same way they have touched mine. If you enjoyed this book and have a minute to spare, I'd really appreciate a short review on the page or website where you purchased *Maggie's Montana*.

It is with much heartfelt gratitude, I thank you.

Sincerely,
Linda

Website: www.LindaBradleyAuthor.com
Facebook: https://www.facebook.com/Linda-Bradley-389688594534105/
Twitter: @LBradleyAuthor
Link to my Amazon page: http://www.amazon.com/Linda-Bradley/e/B00JUIS2FS
Link to my Barnes & Noble page: http://www.barnesandnoble.com/w/maggies-way-linda-bradley/1122880519

Also by **Soul Mate Publishing** and **Linda Bradley**:

MAGGIE'S WAY

Middle-aged, Maggie Abernathy just wants to recuperate from cancer during the solitude of summer vacation after a tiresome year of teaching second grade.

Maggie's plans are foiled when precocious seven-year-old Chloe McIntyre moves in next door with her dad, John. Maggie's life changes in a way she could never imagine when the pesky new neighbors steal her heart. With Maggie's grown son away, her ex-husband in the shadows, her meddling mother's unannounced visits, and Chloe McIntyre on her heels, somehow Maggie's empty house becomes home again.

Available now on Amazon: http://tinyurl.com/jowuly4

MAGGIE'S FORK IN THE ROAD

Maggie Abernathy learns that pesky neighbors John and Chloe McIntyre are moving to Montana. The only problem is…she can't fathom living without them now that they've stolen her heart. While trying to digest the news and accept John's decision to leave Michigan, Maggie ventures to Chicago with Chloe to see Chloe's Hollywood mother in a photo shoot, where the three kindle a quirky bond making it even harder for Maggie to say goodbye. With the support of Maggie's meddling mother, her best friend Judy, and a surprise visit from Montana rancher Winston Ludlow McIntyre, Maggie begins to wonder which fork in the road leads home.

Available now on Amazon: http://tinyurl.com/z9dbsyd